Dane knew ... her, to kiss her, t... ... ... wanted to be taken.

And the next time, because now she was sure there would be one, she would return the favor, calling up everything she'd learned of him, of what he liked, to make sure he would be the one driven mad. She would show him she understood, that she knew what they'd nearly lost, how rare and special it was.

And then he was easing into her, hot and hard, slow and taunting, and rational thought fled. Her body arched in eager anticipation as he slid home bit by bit, and the low groan that broke from him, the first sign he wasn't as completely in control as he'd seemed, made her every muscle clench.

He lifted his head, looked straight into her eyes. "Don't throw this away, Kayla."

She tightened her arms around him. "No more taking for granted," she said.

Her words were apparently what he'd needed to hear, because he abandoned all efforts at teasing slowness and began to move with an urgency that was no less compelling. Kayla gave herself up to the driving stroke of his body, let slip all restraint and reveled in the sweet, delicious fact that he was hers again.

For now.

Cutter's Code: A secret network of operatives specializing in lost causes.

Dear Reader,

Writers are strange people. I say that with full knowledge
that I fall squarely in that category. I have a motto that in
various forms is espoused by many writers, I'm sure: "It's all
research." I'm certain of this because of all the tiny bits and
images that clutter my mind, making me a wiz at *Jeopardy*
but not so hot at things like, oh, remembering birthdays.

Many of these little bits and images fade over time, but
some do not. One day, long ago, I was picking up mail from
my post office box. As I went inside, I saw a young man,
jaw tight, eyes suspiciously wet, wad up a piece of paper
and an envelope and throw them somewhat energetically
into a trash can as he stalked out of the building. As I came
back moments later, hands full of mail, there he was again.
Only, now he was digging through the trash to retrieve that
wadded-up letter. He took it to the nearest sort counter and
tried to smooth it out, then folded the wrinkled paper and
envelope neatly and put it in his pocket before leaving again.

I've lived with that image for all these years, wondering
what the story was behind it. I'll never know, but with a
little tweaking and some role-reversal, I've finally unloaded
that image. It's yours now, and I hope you enjoy the story!

Happy reading,

Justine Davis

JUSTINE DAVIS

Operation Reunion

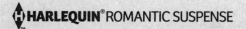

HARLEQUIN® ROMANTIC SUSPENSE

Recycling programs
for this product may
not exist in your area.

ISBN-13: 978-0-373-27815-2

OPERATION REUNION

Copyright © 2013 by Janice Davis Smith

Printed in U.S.A.

Books by Justine Davis

JUSTINE DAVIS

Justine Davis lives on Puget Sound in Washington State, watching big ships and the occasional submarine go by, and sharing the neighborhood with assorted wildlife, including a pair of bald eagles, deer, a bear or two and a tailless raccoon. In the few hours when she's not planning, plotting or writing her next book, her favorite things are photography, knitting her way through a huge yarn stash and driving her restored 1967 Corvette roadster—top down, of course.

Connect with Justine at her website, justinedavis.com, at Twitter.com/Justine_D_Davis, or on Facebook at Facebook.com/JustineDareDavis.

Cedar was intelligent, inquisitive, willful, demanding, bratty, expectant, a dragon in a golden retriever's body. She never met a stranger and fully expected everyone she met to love—and pet!—her, and they generally did. She was the perfect travel companion, the consummate hostess, an intuitive and compassionate friend. She always had a twinkle in her eye and a smile on her face. She always got the last bite of everything I ate and took her duties as pre-wash cycle for the dishwasher very seriously. She loved when I bought a Kindle because it gave me one more hand available to pet her with while I read. She loved to go to the dog beach—not for the dogs, or the beach—but for the pets she received from all the dog-friendly people there; a roll in a dead crab and some seaweed was always a bonus. Her favorite thing in the world was a good roll in some scratchy grass, even better if some wild creature had left something good and stinky there first. She was a force of nature who has left very big paw prints on our hearts and a huge hole in our lives. I miss her every day.

Sharyn Cerniglia

Cedarzmom

Chapter 1

Kayla Tucker stared at the note in her hand. She was barely aware of the woman opening the post office box next to her, stepped out of the way of the man emptying trash, ignored the girl chattering loudly into her cell phone, all without looking up from the page obviously torn out of a spiral notebook.

The note wasn't signed. If it had been printed, she could have pretended it was a mistake. That he hadn't written it. But there was no mistaking the handwriting; the slightly crooked hand, falling off the lines in her brother's typical way, was definitely Chad's.

Of course it was, just like all the others.

The writing blurred suddenly. She blinked, once, twice, then a third time. The last line swam, then cleared.

I'm sorry. I love you, sis.

She swore inwardly. "Then why did you leave, damn it? We could have fought this!"

Furious, mostly at herself for letting this latest in the long line of notes get to her, she wadded the ragged-edged piece of paper and the envelope into a tight ball. Dane would be unhappy yet again, she thought.

No, she thought as the memory stabbed at her. Dane Burdette would not be unhappy. Because he wasn't around anymore. He'd given up on her at last.

His image shot through her mind, vivid and painful. Tall, lean, dark, silky hair that kicked forward over his brow, golden eyes alight as he looked at her, flashing his killer smile. The smile that had grown rarer and rarer as the time passed.

Smothering the usual ache at the thought of the man she'd once expected to spend her life with, she slammed the small metal door of the post office box closed, turned the key and yanked it out. She turned on her heel and walked toward the door. She tossed the wadded up note into the trash can just outside.

"Kayla!"

The last thing she wanted to do just now was talk to someone. But she thought she recognized the voice, so she stopped, turned. And was enveloped in a huge hug.

"I'm so glad to run into you this morning. I was going to call and tell you—Leah and I actually went out to dinner last night."

Kayla managed a smile for the older man who several weeks ago had brought his reluctant wife to the counseling group she ran. "I'm glad to hear that, John. How did it go?"

"Not perfect, but better than I expected. And she's encouraged enough to try something else now."

"That's good to hear. Very good."

She meant it. She'd started the group for victims of violent crime as a means to help herself after the brutal murder of her parents, but in the process she had found a calling. She'd even gone back to school so she could be certified. And moments like this were why. Leah Crandall had been mentally immobilized after her son had been killed by an armed robber at a convenience store, and this was the first time she'd done anything socially normal in more than a year.

Kayla hoped they would make it, she thought as John promised he and his wife would continue with the group and would see her at the next meeting. So many marriages didn't survive the death of a child; the murder of that child only made it worse.

The overcast morning matched her mood as she headed for the parking lot. She glanced down the row of parked vehicles toward her own, the little blue coupe Dane had always kept in perfect shape for her. She spotted a familiar motorcycle parked across from it and slowed her steps. Rod Warren truly was the last person she wanted to see now. Or ever. She'd had an aversion to him ever since she'd found him trying to burn holes in the wings of a living butterfly with a magnifying glass when they were kids. She'd tried to stop him, even though he was older and bigger, and had in return been pinned against a wall and groped in a way she was too young to completely understand.

But Dane had, and when she'd told him about it, Rod had later shown up with a split lip and a black eye, and he'd kept a wide berth from then on. Still, she'd never forgotten the repugnance she'd felt. But the rider of the motorcycle with the picture of a nude female arranged in a particularly obscene way on the tank was thankfully nowhere in sight, so she kept going.

She was almost to her car when she changed her mind.

She should keep the note. The envelope with the postmark at least; this might be the one time when it helped. She turned around and began to walk quickly back. She felt the breeze of her own movement edging her tears sideways across her cheeks.

A loud clank echoed against the block wall of the post office. And the trash can she'd tossed the crumpled note into rolled into her path. She stopped, staring. There was no wind to catch the now-empty metal container, nor anyone to knock it over. The janitor had worked his way around to the other side of the building, and nobody else was even close.

No human anyway.

But there was a dog.

Sitting beside the toppled trash can was a dog, a striking

animal with a thick, longish coat colored black from the tip of his nose past his upright, alert ears all the way down past his shoulders, where the color of his fur changed to a rich, reddish brown.

He was looking at her rather intently.

And he had what she would swear was her note between his front paws. It had to be, she thought. The can had just been emptied before she'd tossed it. The wadded paper and envelope lay on the cement in front of him as if carefully placed. He must think it was some sort of ball to play with.

For a moment she pondered the dangers of approaching a strange dog. He wasn't huge, but he was far from small. Big enough to be intimidating, to make her wary.

And then he grinned at her.

She knew it was silly, but she couldn't think of any other way to describe it. His mouth opened, revealing some formidable teeth, but it was impossible to be frightened when his tongue lolled out on one side and the corners of that mouth seemed to curl upward.

Just when she had decided it might be safe to pet him, at the same time reaching for her note, he moved. He grabbed up the note and she froze. But he was holding it in a way that seemed oddly gentle. Like Dane's sweet Labrador, Lilah, used to hold her pups long ago, so gently there was barely a dent in the fur. The memory made her ache even more for the man who had left her.

And then the dog got up and started to go toward the parking lot.

Angry at herself for tossing the note in the first place, Kayla didn't know what to do. She wanted it back, desperately now, but she didn't want to provoke a strange dog into biting her.

The dog stopped. He looked over his shoulder at her. And waited.

Images from countless movies and television shows flashed through her mind. Was she supposed to follow him? Did dogs really do that? He took a couple of steps, still looking at her, the note still held almost delicately in his mouth.

She followed tentatively. He started off again. Not running, not teasing her as some dogs did, playing a canine version of keep away; he just trotted off. He headed into the half-full parking lot, past the obscene motorcycle and toward the second row of vehicles. When he looked back yet again, as if to be certain she was following, she could have sworn his dark eyes were urging her, compelling her somehow.

Kayla shook her head sharply.

"It's a *dog,*" she muttered under her breath.

She picked up her pace, determined now to retrieve the note. She'd only thrown it away in the first place because she was so upset over Dane.

She passed her own car, then the big pickup parked next to it and the tiny electric car next to that. With her mind distracted for an instant by the absurd contrast between those two vehicles, she was late to realize the dog had come to a halt beside the driver's door of the next car in the row, a dark blue SUV that was a few years old but looked in perfectly maintained condition and had the glass hatch in the back raised up.

Her breath caught as the driver's door swung open and a man slid out. She stopped sharply, momentarily unable to move. He was tall, lean, hair as dark as midnight, with a forbiddingly strong jaw. But that jaw was unshaven, and his tousled hair spoke of a hurried morning rather than trendy style. Still, she took a step back instinctively.

He hadn't seen her yet. He crouched down beside the dog, who was fairly wiggling with pleasure yet holding gently on to that ball of paper. Kayla felt her anxiety fade as the man smiled and reached out to scratch below the dog's right ear.

"That'll teach me to leave the back window open. What'd you find, boy?"

The man's voice was low, steady, strong. He took the paper wad from the dog, who surrendered it easily and looked almost humanly satisfied, as if at a job well done. And then the dog looked back at her, staring in a way she'd never seen from any animal. She felt pinned in place, for a moment helpless and unable to move.

Meanwhile, the man had taken the note out of the crumpled envelope. *Her* note.

The spell broke. "That's mine," she said, afraid after she'd spoken that she'd sounded like a spoiled child who'd had a toy taken from her.

"I gathered," he said, and she realized she'd been wrong; he'd known she was there all the time.

And then he straightened. And she realized just how tall he was.

Most men seemed tall to her, at five-three. But this one had to be at least six feet, and something about the way he held himself made him seem even bigger. That he was obviously fit and strong only added to the impression.

She sucked in a breath, trying not to be intimidated. Nothing would happen here, in such a public place as the post office parking lot.

Then his face changed, softened, and his icy blue eyes warmed.

"Hayley," the man said, his voice raised just slightly.

Kayla frowned, puzzled. Then had her answer as a woman stepped past her, a post office receipt in one hand.

The dog greeted the woman effusively, on his feet, tail wagging madly. The woman reached to scratch the same spot the man had as she glanced from dog to man to Kayla. Mirth was in her voice and echoed in vivid green eyes as she spoke to the animal.

"And now what have you done, Cutter, my lad? And why are you running around loose anyway?"

The dog yipped, short and sharp.

"He jumped out the back and took off like…a dog with a mission," the man said as he lifted one arm toward the woman. She stepped into the shelter of it so naturally that Kayla knew these two were together in a way few people were. She could feel it, coming off of them in waves, could see it in their faces—love, respect, comfort and, in the glance they exchanged, passion.

She smothered a sigh. She'd known all that once. She'd had a place like that at Dane Burdette's side, a warm, safe, welcoming place. And she'd thrown it away. Dane was a man of near-infinite patience, he'd proven that for years, but she'd pushed and pushed until she'd finally found his limit.

The pain of losing him wasn't just emotional; it was a harsh, physical hurt, an aching for him with heart, mind and body. Oh, yes, body, she thought with an inward moan. Sometimes at night she would curl up into a ball and weep for missing him beside her, loving her. She gave herself an inward shake; if she let herself slide back into that morass of pain and loss, she'd break down sobbing right here in public, in front of these total strangers.

Belatedly she realized she'd seen the woman inside the post office, that she'd walked past her on her way to her post office box. She'd been comparing the woman's warm, auburn hair to her own shorter, dark-brown bob, wondering if a change would help her outlook.

Not that anything could help because Dane had walked out of her life.

"I was just about to go round him up when he came back," the man said, gesturing with the note. "It seems he stole this."

"Stole?" the woman named Hayley asked as she looked at

the balled-up paper. "Can you steal something someone obviously didn't want?"

Kayla tried to explain. "I…"

The man looked at her, and she hated the way her voice faded into nothing. But it was too big, too complicated to explain. Still, there was something oddly calming in this man's eyes, as if he'd reached out a hand to steady her.

Kayla tried to get a grip; whoever these two were, they clearly weren't a threat. Stick to the simple facts, she told herself.

"I didn't mean to throw it away." She sighed, corrected herself. "I mean, I did throw it away, but I shouldn't have. I'd like it back."

"Of course."

He handed it back without hesitation, reassuring her further. She smoothed out the note, realizing after a moment that the paper wasn't even damp from the dog's mouth. She glanced at the animal, who was looking up at her intently. She'd never had a dog, and suddenly she wondered if this one would have the same effect on her if she was more familiar with them. Or if it was just this dog who could look at her in that piercing way that made her feel as if she shouldn't move.

"He's…a beautiful dog."

"He is," Hayley said. "And clever enough to be amazing and annoying by turns."

Kayla smiled at that. She thanked the man, nodded at the woman and turned to head back to her car.

The dog stopped her.

Not aggressively—in fact, he was looking up at her with the same tongue-lolling grin she'd seen before. She tried to walk around him, but he moved to block her again.

"I'm sorry," Hayley said quickly. "He's a herding dog by breed, and it's his nature."

She reached for the dog's collar. Before she could grasp

it, the dog dodged slightly, the bright blue, boat-shaped tag Kayla had caught a glimpse of rattling. Cutter, she thought. Hayley had called the dog Cutter. As in coast guard cutter? Was that why the man looked so imposing, some military background?

The dog yipped again, now looking from her to his owners and back. He clearly wanted something, but—

He snatched the note again, right out of her hands.

Kayla let out a startled yelp that probably sounded like the dog's yip. This time the animal didn't run off. Instead, he turned and with a startling sort of delicacy, presented the note to the woman, who glanced at it, then up at the man beside her.

"Uh-oh," the man said.

"So it seems," Hayley agreed.

Kayla had no idea what they were talking about, what was going on, but it was all starting to make her nervous again. And no amount of telling herself she was perfectly safe here, out in the open in a public parking lot with people coming and going around them, seemed to help. Without Dane solidly by her side, she felt vulnerable.

She summoned up all the old coping tricks she'd been taught in the days after her world had been shattered. It was only normal she be nervous around strangers, even after all this time, she told herself. And she knew how to deal, really she did.

"Please," she said, trying to sound merely polite instead of pleading, "that's personal."

"Someone's in trouble," the woman said. It wasn't really a question. But her voice was so soft, so gentle, it eased Kayla's rising anxiety.

"Yes," she admitted. That much was clear in the note now open for all to see, so there didn't seem much point in denying it.

The man spoke. "Time for names, I think. I'm Quinn Fox-worth. This is my fiancée, Hayley Cole."

"Congratulations," Kayla said, not sure what else to say in this odd situation.

"And this rascal," Hayley said, scratching the dog's ear again, "is Cutter."

"Nice to meet you."

It was automatic and sounded utterly inane. She needed to get out of here, collect her thoughts. But first she had to get that note back.

On the thought the dog moved once more, this time closer to her. And then he was leaning against her leg, looking up at her with what for all the world looked like reassurance.

"What an…unusual dog," she murmured, half to herself.

"You have no idea," Hayley said, her tone wry.

"He has a nose for trouble," Quinn agreed. "In this case, apparently, yours."

She looked up at the man then. And read the same kind of reassurance in his eyes that she'd fancied she'd seen in the dog's.

"It's my brother's trouble, really."

Now why had she said that? She didn't make a habit of discussing her ugly family history with strangers.

"And now ours," Hayley said quietly.

Kayla blinked. "What?"

The woman gestured at the dog. "This wasn't coincidence. But we'll explain all that later. In the meantime, let's go some-where where we can talk and figure out what to do about your problem."

Kayla took a step back. Or tried to. The dog, once again, was there. He seemed uncannily able to sense her every move before she made it.

"Who are you?" she asked, something dark and unsettling churning in her stomach.

"Friendlies," Quinn said, as if he'd sensed her fear.

"We just want to help," Hayley said. She glanced at Quinn, such pride in her face that it went a long way toward soothing Kayla's nerves. "It's what we do."

"You can't help. Nobody can."

Bitterness spiked through Kayla. She'd accepted the lost years, the thrown-away money, but Dane.... Losing Dane was—

She cut her own thoughts off.

"This is beyond anyone's help," she said. "It's a lost cause."

"Well, now," Hayley said, "isn't that convenient? Lost causes are our specialty."

Chapter 2

Dane Burdette paced the width of his home office, turned, made the return journey, then turned again. Although the apartment was large enough, this den was a small space, one that overflowed with equipment that now also filled the adjoining dining area.

A sound from outside brought him out of the reverie he'd slipped into and back to reality. A reality that, for the first time in more than a decade, didn't have Kayla in it.

His jaw tightened. He rubbed at the back of his neck, trying not to think about Kayla doing the same, as she so often did when he'd been working too many hours. And he barely managed not to look for the hundredth time this morning at the photograph on his desk, the picture he'd taken at the Washington coast last year, catching her at her most beautiful, happy, smiling, looking almost carefree. It was clear to even the most casual observer that the love and warmth in her eyes was aimed at the person behind the camera.

It nearly ripped his heart out every time he looked at it. He'd done the right thing. Finally. He'd meant what he'd said—he couldn't go on like this. Ten years was enough.

Too bad knowing that didn't stop the urge to give in, to go to her and patch things up. Again.

But he'd meant it this time. He'd spent too long living with her obsession. She'd idolized her big brother, believed completely in his innocence and had never given up trying to find him. She'd traveled thousands of miles, going every time one of those damn notes arrived, chasing postmarks. And every time it came to nothing. She'd spent time, money and much of her energy on the quest, and there was no end in sight.

He glanced at the heavy dive watch Kayla had given him for his twenty-fifth birthday. She'd be at the post office even now; she went every Friday to pick up the mail for her counseling group, but in truth she was both hoping for and dreading the arrival of another communication from her brother. Dane himself was long past hoping; he was firmly in the dread category.

He needed to quit wearing the watch, he thought. Even though he liked the solid weight of it on his wrist, that Kayla had chosen it and given it to him—and the passionate night that had followed—was not something he wanted to be reminded of at every move.

"I had to do it," he muttered under his breath, as if actually saying the words would be more convincing to a heart and mind that felt as if something vital had been torn away.

At this point, Chad Tucker's guilt or innocence didn't matter much to him. What mattered was that Kayla couldn't seem to move on. It wasn't that he didn't understand—he did. He'd been there that night, in the bloody, awful aftermath. He'd been the one to hear her scream, the one to run to her, to pull her out of the room that held the nightmare. To this day he couldn't imagine what it must have been like for the teenage girl to walk into that hell.

That it was a girl he cared about made even thinking about it difficult. And he had cared about Kayla since the first day he'd seen her, a slight, fragile-looking fourteen, sitting on a limb high up in the old tree between their houses. She had been staring downward, turning her head this way and that, and he'd realized after a moment what was going on.

"Stuck?" he'd called to her.

"Not yet," she'd answered, making him laugh.

She'd been in his life one way or another ever since that day. Until now. Until he'd had to leave her, had to walk away. Even though it was like leaving a part of himself behind. But he knew—

"Dane?"

He spun around, a little embarrassed that he hadn't realized his roommate and business partner Sergei was standing there. He needed to get his head back in the game.

"I need to go if I'm going to make it on time. Don't want to speed out of here because our downstairs neighbor the cop is out washing his car. Is what you sent last night the final cut?"

"Yes."

"I'll be on my way then," his partner said.

But he stopped in the doorway and looked back. He and Sergei Kesic had built their small, digital video promotion company from nothing to a going concern, thanks to Dane's knack for tailoring the product to individual customer needs and Sergei's no-nonsense, bottom-line sales approach that appealed to companies in a belt-tightening era.

"You sent it at 3:00 a.m.," Sergei said.

"Did I?"

"You're keeping some pretty long hours, buddy."

"Don't be late," Dane said. The last thing he wanted was to get dragged into discussing the reasons behind his late nights and lack of sleep. Sergei hadn't asked why he'd suddenly taken to sleeping here instead of at Kayla's, and he didn't want that conversation to start now.

He had to put it out of his mind, he told himself as Sergei shrugged and left. There were decisions to make, plans to go over.

A sour laugh escaped him. Plans. Yes, indeed, plans. He'd had a lot of those.

He yanked the watch off his wrist, opened a desk drawer, shoved it in the back and slammed the drawer shut. One more step, he thought. And he should do it now, when he knew where she'd be, at the post office checking for another one of those damned notes. He would go over to Kayla's and pick up the last of his stuff.

And leave his key.

He winced at the thought but shored up his determination and grabbed his key ring from the desk. He pried the ring open and worked the gold key off, fighting memories of the night she'd given it to him.

He shoved the key in the watch pocket of his jeans.

With a final glance at the photograph, he headed for the door. That picture was going, he told himself firmly. As soon as he got back.

This was crazy.

Kayla stared at the business card in her hand. It looked official enough, but anybody could churn out a good-looking business card. And there was no indication on the card of exactly what the "Foxworth Foundation" did.

They had walked across the street to the small city park and were seated on the stone wall that surrounded the kid's play area, deserted now at this morning hour. The dog that had started all this was sprawled in the grass, basking in the morning sun and looking decidedly smug.

"Does he do this often?" she asked.

"Cutter?" Hayley said.

"Yes. Does he drag total strangers with a problem to you?"

"As a matter of fact, yes."

Kayla blinked. Hayley smiled.

"He has a knack," she said. "I don't know how he does it, but he seems to know when people are troubled."

"And he brings them to you?"

"It's not usually as…neatly as today," Quinn said with a wry smile. "But yes, he does."

Kayla glanced at the dog, who seemed blithely unconcerned about the entire situation. As if his job was done, she thought, even as she realized she was going a bit overboard with the anthropomorphism.

"And he makes it pretty obvious," Hayley said, "that he expects us to fix whatever's wrong."

Whatever's wrong, Kayla thought. And lost causes are their specialty?

I love you, but I won't—I can't—stay and watch you throw the rest of your life away on a lost cause.

Dane's final words as he had walked out her door echoed in her mind, drowning out every other thought. He'd been upset with her before but always seemed to find a reserve of patience she marveled at even as she used it up. But this time had been different. She'd heard the finality in his voice, seen the sadness in his eyes. The man she'd loved since she was fourteen had finally had enough. His departure had left her bereft and a little stunned at how completely off balance her already damaged world now felt.

"Whatever it is," Hayley said softly, "let us help. It's what we do."

Kayla looked up. "Lost causes?"

"Yes."

"Who are you?" She glanced at Quinn, gestured with the card, remembering his introduction. "You're the Foxworth."

"One of them," he said.

"What's this foundation do?"

"What should be done but isn't," Quinn said, with a warm glance at Hayley that made Kayla miss Dane all the more.

"They—" Hayley caught herself, smiled and went on, showing Kayla she wasn't used to saying it yet, "*we* work for people in the right who don't have anyone else to help them."

Curious now, she looked at them both. "Who decides who's in the right?"

Quinn grinned suddenly. Kayla could have sworn she heard Hayley's breath catch; she didn't blame her, it was a killer grin. Nothing on Dane's, of course, but still....

"That's the joy of being privately funded. We decide. We have a crack research team to help in that."

"Research team?"

"You'd be amazed," he said, his voice taking on a wry note, "how many people sound like they're in the right until you look into the other side."

Kayla sighed. "Then you won't want to help me," she said.

"Why do you say that?"

"Because the other side is the police, and when you look into it you'll probably find some notes saying I'm delusional, disturbed or maybe just crazy."

"Are you?" Hayley asked, sounding merely curious and not at all bothered by the mention of the police.

"No!" Kayla stopped, sighed. "I'm...determined. Dane thinks I'm obsessed. But he and Chad never got along anyway."

She realized she was starting to sound a little mental, talking to total strangers about people they didn't know. She should get out of here. Whoever these people were, they couldn't really do what they said they did. People didn't just help strangers like that. Did they?

And even if they did, what she'd said was true. If they looked into this they'd find all the evidence the police had pointing to Chad and probably some mentions of his sister. Not nasty ones, she didn't think; they had been kind, if unbelieving. They'd probably just gently suggested, in some police jargon, that the suspect's little sister was a bit nuts, driven to the edge of insanity by what had happened.

She needed to get out of here. Getting one of these notes always revved her up, and she needed to calm down, to think. How she was going to do that when she no longer had the option to go to the one person who had always helped her with that, she wasn't sure.

Oddly, the moment she decided to get up and leave the dog awoke from his snooze and scrambled to his feet. Before she could rise he was there, as if he'd somehow read her mind and was once more preventing her from leaving. The animal leaned into her, resting his chin on her leg as he stared up at her. And suddenly it was impossible to move.

"Why don't you start at the beginning?" Quinn suggested.

"And pet Cutter," Hayley added. "It's remarkably soothing."

Kayla nearly smiled at that; people got so silly about their animals. But maybe if she did pet the dog, he'd be satisfied and get out of her way. She lifted a hand and ran it over the dog's head, then, remembering what Quinn and Hayley had done, added a scratch below his right ear. The dark eyes never wavered, but he let out a sound that was amazingly like a happy sigh.

It was soothing, she thought, startled. She felt calmer, steadier. And when Quinn again suggested she start at the beginning, to her surprise, she did.

"Chad is my big brother. We moved here when I was fourteen. He was sixteen. Two years later, ten years ago, our parents were murdered in a home invasion robbery. The police suspected Chad. He ran. I haven't seen him since."

"Well," Quinn said to Hayley without any of the horrified reaction Kayla was used to whenever she told the tale, "that could give Rafe a run for his money for succinctness."

"I'm sure she's had to tell it a few times," Hayley said.

Although there was a world of sympathy in her voice, the auburn-haired woman didn't gush. Nor did she recoil from the blunt, grim story. Kayla was a little amazed at how comforting that was. Like petting this darn dog, a motion she only now realized she'd continued the entire time she'd been speaking. And it really did soothe her at a time when she needed it.

"That," Quinn said, gesturing at the note that began it all, "is from him?"

She nodded. "I get one every few months. He never says where he is, or has been, just that he's sorry he had to leave, he didn't do it and he loves me."

"Where do they come from?" he asked.

"Oregon. Northern California. Idaho. Montana once."

"So he stays in the northwest, generally."

She nodded.

"And what do you do when you get one?" Hayley asked.

Kayla shrugged. "The only thing I can do. I go there, wherever he sent it from."

"Have you ever found anything?"

She sighed. "Nothing useful. I don't have a current photo, obviously. I tried an agency that aged up an old one for me, but it didn't help. A few times in the beginning someone thought they remembered seeing him, but most times it's like he was never there."

"He's gotten better at it," Quinn said, sounding thoughtful.

They both seemed so open, so willing to listen, unlike the police, or even Dane, who had grown so weary of it all.

"I set up a page on a couple of social media sites," she said, "but it's the same problem. And I got more junk than genuinely helpful stuff. Even got some real creeps, pretending to want to help."

She shivered at the memory; if Dane hadn't insisted on going with her every time who knows what would have happened. Twice, guys who looked nothing like their own profile photos, had shown up obviously with something other than help in mind. They'd taken one look at Dane and departed hastily.

"It's definitely a cold case after all this time," Quinn said.

"That's what the police say, too. So why would you help me?"

"I know something about worrying about a brother," Hayley said. "I have one I haven't heard from in months. Walker's not on the run, or in trouble that I know of, but I don't know where he is or how he is."

So the empathy in the woman's voice had been real, Kayla thought. It helped her decide.

"I believe Chad. He didn't do it. I don't care what the police think they know—I know he didn't. He couldn't."

"If it's true, then we'll prove that," Hayley said. "You're not alone any longer, Kayla. You have—"

She broke off as Cutter's head came up suddenly. His eyes had been closed as Kayla petted him—in fact, he'd seemed to be snoozing as she stroked her fingers over his soft fur—but something had clearly brought him to alert. She'd heard nothing, but her ears weren't as keen as a dog's. As Kayla glanced around, she saw nothing different than it had been moments ago. There had been a few people coming and going while they'd been here, and the dog hadn't reacted at all.

She would have written it off to unfamiliar dog behavior if not for two things; Hayley never finished her sentence, and Quinn immediately stood up. And suddenly he was no longer the friendly man with the nice smile, but someone altogether different, alert, ready and capable. He glanced around much as she had, but then he looked at the dog, watching, waiting, as if for some signal.

Cutter's head moved sharply in what looked, impossibly, like a nod.

"What have you got, boy?" Quinn's voice was low, and Kayla heard something in it that hadn't been there before, some edge that made her think Quinn could be a very dangerous man. The dog made an answering sound she couldn't quite describe. Hayley stayed silent, her gaze flicking from man to dog and back, waiting.

The only thing Kayla was sure of was that this, or something like it, had happened often enough that none of the three found it unusual.

She shifted to look around again, wondering what had set the dog off. He seemed to have settled on a direction now, looking out toward the street. And then, unexpectedly, his tail began to wag just slightly. She looked that way and saw nothing amiss—an older couple walking arm in arm, a kid on a skateboard, a man crossing the street from the post office parking lot, a car—

Her gaze shot back to the man. A man heading quickly toward them. The way he moved, with that easy grace and long stride, the way he held his head, the gleam of the morning sun on dark hair....

Dane.

Her pulse kicked up, as it always did at the sight of him. But how had the dog known, of all the people around this morning, that this was the one? And what was he doing here anyway?

Hope leaped in her, but she quashed it; Dane hadn't been angry when they'd parted, or she would have nurtured that hope that he would, as he always had before, get over it. He'd been quietly weary in a way that told her as nothing else could that he was done.

"It's not that I don't admire your loyalty," he'd said. "I do. I just could have used a little more of it myself."

She shivered at the memory of the words and of her own freezing reaction when she'd realized, for the first time, he'd used the past tense.

"You know him?" Quinn's voice broke through the awful memory, and that edge in it shook her back to the present.

"Yes," she whispered. She couldn't think of another thing

to say that would explain who this man was to her. There were no words that were adequate. But as she looked at Quinn, then Hayley, she realized she didn't have to.

They knew.

Chapter 3

"Who the hell are you?"

Dane stared at the man standing between him and Kayla. The guy looked tough, solid and ready for anything. Just about matched his own mood, Dane thought. Which made no sense; who Kayla hung out with wasn't his business anymore. Not that that had stopped him from bolting over here when he'd spotted her with two strangers.

"He's my fiancé." Dane's gaze snapped to the woman who had been sitting beside Kayla. It was further evidence of his mood that he hadn't really focused on her before; she was lovely, and if her words hadn't completely disarmed him, her smile might have. "I'm Hayley Cole, and this is Quinn Foxworth. Behave, both of you."

Dane wasn't sure if she meant him and Quinn or Quinn and the dog. The dog who was looking at him in the oddest way. Not in the love-filled, melt-your-heart kind of way Lilah always had, but with an intensity that spoke of a clever brain behind those amber-flecked dark eyes.

"And you, I gather, are Dane."

The man's voice was steady, with no particular inflection, but Dane couldn't help thinking this was a man who would react quickly and effectively if necessary.

It hit him somewhat belatedly that this stranger had known who he was. And the only way that could be was that Kayla had told him.

His gaze shifted quickly to the woman who had been part

of his life for so long. Had she really told these strangers about him? Maybe even how he'd walked out on her, telling her wrenching story, making anybody who hadn't lived it with her over the past ten years wonder what kind of heartless bastard left a woman whose life had been torn apart like that?

A sense of betrayal filled him, and he took a step back. But it turned out to be only a half-step; somehow the dog had gotten in his way and he had to stop.

"I thought you were through with me," Kayla said. Her voice was quiet, unemotional. And that sparked a new feeling in him, one that was almost anger. She didn't even think they were worth fighting for?

That he didn't want to fight with her, that he never had, was something he cast aside just now. He focused on the fact that she sounded so calm. As if she'd processed that it really was over. And instead of crying over it, or getting angry at him, she was…accepting?

"So that's it?" he said sharply, ignoring the three unknown onlookers. "You just quit on us?"

"You're the one who left." She gestured with the note. "And he's still out there, Dane."

"Yeah. And I'm here. I've done nothing but support you and love you and help you for ten years, while that spoiled, manipulative brother of yours plays with you, taunts you, but is too big of a coward to come back and deal with the mess he left you with."

"Dane! He's not—"

He held up his hands; he really had had enough.

"He always skated by on his looks. He used you, took for granted that you'd always worship your big brother." Dane grimaced. "And I guess he was right about that."

His anger faded as once more the reality hit him in the face. This time she was silent when he took a breath. And he realized he had no right to stay upset at her for talking about them—and him—to strangers when he'd just dumped a pile of dirty laundry in front of them. To their credit, they'd said nothing, but they hadn't left them alone either.

"I tried, Kayla. I really tried." He heard his own voice, realized he sounded as tired as he felt after that last burst of pained rage and resentment. "But I can't play second fiddle to your fixation any longer. I won't. The woman I…loved is buried beneath this obsession and I can't find her anymore. You're on your own."

"That's just it," Kayla said, showing a spark of spirit now. "I'm not on my own anymore."

She waved toward the couple standing a couple of feet away in a gesture that seemed to include the dog.

"They're going to help find Chad."

Suspicion bit as hard and deep as that dog probably could if motivated. Ignoring the jab of pain at the reminder that, although she'd given up on them, she obviously wasn't about to give up on her obsession, Dane spun on his heel to stare at the trio. On the surface they looked harmless enough— handsome guy, beautiful woman, nice-looking dog. Quite the picture they presented.

He didn't believe it for a minute. And he hadn't forgotten his first impression of the man as someone not to take lightly.

"Are they?" he said, focusing on the man introduced as Quinn. "And just how much do they want you to pay for this 'help'?"

One corner of Quinn's mouth quirked, and Dane saw something flicker in the man's eyes, something that looked strangely like approval.

"Nothing," Kayla said.

Dane turned his head to look at her. "Haven't you learned? Didn't that phony P.I. and that guy who took you for five grand in California teach you anything?"

Kayla flushed. He hated doing it, but somebody had to

protect her from herself, and right now he was the only one around.

The dog moved and, oddly, came to sit between him and Kayla. The animal looked from him to her and back, with an expression that looked for all the world like impatience. Dane shook his head; he loved dogs, but he didn't usually impart human qualities to them.

"Quinn?"

It was the other woman who'd spoken, drawing his gaze. She looked the picture of innocence, which made him even more suspicious.

"Yes," the man said. "I think so."

Another stab of pain shot through him. He and Kayla had been like that once, able to communicate without words. But lately he'd quit trying, or even asking what she was thinking, because his gut knew one more admission that she was worrying about her brother would send him over the edge.

And it had.

"Walk with me," Quinn said. Dane eyed him warily. "You have questions," the man said in answer to his look. "I'll give you all the answers you want."

"And I'm supposed to just believe you?"

"No," Quinn said. "I expect you to do your homework and then decide if you believe us."

That surprised him enough to make him follow the man's lead. And if he wanted to be out of earshot of Kayla, it could mean he wanted to hear the other side of the story.

"That note she got today…" Quinn began as they neared a stand of cedar trees along one edge of the park.

"Don't bother. I know exactly what it said. 'I didn't do it. I love you. I'm sorry. Forget about me.' Even as he keeps sending them so there's no hope she ever could."

Quinn stopped walking and turned to look at him.

"I know that sounds harsh," Dane said, "given what she's been through."

"Crimes like that have a far-reaching ripple effect," Quinn said. "They touch many more lives than just the immediate family."

The rather detached yet undeniably true observation made Dane take a second look at the man. He was as tall as he himself, and while Dane biked and ran to keep in shape, he doubted he was as strong as this guy looked. He'd been thinking of adding some weights to his regimen, and just looking at the arms on this guy was enough to convince him.

"Look, I know she loved Chad, but he was…"

"Spoiled and manipulative?"

Dane's mouth tightened. "Yes. Chad never once had to suffer the consequences of his actions in his entire life."

"His parents protected him?"

Dane nodded. "He was the firstborn, and he was spoiled rotten. Until Kayla came along. He was jealous at first, but she adored him so much he finally decided he liked it. She would do anything for him, and he wasn't above using that."

"You didn't know them back then."

He didn't sound particularly accusatory, but Dane was raw enough that he answered a bit sharply.

"Their father told me the first part. The last part I saw for myself. Chad used Kayla from the day he realized she was smarter than he was. I don't know how many school papers he conned her into writing for him, even though she was two years younger. Or how many times he convinced her to lie for him, cover for him, with their parents. A couple of times she even took the blame for something he did when he was skating too close to the edge with their father."

"How long did that go on?"

"Until I was able to convince her she wasn't doing him any favors."

Again Quinn studied him for a moment. "You've always had her best interests at heart."

It didn't seem to be a question, but it reminded Dane he should be worrying about those best interests now. "Who are you? And what's all this crap about helping Kayla find Chad?"

"It's what we do."

"Find missing persons? You some kind of private investigator? Because she's been there, and she got taken. I proved that and convinced her to give up on them," he ended with a pointed glare at Quinn.

He didn't mention the large insurance policy their parents had had, with Kayla and Chad as sole beneficiaries. It wasn't a huge fortune, but it was enough to tempt unscrupulous types. Hayley Cole seemed innocent enough, but there was an edge about this man that made him wonder. He just hoped Kayla hadn't been foolish enough to say anything about the money. He didn't think she would; she might be foolishly obsessed, but she was far from a fool, and she'd learned her lesson after that P.I. ripped her off.

Of course, he also didn't know how much of that money was left after ten years of pouring it into her endless search.

"No, we're not private investigators," Quinn said. "We don't work for just anybody. Only people we believe in."

"And you do it for free? Right." He'd slipped from skepticism into outright sarcasm, but Dane didn't care. He might be through with Kayla, but that didn't mean he didn't care at all; he couldn't turn it off like a faucet.

"That's why we're very particular about what we take on." The man's mouth quirked wryly. "Unless it's somebody Cutter brings to us."

Dane blinked. "The dog?"

Quinn sighed. "It's a long story. But the bottom line is, he's better than a lie detector."

The whimsy of that, coming from a man like Quinn Foxworth, almost made Dane smile. But his own reaction made him even more wary; he knew predators often used animals to lull their targets into trusting them. They didn't seem the type, but did the type ever really seem like the type? He shook his head before his thoughts got even more muddled.

"I think your canine lie detector misfired on this one," he said.

"Kayla mentioned you and Chad didn't get along. Were there other reasons?"

Dane's jaw tightened. "Nothing that has anything to do with this. Why should I believe anything you say?"

Quinn looked at him thoughtfully. He pulled out a business card and handed it to him. "I'm not going to give you answers you'll question. Find your own answers. Do that homework."

"You can count on it," Dane said, letting more than a hint of warning into his voice. "And you stay away from Kayla until I do."

Chapter 4

Dane leaned back in his chair, staring at the computer monitor, tapping his pen on the note pad at his side. The top page was full of scribbled notes; his search had been easier than he'd expected. And quicker. It had only taken him a couple of hours to become convinced.

He'd ignored most of the stuff on the website for the Foxworth Foundation. Anybody, as he knew better than most, could put together a website and put anything they wanted on it. It was a sad fact that if it looked genuine enough, far too many people took it at face value. The Foxworth site gave away very little information, however, as if anybody who went looking for it had to already know what they did.

But he'd noted the areas across the country that had contact numbers for them and then called local authorities in those places. Many had never heard of the foundation and some had heard of them but not had any contact with them, but a few had dealt with them directly, and it was those he concentrated on.

The results were impressive, to say the least. More than one cop or D.A. he spoke to admitted they'd been wary at first, or even irritated that Foxworth was treading their turf, but because most of the cases were cold anyway, they'd decided to let it play out, figuring the amateurs wouldn't be able to do much anyway.

"Boy, were we wrong," one detective told him. "They wrapped up a rape and murder case we'd had to move on from years ago. And they didn't care about taking credit for it either, which smoothed some ruffled feathers around here."

And that seemed to be the theme from the official side. And there were enough stories like that to make him begin to believe the Foxworth Foundation might be for real. So he'd gone on to track down stories about those cases and then find some of the people involved, the people who had turned to Foxworth for help.

The stories there were even more impressive, and the praise imparted was heartfelt and moving. Not only for the success rate, but for the kind of things they took on. From reuniting long separated family members to helping a troubled teenager find the right path, from giving a lost soul a new lease on life to giving a grieving family a reason they could bear for someone's suicide.

And then there was the stolen locket. It was the only memento an adopted child had had of her real mother, and it seemed Foxworth had set upon finding that as wholeheartedly as they had what some would consider more important cases.

He shook his head and sat upright. What he should be focusing on, he told himself, was the fact that on more than one occasion, Foxworth had been instrumental in proving the innocence of people suspected of crimes. Nothing quite as grim as Kayla's parents' murders, but still....

Maybe they could. They seemed to be very good at what they did, and he couldn't deny he liked the idea of what they did.

He picked up the business card and looked at it for a moment. He thought of the stories he'd heard, how many people had said simply, "Someone gave me their card and told me they could help."

He picked up the phone again. This time he dialed the number on the card. To his surprise, Quinn Foxworth himself answered.

"It's a policy we have," the man explained. "Each card has our own number on it. We like to maintain consistency of contact."

"Don't you get a lot of spam calls that way?"

"Some. Better that than make somebody who's feeling helpless jump through the hoops of a big phone menu system."

He heard sounds in the background, some equipment running and the familiar harsh honk of a heron passing overhead; Quinn was obviously outside.

"What if you can't answer right then?" he asked.

"Then it rolls over to our head office. But a live person will always answer."

"That's in St. Louis?"

"Been doing that homework, I see."

"Yes. Detective Saunders in Phoenix says hello, by the way, and Mrs. Louis sends her love."

Quinn laughed. "I thought you might be thorough."

"Yes."

He heard the sound of a door and the background noises ended. Dane wondered where Quinn was, where he'd stepped inside.

"So have you decided we're who we say we are and do what we say we do?" Quinn asked.

"Let's just say I'm open to the idea."

"Fair enough. And I'm ready to believe that you had nothing to do with Kayla's murders."

Dane went still. "What?"

"Your alibi was solid."

"Yes, it was." He'd been with five other kids and a teacher at a college prep study session at the time of death, and he'd never left or been out of sight. He had been home barely fifteen minutes when Kayla's horrific screams from next door had sent him racing over there. "What the hell are you doing investigating me?"

"We're working for Kayla. We'll do whatever it takes to get her the answers she wants."

"Even if it means wasting time on innocent people?"

"If Kayla's right, that means the real guilty person is still out there."

Dane couldn't argue with that. It was something he thought about often, even if Kayla didn't seem to.

And it was the size of that "if" that always threw him.

"Ready to tell me why you and Chad Tucker didn't get along?"

"Hasn't Kayla already told you?"

"I'd like your version."

"Why?"

"We don't build the kind of success rate we have by only listening to one side."

"Fair enough," Dane said. "I didn't like him. Part of it was that in school I was one of the nerdier kids, and Chad was one of the cool guys."

"You don't look like much of a nerd."

"That's because Kayla challenged me to change that."

"Challenged you?"

"She said we couldn't change the fact that people judged on appearance and bought into stereotypes—except by breaking that stereotype. So I started running, lifting weights to get into shape. Found I liked it, and it cleared my head for the tech stuff. And she was right. People looked at me differently, tolerated the…geek in me because that wasn't all I was."

"So she's as wise as she seems."

"Wiser. She was fourteen at the time. Still just the girl next door, who felt like the little sister I never had."

"But she already had a big brother."

"Yeah," Dane said, his tone sour. "And Chad didn't like me either."

"Not surprising, if you saw through him."

Quinn really was open to the idea that Chad might not be the good guy Kayla insisted he was, Dane thought. So he'd meant it when he'd said they weren't taking her viewpoint as the only one. Encouraged by that, he went on.

"When Kayla turned sixteen and her folks let her date, Chad kept trying to set Kayla up with his best friend, Troy Reid. I'd started to look at her differently then, and he wanted to get her away from me. Her folks went along with him—they adored Troy, he was the catch of the whole town, and they thought I was too…something. Her mom, especially."

"But it didn't work. Kayla stayed with you."

"She's incredibly…loyal."

He stumbled over the word, remembering how he'd thrown the word at her the day he'd finally walked away.

"Were there other reasons Chad didn't like you?"

Dane had the uncomfortable feeling Quinn already knew. What was that they told lawyers, about never asking a question you don't already know the answer to? Hell, maybe this Quinn was a lawyer, for all he knew.

"He got into some trouble, a couple of times, right after they moved here."

"Stole a bike, joyriding in a senior citizen's car, breaking into a convenience store for cigarettes?"

So he did know. Dane filed that away to remember when dealing with this man.

"The bike was mine."

"And you reported it."

"My folks did. I didn't care all that much by then—I'd started to drive, but it was a really good bike. And I remembered Chad asking how much it was worth."

"And you told the police that?"

"Yes. And they tracked it down, found who he'd sold it to." Dane jammed his fingers through his hair. "Even then he blamed somebody else. Said Rod Warren, a local punk, had put him up to it. But Chad was no angel, no matter what Kayla thinks."

"Do you think he could have killed them?"

Dane sighed. How long had he been wrestling with that thought? How many times had he been on the verge of telling Kayla just that, only stopping himself because he couldn't bear to see her face if he turned on her. Because that's how she'd see it, he was sure.

In the end, he gave Quinn the answer that had always been his bottom line, even as he realized it stemmed more from his love for his own parents and an inability to relate to the idea of parental murder, than a real belief in Chad's innocence.

"He had no reason to. They were good people. They loved him."

"The police seem pretty certain. He was their only real suspect."

"I know. After he ran, I don't think they ever really focused on anyone else."

"They're a small department, overloaded, and they labeled the case cold fairly quickly. Not their fault—they just don't have the manpower."

"Kayla keeps pushing them, but…"

"They're down to wanted posters and flyers and the occasional search of criminal databases, probably spurred by her pushing."

"And everything is still focused on Chad."

"Yes."

"But Kayla's right about the fact that there's an innocent explanation for all the evidence," Dane said, feeling the need to be fair despite it all. "They found cigarette butts with his DNA outside, but he always snuck out there to smoke. His fingerprints were on the den window, but that's how he always snuck out."

"All true."

"But he ran," Dane said, coming down to the final, damning fact.

"Never a good sign." Quinn sounded completely neutral, like a man who truly hadn't made up his mind. "If it wasn't Chad, who do you think it could have been?"

He had spent literally years batting that one around in his mind. "The only one who ever seemed likely to me was Rod. He tried to hang with Chad, but Troy was too straight-arrow to like him, so that got in the way. For that matter, I always wondered why Troy hung with Chad—they were so different."

"Why did Rod seem likely?"

"He scared Kayla once when she tried to stop him from some kind of twisted experiment with setting butterflies on fire. He...touched her."

Quinn was silent for a moment. "And did he ever again?"

"No. He did not even go near her. Ever."

"I see," Quinn said with what sounded like amusement and understanding. "So, is this Rod still around?"

"Yeah. And he's been in trouble a few times. Breaking into houses and stealing cash."

"Sounds promising. Did the police look at him?"

"They did," he admitted. "But he gave them an alibi they believed."

Quinn didn't miss the inference. "But you didn't?"

"The alibi was that he was with another kid. One he used to harass. Unmercifully. Really harsh stuff. But the kid swore Rod was with him. The cops bought it, figured the kid had no reason not to but every reason to finger Rod if he could."

"But?"

"After that, the harassment stopped."

"So you think he made a deal with the kid?"

Dane shrugged. "Couldn't prove it, but it seemed...coincidental, to say the least."

"We'll check him out," Quinn said.

"What the hell can you do that the cops can't?"

"We have resources. And sources. Time. The manpower. And we have an open mind about Chad's guilt."

"What if you come to believe he's guilty?"

"Then we'll tell Kayla just that. Gently but honestly. Hayley's good at that."

A memory of the couple as they'd stood together this morning in the park shot through his mind. Quinn had constantly been touching Hayley, and vice versa. Little brushes, a touch on the arm, brushing back an errant strand of hair. Even when they were clearly focused on something else, they were still touching, even if it was as simple as standing so close their arms touched. Not quite joined at the hip, but close.

Dane recognized it because he and Kayla were the same way.

Pain jabbed through him, knotting his gut. He and Kayla *had* been the same way.

"Can you really do this? Can you put an end to this one way or another?"

He didn't care that he sounded angry. And he knew quite well he wasn't asking the real question. Asking that would sound more pitiful than he was willing to sound before a man like Quinn Foxworth.

"We can. And we have people who will help Kayla deal with whatever we find."

His confidence was bracing. Dane had spent so long being unable to do anything, about Kayla or her obsession, that he'd slid into unfamiliar territory—hopelessness.

If what he'd learned today was true, these people were the best and brightest at what they did. If they couldn't find Chad, maybe Kayla would finally admit it was over, maybe she would finally move on.

Maybe he'd moved his things a bit too soon. He tried not to let hope rise too far. But it was one last shot, the last chance for them, and he couldn't say no.

Chapter 5

Kayla tried to tamp down her excitement as she hurriedly made her bank deposit. She wouldn't have stopped at all if her mortgage payment wasn't set to go out in three days. But Hayley was gracious about the errand, waiting in her car, and as soon as Kayla was done here, they'd be on their way to what Hayley called the Foxworth building.

After a friendly goodbye to the teller, who happened to be her neighbor's niece, Kayla stuffed her deposit receipt into her purse as she groped for her keys and the fob that would unlock her car door. At the same time, she tried to shoulder the heavy glass door of the bank open.

The door suddenly swung open. "Hey, pretty lady," a familiar voice said, "let me get that for you."

She looked up into the face of Chad's best friend.

"Hi, Troy." Troy Reid gave her a wide smile as he held the door for her. "How are you?" she asked.

Troy had been part of the fabric of her life ever since they'd moved here and he and Chad had become fast friends. Her parents had both liked him, and she suspected they'd secretly hoped some of his charm and friendly manner—and his politeness with adults—would rub off on her brother.

He shrugged. "Things are pretty grim here. I'm thinking of leaving soon."

Kayla felt a surge of empathy. "I understand."

"I admire you, Kayla. It takes courage to stay in the place that has so many ugly memories."

"I'm in a different house, different neighborhood. That helps. But this is home for me. You always wanted to get out of here."

"And I did, for a while," he said with a wry smile.

"Did I ever tell you how wonderful I thought it was that you came back to take care of your mom after your dad died?"

"Yes," he said, then with a smile added, "but you could tell me again."

"It was."

She meant it. It wasn't just guilt that made her say it; she hadn't made it to Troy's dad's funeral. It had been less than a month after the murders, and she just hadn't been able to face it. Troy understood, had been more than kind about it— something she'd always appreciated.

"But not wonderful enough to pry you away from Dane."

She was sure, after all this time, the irritation in his voice was feigned. His laugh a split-second later proved it. And Dane was not a subject she wanted to discuss just now.

"So, you'll be leaving again now?" she asked hurriedly. "Nothing really holding you, if you want to leave, I mean, with both your folks gone."

Well, that was tactful, she thought. Teach her to dodge without thinking.

"And my best friend," Troy said. "Don't forget that."

Kayla blinked. As if she could forget. But until it had come together like this, she hadn't quite realized just how many losses Troy had suffered. As many, in fact, as she had, albeit not in such an ugly way.

"You know, I still don't believe it," he said. "I know what the police think, and he ran and all, but I still can't believe Chad really did it."

The words, from someone who knew Chad almost as well as she did, were balm to her battered spirit.

"Thank you," she said fervently.

He studied her for a moment. Then, gently, he asked, "You still don't believe it either, do you?"

"No. No, I don't. Chad couldn't. Wouldn't."

"I agree." He sighed. "I'd have been trying to prove it myself, if it hadn't been for my dad, then my mom getting sick."

"I know you would," she said.

"Are you still looking for him?"

She nodded. "And I have some help this time. Some people from the Foxworth Foundation."

He blinked. "Who are they?"

"They specialize in helping people when no one else will. Especially with what they call lost causes."

"Never heard of them. Are you sure they're legit? I wouldn't want you getting taken."

You and Dane, she thought. "Thanks for worrying," she said.

Troy reached out and touched her shoulder comfortingly. "If there's anything I can do," he said.

"They may want to talk to you, since you were Chad's best friend."

"Send them around. I'll be happy to talk to them."

"Thank you, Troy."

She felt much better now, she thought when Troy had gotten into his car and gone. He had that knack. And knowing she wasn't the only believer in Chad's innocence helped.

If only Dane felt the same way.

"You really don't know where your brother is?"

Kayla looked at the woman across the table from her. Hayley shook her head. "No. But Walker is just a born wanderer, I'm afraid. I know he loves me, and I love him, but he just has this need see what's over the next mountain. And eventually, he always calls." She smiled then. "But now it feels like I have a ton of siblings. Everybody at Foxworth seems to think I need looking out for."

Kayla couldn't help smiling at her tone of mock grievance. "Is that good or bad?"

"Mostly good."

"You don't seem like you'd need a lot of protecting."

"I don't," Hayley said. "But they love Quinn, and he loves me, therefore…"

She ended the simple yet moving statement with a wave of her hand.

"Nice," Kayla said, trying to quash the now familiar ache that was always threatening to crush her, making it hard to breathe.

"Very. And unexpected."

Hayley's cell phone chirped the arrival of a text message. She excused herself to glance at it. Kayla guessed, from the way her mouth curved into a soft smile, that it was from Quinn.

Kayla glanced around, looking for distraction from the pain that was so close to the surface. She'd been surprised when Hayley had directed her so far out; in fact, she had begun to feel a little leery the farther they'd gone. She supposed that was why it was Hayley, because if she'd been riding with Quinn, she would have been a lot more nervous; for all his offering to help he was still a stranger.

At just the time she really began wondering if she'd made an awful mistake, they'd arrived here. They'd left the city limits of Redwood Cove and entered a more rural county area. The three-story green building was somewhat isolated in a clearing hidden by a thick stand of tall evergreens. The color blended with the trees, making it even harder to spot. There were no markings, not even a street number or name.

"Sometimes we make people unhappy with us," Hayley had explained. "So the less obvious we are, the better."

Off to one side was what looked to be a large warehouse, and on the far side of that, a flat concrete pad with markings painted on it, and an orange wind sock that had been barely stirring in the minimal breeze. A landing site for a helicopter.

"I would have thought you'd have an office in Seattle," she had said.

"Quinn picked this one, and he's not a city boy at heart," Hayley had answered.

No trace of the city here, Kayla thought now as she sat at the large table. The windows here in the top-floor meeting room were large, giving a full view of the rest of the clearing, the trees that ringed it and the sky above. Which was blue today, a clear early-summer day that made the long gray days of winter seem worth it.

Something moved in one of the trees, a large maple amid the firs. Kayla leaned forward, curious, and her breath caught when she realized it was a bald eagle. No, two of them, she thought, a pair, looking as if they were snuggling together on the sturdy branch.

"And that," Hayley said, "is one of the reasons Quinn set up on the third floor even though we're only using half of the first and the second not at all. They come here often."

That bit of information reassured her in a way nothing else could have; the idea of a man like Quinn choosing to situate his office up two flights of stairs just to watch birds—albeit glorious, magnificent birds—was somehow very comforting.

"Tell me about Dane."

Kayla stopped breathing altogether for a moment as the pain she'd quelled for a moment rushed back. Was she that easy to read? Or was Hayley just that perceptive? Probably both, she thought.

"He's obviously crazy about you," Hayley said.

"He was." Even Kayla could hear the ineffable sadness in her voice. Just the sound of it made her sadder still.

"And you?"

"I've loved him in one way or another since I was four-teen."

Hayley simply waited. Kayla sighed.

"That's when we moved here. I met Dane the next day. I climbed the tree between our houses and couldn't get down."

"So he is literally the boy next door?"

"He was then, yes. And he was…wonderful."

She hesitated. She didn't want to say anything that made them think badly of Chad, not when she was asking them to believe her and help prove him innocent, but she also couldn't not give Dane his due. He might have given up on her, on them, but she couldn't deny he'd stuck with her longer than anyone else would have, that he'd been there for her every step of the way until even his considerable patience ran out.

"He was like a brother at first," she said. "Only nicer." The subtext "compared to Chad" was there, and she guessed Hayley knew it, but she couldn't bring herself to say it aloud. Besides, didn't all siblings abuse each other in that familial sort of way? "Dane laughed with me, not at me, for being a skinny, bookish girl with braces. He knew how it felt to be the odd one. You wouldn't believe it now, but he was kind of a geeky-looking guy back then. People teased him, so he understood how I felt."

"He certainly grew up nicely."

She smiled. "Yes, he did. We kind of made a pact. To work on ourselves, but not to let them change who we were inside. We couldn't change other people, but we could change our-selves, challenge the stereotypes."

"That's pretty deep."

"That's the kind of thing we talked about. We used to have long, esoteric conversations about the state of the world and how to fix it, what era of time we'd like to go back to and why, that kind of thing. Even though he was a couple of years older, Dane never treated me like a dumb kid who didn't know anything."

She missed those days, she thought. And wondered if Dane did, too—missed those long talks about everything but themselves because they were fine and destined for a long, happy life together.

"So, you set out to what, change what people assumed?"

Kayla nodded. "Dane started working out and found he actually liked it. Pretty soon he was so fit and strong nobody bullied him to his face anymore. He could throw a football better than any guy in school, but no matter how much they recruited him he wasn't interested. That caught people's attention. He never changed who he was. He was still into computers, but he was making *that* cool."

"And you?"

"I swore I'd never be ashamed of being smart. Never try to hide it. I'd kind of started to do that because I thought the cool kids might like me better."

"It's been my experience," Hayley said with a wry smile, "that most of the 'cool kids' are in fact anything but."

Kayla laughed. "That's what Dane said."

"When did he stop being your surrogate brother?"

Kayla blushed. "I always had a crush on him. But he... well, I was just a kid. The difference between fourteen and sixteen is a lot bigger than sixteen and eighteen."

"Is that when it changed?"

"Sort of. At least, it started to, and then...my parents were killed."

"And Dane was there for you."

Kayla nodded. "Every minute. He never left my side. He took care of things I couldn't, did things I didn't have the presence of mind to even think of."

She fought off the memories, trying not to let them swamp

her. It didn't happen often anymore, but when it did, it was as fresh and vivid and horrible as if it had been yesterday.

She felt the warmth of a touch and realized Hayley had reached across the table to put her hand over hers.

"I can't imagine." Those vivid green eyes were fastened on her and full of warmth and concern. "That you're even upright is a testament to your strength."

"Dane used to think that," Kayla said with a sad smile. "Now I'm afraid he just thinks I'm crazy."

"Ten years is a long time." Hayley's voice was very even, and Kayla wondered how hard she was having to try to keep it that way.

"So I should give up on my brother?"

"I didn't say that. You are between the proverbial rock and a hard place."

"Chad has his flaws—I'm not blind—but he's no killer. I can't just quit on him. People say I should forget about it, but—"

"You can't."

"No."

"That's always irritated me," Hayley said, as casually as if they were discussing the weather, "when people say forget about it, put it out of your mind. Like the memory is a physical thing you could grab and shove in a box and hide. You can't. But you can reduce the time you spend on it, and the only thing that can do that is time."

"Dane says quit feeding it."

"Good way to put it. But it still takes time. You can not dwell on it, you can have other things ready to supplant it for when it pops into your mind, you can keep busy to distract yourself, but you have to do all that long enough that it recedes from the front of your mind. And you can't when these notes keep coming."

Kayla was so grateful Hayley seemed to understand that she felt her eyes begin to tear up.

"Thank you for understanding." Something occurred to her, and as she looked at Hayley's gentle smile—no wonder her Quinn adored her, she was wonderful—she decided to ask.

"You've been there, haven't you?"

"Yes. My mom died last year, of cancer. And my father was a cop. He was killed in the line of duty when I was twelve."

Kayla's breath caught. "How awful."

"That's how I know forgetting's not possible. Just like Quinn does."

"He…lost someone, too?"

"He was younger than you were. Just a little guy. His parents were both on that airliner a terrorist brought down—bombed—over Scotland in 1988."

Kayla gasped. "I remember my parents talking about that, on the anniversary of it, when I was little. They were horrified, all those innocent people. They thought it was one of the worst things that would ever happen."

"I wish they'd been right," Hayley said quietly.

The unmentioned memory, of the even more hideous attack that had happened thirteen years later hung between them for a moment.

"That was, in essence, the reason our foundation exists. When they turned the man who did it loose, the injustice of it, when those men in back rooms who had never suffered the loss made that decision, Quinn made one of his own."

"And started the Foxworth Foundation?"

Hayley nodded. Kayla understood.

"September 11 was one of the reasons we moved here," Kayla said. "My parents wanted to be out of the city. My mother couldn't even bear to look at a skyscraper, and my dad would stare at every jet that flew overhead until it was out of sight."

She stopped abruptly, the old, sad irony battering at her. She heard a bark from outside and wondered vaguely if it was Cutter.

"And two years later, they were dead anyway."

Hayley's words would have seemed cold, harsh even, had they not been spoken in such a gentle voice. And if they hadn't been exactly the words Kayla had been thinking herself.

She tried to pull herself together. Everything seemed so much closer to the surface than it had been for a while. It was like that whenever a note came, but she had to admit this was more. Because this time she was dealing with it without Dane's help, without his steadying presence, without his un-wavering strength bolstering her.

"Yes. They were."

"What happened to you? At sixteen, you were too young to be on your own," Hayley said.

"My dad's sister happened, bless her. She took me in until I went off to college. Aunt Fay never had kids of her own, couldn't, but she loved me. She did her best, we got along great, she was fun and smart and the best thing that could have happened to me, under the circumstances."

"Dane," Hayley said.

"He was already in college by then. I—"

"No. I meant…" She gestured toward the door to the meeting room. Kayla turned.

He was here.

Chapter 6

Quinn, who had come into the room right behind Dane, signaled to Hayley and they left them alone to talk. It was, oddly, Cutter who seemed most reluctant to go. The dog, who had arrived with Quinn, lingered in the doorway, looking from Kayla to Dane as if he didn't want to leave them alone.

Maybe he thinks we'll start fighting, Kayla thought with a sigh.

But when Dane crossed the room and sat in the chair Hayley had vacated, she realized that, although he seemed tense, he wasn't angry. She could read his mood almost as well as her own, sometimes better, and he wasn't angry. Because he'd given up? Had he let all the anger go when he'd walked away?

"I checked them out," he said abruptly. "From what I could find, they seem to be who they say they are."

Kayla went still. If he no longer cared at all, surely he wouldn't have bothered, right? She didn't ask, mainly because she wasn't sure she wanted to hear the answer. She didn't know why he was here, and she didn't want to ask that either. Instead, she explained what Hayley had told her about the founding of Foxworth.

"So Quinn was a victim," Dane said.

She heard the musing note in his voice and understood; it was hard to picture today's strong, tough Quinn as any kind of victim.

"He was only ten," Kayla said. "And Hayley's father was a police officer who was killed when she was twelve."

He drew back slightly. "Is that why you trusted them both so quickly? You felt connected because of all that?"

"I didn't know all that then. But I knew they understood."

"And I don't."

"I didn't say that. I've never said that."

"But I'm lucky, right?" He was starting to sound confrontational. "I'm not a member of the club. I'm the only one here not damaged by tragedy."

She winced at the oblique reference to her counseling group. She'd called it Collateral Damage because that's what they were. Just as wounded as the actual victims, yet still up and walking around. She'd thought of Walking Wounded, but that didn't make the point she so strongly believed in—that the perpetrators didn't care who else they hurt. In war, it was an expected part of the grim business. But for civilians, it was the ugliest of side effects.

"Believe me, it's a club you don't want any part of." She took in a quick breath. "Besides, I always thought you'd been damaged by mine. Because you loved me."

As quickly as that, his demeanor changed. He let out a long, compressed breath.

"All right," he said. "If these people are as good as they say, maybe they can do something."

Her heart leaped in her chest, and hope sparked to renewed life.

"Dane!"

He reached across the table and took her hands in his. The touch, the contact, made joy well up inside her, as if some vital part of her had been restored.

"Listen to me, Kayla. I'm willing to give them a chance. Everything I've found indicates they are really good at what they do."

"Yes," she answered, tightening her fingers around his, feeling an elemental fear that if she didn't hang on, he would somehow vanish again. "Yes, I think they are. Maybe even the best. Hayley showed me some of their case records. No names, but—"

"Then if they can't find Chad, it's likely nobody can."

She saw suddenly where he was going. And knew his next words would require a decision from her. A difficult one. But nothing could be more difficult than his absence from her life the past two weeks.

"Yes," she finally said.

"Then if they can't, if this comes to nothing, will you quit making this the sole purpose of your life?"

She drew in a deep breath. She'd had a brief taste of life without him, and it had been immediately clear that it was worse, much worse, than life without knowing how and where Chad was. And she knew Dane, knew she'd pushed him to the edge, and that he was here now at all was a testament to the power of what they'd built together from the day he'd climbed up that tree to sit beside her. He'd understood her even then, that what she'd wanted, needed, wasn't someone to come along and rescue her, but someone to help her figure out how to rescue herself.

She knew what she would be promising if she said yes.

"I won't ever stop wondering, or worrying," she said, wanting it to be perfectly clear.

"I wouldn't expect you to. I just want to know that you won't obsess over it anymore, that you'll take back your own life. Our life, together."

He didn't say, "Or it's over," but the words hung in the air between them as clearly as if he had.

"Will you give them a real chance and enough time?"

"I'll give them a full, honest chance, if you'll agree to accept whatever they find."

Still feeling torn, she nevertheless gave the only answer she felt possible.

"All right," she said.

Dane let out an audible breath. And then he was on his feet, pulling her up and into his arms. Kayla nearly wept at the rightness of it. She clung to him, trembling at how close she'd come to losing this, losing him, forever.

She didn't know how long had passed before she heard a slight jingle from the doorway. She looked up and saw Cutter trotting into the room, tail up and waving slightly. The dog came to a stop before them and sat down. He looked at them both, with an expression Kayla would have sworn was satisfaction.

Quinn and Hayley followed the dog into the room.

"Why Cutter?" Kayla asked.

"He came with the name," Hayley said, reaching to scratch the dog's ear. "He turned up on my doorstep with only that tag. I tried but never could find out where he'd come from."

The dog tilted his head way back to look at Hayley without changing position, looking so comical as he did it that Kayla couldn't help but laugh. She heard Dane chuckle beside her and savored the sound of it; she'd missed his easy laugh, not just in the past two weeks but, she had to admit, for much longer. She'd caused that, she realized regretfully.

"I spent some time with a friend of mine this afternoon," Quinn said in a back-to-business tone as Hayley gestured everyone back into the chairs around the table. "Sam works for the local sheriff's office."

Kayla sank down into the chair Dane held for her, feeling suddenly wobbly. This all seemed to be happening quickly now that it had begun. She'd only met them this morning, yet Quinn was already on the move.

"The sheriff's office? But the Redwood Cove police handled the case."

"Yes, but the sheriff's office did most of the forensics. Redwood Cove doesn't have its own lab."

"Oh. Yes."

"Sam was able to pull up the reports for me, at least the basics. The locals trust this guy. He can get answers that others can't because of that."

"Meaning distraught, crazy family members?" Kayla knew she sounded bitter but couldn't help it.

"They never thought you were crazy. And if you were distraught, they knew you had good reason."

She sighed. "To be fair, they never said so. In fact, except for a couple who got sharp about it, told me they had their suspect and to give up, they were unfailingly kind. Even though I knew they hated to see me coming."

"Cops get that way when they can't help any more than they already have."

"But they could have. They could have looked for other suspects, they—"

She stopped herself before the whole, long, painfully familiar spiel unwound.

"You know what the evidence was," Quinn said gently. "It's pretty conclusive that Chad was in that room either during or shortly after the murders."

"The bloody fingerprint," Dane said.

Quinn nodded. "He's certain it was left while the blood was…"

Quinn's voice trailed off as he looked at Kayla.

"Still wet," she finished for him. "Fresh. I know. I've heard it a hundred times. I'm used to it."

"It's still awful," Hayley said. Her tone was comforting, but nothing made Kayla feel better than Dane's arm tightening around her.

"Yes. But I'm not going to fall apart talking about it. I really don't wallow it in every day."

She managed not to glance at Dane, although that wasn't

really fair; he'd never accused her of wallowing, only of letting this overwhelm her own life.

"I never disputed that Chad was there," she said. "He still came to the house often, even though he'd moved out. He'd sneak in through the den window and then head to the kitchen to get food."

"So you think that's what he intended that night? To raid the fridge?" Quinn asked.

She nodded. "And he found them lying there in the den, panicked and ran."

"Leaving you to deal alone, as usual," Dane said.

Kayla stiffened. Dane let out a compressed breath. "Sorry," he muttered. "I'll stop. I promised you one last shot, and I meant it."

Neither Quinn nor Hayley commented on the moment of tension, although Cutter let out a low whine as if he'd sensed it and didn't like it. After a moment, Quinn nodded.

"I'll need some things from you," he said. "Names of Chad's friends, his interests. Then the same about your parents."

Kayla frowned slightly. "That was all in the reports."

Quinn smiled. "Sam bends the rules occasionally, but letting those reports leave the building without me jumping through all the hoops would be outright breakage. That we'll have to do through regular channels."

"Sorry," Kayla said. "Of course."

"Plus, I'd like to save bugging the local LEOs for things we can't get anywhere else. They're a bit understaffed."

"Back at the time, they were thinking about dissolving the department and going back to contracting with the sheriff because they were so strapped and short-handed," Dane said. "Maybe that's partly why they didn't pour a lot of energy into this after Chad ran."

Kayla wanted to hug him for that; it was the most supportive thing he'd said lately.

"I know once they verified where I'd been at the time of
the murders," Dane went on, "they didn't have time to talk
to me much."

"Except when you'd push them, for me."

He deserved that acknowledgment, Kayla thought. For a
long time, longer than most would, Dane had been right there
with her, at the forefront, pushing, nagging, pressing the police. Dane gave her a smile that further warmed a heart that
had been nearly frozen by his departure two weeks ago. He'd
really asked so little of her, she thought. And she'd abused
that.

"It got so they hated to see us coming," Dane said.

"Can't blame them," Quinn said. "It's a small department,
they've got a huge case on their hands and they have no resources or experience dealing with that kind of thing. Sam
said Detective Adams was a good guy, but he was out of his
depth on this. And by the time he asked for help, what trail
there was had gone cold."

"He knows that," Kayla said quietly. "He admitted that to
me last year, when he retired. He feels guilty about it."

Dane gave her a sideways look. "You never told me that."

"You didn't want to hear anything about it by then," Kayla
said, carefully keeping any sort of accusation out of her voice;
Dane was back at her side, and she simply had to keep him
there. She knew that now, that nothing mattered more.

"I'll need the same info from you, too," Quinn said to
Dane. "Anything and everything you can remember."

Dane nodded.

"And no comparing lists," Hayley said. "You each have
your own memories and viewpoint, and we need them as
pure as possible."

Kayla nodded, although the words made her a little nervous. Dane and Chad's mutual dislike was going to color Dane's recollections. But he was doing it, cooperating, which was more than she'd had this morning. She didn't ever want to feel that alone again.

She would keep her promise as Dane was keeping his, she vowed. She would pour all she had into this last-ditch effort, she would do whatever Quinn and Hayley said was necessary and, in the end, she would accept the results.

And then, she swore silently, she would do what Dane had wanted her to do for a very long time now.

She would move on.

Chapter 7

Аll the way back to her house, Kayla fought the memories stirred up by spending two hours writing down everything she could think of—the name of every one of Chad's friends, descriptions of those she couldn't remember the names of, every place he used to hang out and putting a star on the most frequent, even listing the times he'd gotten in trouble and with whom. She didn't want to sugarcoat anything.

Dane had commented on that, when he'd seen her list after finishing his own, shorter one and going over it with Quinn; Hayley had taken Cutter outside for a run while they worked. Kayla had been grateful for that; the dog was almost spooky in the way he looked at them, the way he seemed to sense every change, every shift in mood, and understand it in a way that had to be impossible for a dog.

"You told them about when he got arrested twice," Dane had said.

"Yes." She'd stood up to face him. "Once, all I wanted was to prove Chad innocent. Now I just want the truth."

Dane had blinked, clearly startled. "When did that happen?"

"About two weeks ago," she had said, knowing he'd understand. "Everything changed two weeks ago."

They'd agreed at the Foxworth facility that they'd spend some time searching their memories for anything they might have forgotten, any additional details that might help.

She pulled into her driveway now and for a moment just sat there.

She had considered, seriously, that she might have to sell her beloved little house. She'd bought it with the cash from the sale of her parents' home, a place she had known she could never set foot in again. She didn't want to move again, but she didn't think she could bear to live here without Dane. They weren't living together in the usual sense—he still had his place, but he also ran his business out of the den, and the work tended to spill over into the rest of the house. So he spent most nights here unless he was on a major project and working eighteen-hour days.

That boy'll go far. He's not afraid of hard work.

Her father's words echoed in her head. As did his tone, touched with a sadness it had taken her a few years to figure out was over not being able to say that about his own son.

Her father had liked Dane, although that hadn't stopped him from keeping a close watch when Kayla had been younger. But he'd soon been convinced Dane looked at her like a little sister, and sadly, he was a much better protector than Chad was, standing up for her more than once when those who thought her too studious and odd started harassing her.

And then Dane was there, pulling his compact SUV in beside her, and her world snapped back into balance. For a moment the relief that he was back swamped her, making it impossible for her to move.

He waved at her next-door neighbor, Mr. Reyes, who was out working in his yard as usual. The man called out a cheerful hello and went back to trimming his hedge. It was a measure of how distracted she was, Kayla supposed, that she hadn't even noticed him there.

Dane came over and opened her driver's door.

"You okay?"

"I will be," she said, meaning it.

But when they got inside, it didn't take long for her improved outlook to be shaken. She noticed first one thing, then another, ran to the bedroom then the bathroom and finally turned on him.

"Your things are gone."

He didn't deny the obvious. "Yes."

"They weren't this morning."

"I knew you'd be gone this morning so I came over and got them. I didn't want to fight."

The same sort of creeping chill that had overtaken her when she'd realized he was serious this time began to envelop her again. He really had left her. He'd packed up all of the things that had gradually made their way over here—toothbrush, clothes, books, razor, the laptop he kept here in case something came up that was too much to handle on his tablet, all of it was gone. The reality pounded at her in a way it hadn't when his familiar things were still there, and she realized she hadn't really accepted it, investing hope in those inanimate objects, hope that he didn't really mean it.

Now she knew he had. And was thankful he hadn't done it before.

"Then why," she said when she thought she could speak without her voice wobbling, "did you show up at the post office?"

He didn't dodge that either. But then, this was Dane, who was utterly honest, forthright and occasionally blunt. As he was now.

"This," he said, reaching into the watch pocket of his jeans and pulling out the square gold key that had been on his key ring since the day she'd given it to him five years ago.

A shiver went through her. "Dane—"

He waved a hand. "Let's not. We're going to deal with this, give it our best shot, and then…then we'll see where we are."

Slowly, reluctantly, she nodded. She wanted to know now, wanted to hear him say he was back, that things would be fine, that they would pick up their old, familiar life.

He didn't say any of it.

He's an honest one. Doesn't just tell you want you want to hear. I admire that.

Again her father's voice echoed in her head, as clearly as if he were standing beside her.

And she wondered if she'd really gotten Dane back at all.

Dane watched as she turned the pages of the old scrapbook she'd dug out of a box in the back closet. It seemed a good idea, to help stir any memories that might help.

He'd seen it before, had gone through it himself, because he wanted to know everything about her and loved seeing the early pictures of a wide-eyed, dark-haired pixie who had seemingly faced the world with an endless wonder.

There were several of her and her brother together, with Kayla generally staring up at him adoringly while Chad looked annoyed and sullen. They were eighteen months apart, Dane knew, and he'd often wondered if things would have been different, if Chad would have acted differently toward her, if it had been more.

She turned another page and there was the photograph he'd been waiting to see. Kayla, now a brand-new junior, off to her first school dance. A worldly high school graduate himself now, about to leave for college, he'd come by to return a borrowed book that evening and found her father chuckling over the fact that she and her mother had been holed up all afternoon, preparing.

But when Kayla, barely sixteen, had come down the stairs, Dane wasn't chuckling at all. His odd, shy, bookish, tree-sitting buddy was nowhere in sight. Instead he saw a young, slender woman with graceful curves highlighted by the fitted, strapless, shimmery dress she wore. Her hair was smoothed into a sleek sweep, her eyes seemed huge and luminous, her mouth touched with a color that made him wonder what it would be like to kiss it off.

And that had taken his breath away.

She'd come to a halt at the bottom of the stairs and given him an impish smile.

"Did it work?" she asked.

"I— What?"

He knew he sounded like he felt—gobsmacked.

"I promised you I was going to play the game, do all the girly stuff, just to show them I could if I wanted to."

"Kayla." It was all he could get out, even though she was suddenly looking anxious.

"It's like we talked about," she said, the anxiety echoing in her voice. "Show them I can, then when I don't, they know it's because I don't *want* to. My choice. Just like you did, making the football team, getting everybody fired up about how good you are, then walking away because it was your choice not to play their game."

"And that had its down side, if you recall." He'd proved his point, but he hadn't realized some would take it as dissing the whole school by not wanting to play for the team that represented them.

"But they respected you," Kayla had said. "That's all I want."

He didn't remember now what he'd finally said to ease her nerves. But he'd made her smile, reassured, so it had worked. And he spent the remainder of his own evening reminding himself she was still his young, very smart, annoyingly honest and perceptive sounding board. And he was still the boy next door to her, her sounding board in turn, sometimes her protector, but always her listener.

"Dane?"

He snapped out of his reverie.

"I remember that night," he said, unable to help or care that his voice was a little husky. "Two years seemed so little separation and yet so long."

"I didn't ask you to wait until I was eighteen."

"Anything else seemed a little too…predatory to me."

For a moment she just looked at him, and then she smiled, that slow, dawning Kayla smile that always reminded him that there was warmth in the world, no matter how cold it might seem at any given moment.

"You were—and are—a gallant man, Dane Burdette."

Her use of the old-fashioned term made him smile in turn, even though he hadn't felt in the least gallant at the time. Only his vow to wait until she was eighteen had made his new-found appreciation of her as a woman acceptable. Where his eighteen-year-old self had found the will to wait he wasn't sure, although he was ruefully aware that the stigma of dating a high school girl when you'd graduated had played a bigger part than he'd like to admit. With Kayla's support he had flouted the expected norms with some success, but he had found himself unable to get past that bit of peer pressure. And he'd harbored the notion that maybe, if he put her off-limits, he'd just get over her in that two years.

He hadn't.

And then three months after that dance her parents were dead, changing both their lives forever, and self-control was no longer an issue. He would no more risk further damage to her already shattered soul than he would cut off his own arm. He'd shoved his newly awakened awareness of her into a cage and locked it, setting out to be what she needed and only what she needed—a strong shoulder, a comforting ear and a safe place to be.

He'd succeeded, he thought.

He'd just never expected to be in essentially the same place ten years later.

Chapter 8

Kayla woke up screaming. And alone.

The nightmares had, thankfully, become rare. But when they came, they were as vivid and terrifying as ever. And real, all of it—walking into the dark den, hearing the odd squish of the carpet, reaching for the light switch, then wishing she hadn't as the scene flashed into being before her stunned eyes.

Normally Dane was there to hold her, easing her out of the remembered horror gently, not pushing her, not giving her meaningless platitudes, not telling her it would be all right when it never could be, but simply holding her, his strength and understanding flowing to her as if there were a direct connection between them.

But Dane was not here.

He had left early last evening, refusing to settle right back into the routine they had developed over the years. She supposed she should feel hurt, but she was more scared than anything. This further evidence that things weren't the same had rattled her. He was back, and yet he wasn't. It pounded home to her anew that their relationship had been damaged.

Shaking, she reached for her phone. She knew it was late, after midnight, but she couldn't help it—she had to hear his voice. If he was angry that she'd woken him up, so be it.

He answered on the first ring and sounded anything but asleep.

A possibility hit her, biting deep. It was Friday night. And until today, until the Foxworth Foundation had been brought into things, Dane had been through with her.

A date. Had he been out on a date? Was that why he'd insisted on leaving early? Had he already started seeing someone else? He would never have cheated on her; she knew that as surely as she knew his eyes were golden. It just wasn't in him. But he'd told her he was done two weeks ago. Enough time to ask someone else out. More than enough time if he'd already known her, whoever she was.

And whoever she was, she likely had a much simpler life, free of trauma and tragedy. Dane would probably find that wonderfully refreshing, and—

"Kayla?"

Stop it, she ordered herself. Get a grip. "I'm sorry," she said into the phone. "I know it's late."

"Did you think of something?"

It took her a moment to realize what he meant, and the only thing that stopped her from letting out the sound that rose in her throat was the fear it would sound like some crazed woman's maniacal laughter.

"No, but I learned that there's something worse than my old nightmare."

His voice changed then. Went softer, gentler. "You had it again?"

"Yes."

"Not surprising. A lot of old memories were stirred up today."

"Are you one of them?"

"What?" He sounded puzzled now.

"An old memory."

"I know that nightmare shakes you up, but what are you talking about?"

"Did you have a date tonight?"

"What?"

"You insisted on leaving. It's Friday night. It's after midnight and you're wide awake."

She heard him let out a long breath. "So you decided I was out on a date? That's three facts and an awful lot of supposition."

"Not decided. Wondered."

He answered her in typical Dane fashion: honestly and a bit bluntly. "That it's Friday has nothing to do with anything. I'm not there because I'm not sure you can really leave this behind if the results they get aren't what you want, and I'm not going to lay myself out for that kind of pain again. And I'm awake because, damn it, I miss you and can't stop thinking about you."

And in those few words, spoken with an edge in his voice, he blasted Kayla's silly panic to bits.

"Oh."

Her voice sounded tiny even to her. For a long moment, silence hung in the air between them.

"I promised you I would move on after they find…whatever they find."

"I know you did."

"You think I didn't mean it?"

"You've spent ten years on this quest. It's been a huge part of your life—it's sunk into your bones. So I think promising now, and really letting go when it's over, are two different things."

She couldn't deny a single word he said. Nor could she think of a single thing to say that would convince him she'd meant what she'd said.

Maybe he was right. Maybe when the time came, she wouldn't be able to just let it go.

"I'm sorry about the nightmare." He sounded cooler now, less on edge.

"It's all right. Like I said, I found out there's something worse—waking up to the reality that you're gone."

There was a pause before he said quietly, "I just can't slide right back into life as before, Kayla."

"I'm going to start now," she said. Her voice still seemed a little shaky, so she added some emphasis. "Right now."

"Start what?"

"Wrapping my mind around the idea—the fact—that when this is over, if they don't find him, I'm done. I'll always wonder and worry, but I won't lose you over him. Chad's my brother, but you're my life."

Her voice had gotten stronger as she went. As had her resolve.

"I love you," Dane said after a moment.

"I know," she said. "Or you would have walked away long ago."

It was an admission she'd never made to him before, although she'd often thought it, often wondered why he hadn't left her to find somebody without all her baggage. She'd never dared speak it, for fear it might make it really happen. But now that it had, she felt compelled to speak the words.

Now she had to live up to them.

Dane leaned back against the pillow he'd tossed on the end of the sofa in his living room. He'd given up on the bed around eleven, laughing ruefully at himself.

"Can't live with her, can't sleep without her," he'd muttered just before his phone had rung. He'd grabbed it, needing to hear her voice, answering before he remembered he'd sworn not to jump right back into the life he wasn't sure yet had changed at all.

Amazing how one phone call could make everything feel so different. She'd been different, sounded different. And in a good way for him.

...there is something worse than my old nightmare.

He couldn't even begin to describe the feeling that gave him. When he'd walked away he'd been afraid that she would simply go on, filling in whatever empty place he left behind with her quest, perhaps even welcoming his absence so she could focus on it completely.

When it came right down to it, he'd never been sure how big a place he had in her mind and heart. If it was bigger than Chad. Selfish, maybe. But true. He knew she loved him; the question that had always nagged at him was how much.

At the same time, he'd felt he was being unfair. What was she supposed to do—just go on with her life as if her brother had never existed?

He rolled over, punching the pillow with more force than was necessary. He wished now he'd stayed. But the part of him that had been ripped open when he'd finally walked away was still raw, and his fear was real.

He only realized he'd finally fallen asleep when his cell rang and woke him. His pulse jumped, but when he looked at the screen before answering it wasn't Kayla's number.

"Dane? Quinn Foxworth."

"Oh."

He sat up. The crazy thought hit him that they'd already found Chad. He glanced at the time on his phone. Nine-fifteen. The realization that they'd been on the ten-year-old case barely twenty-four hours steadied him.

"I woke you?"

"Sorry. Rough night."

"I can call back—"

"No, no. It's okay. What did you want?"

"I needed to ask you about something. On your list, you said Chad used to hang out with a chop shop guy."

Dane rubbed at his eyes. "Yeah. That's where he met Rod. Rumor was the guy had a place over on Raccoon Bay, an old barn he used. Can't remember his name, but when Chad got nailed for joyriding, I thought maybe it was more than just that."

"You thought maybe he was stealing the car?"

"I wondered."

"Did you tell the police?"

"Not that I suspected Rod. I told them Chad was friends with the guy. They went from there. But they said later they couldn't find any proof Chad had meant to actually steal the car." He felt compelled to be fair and added, "And he was heading back toward where the car had been when they stopped him."

"Did Kayla know?"

"I don't know if she knew Chad hung with the guy sometimes. I never said anything to her about it—she was already touchy enough."

"She truly loves her brother."

"Yeah." Dane hesitated, then asked, "You have any brothers or sisters?"

"One."

"I don't. I figure maybe that's why I don't get it. Maybe I really don't understand."

"It's like any family thing," Quinn said. "Different depending on the people. I've come across some siblings who hate each other fiercely. And some who merely coexist without much interest in each other."

"What about you?"

"I'd die for Charlie," Quinn said simply.

No, Dane thought after he disconnected the call, maybe he just didn't get it. He tried to picture what he'd do if Kayla was accused of something he was certain she hadn't done, but it was a different kind of thing. He thought of Sergei, who had been his friend for years, and helped him start Sound Digital Video. What if he was accused of hacking a bank or something even worse? The idea was laughable. Serge might sneak his way into the hottest gaming company around, but nothing more.

But he tried to imagine the scenario. If Serge vanished after the crime, how would he feel? What would he do? To what lengths would he go to find him and help him?

A long way, he thought. But ten years of unrelenting searching?

It was, Dane thought as he wearily headed for the shower, a lousy comparison. Serge was a good friend but not a brother. And the crime wasn't some computer hacking but a literal hacking, the slaughter of two people.

He thought of his own parents then, all they'd done for him, given him, how they'd supported him, believed in him, even given him a loan to keep SDV going until it started gaining some traction in a crowded field. The day he'd paid them back was one of the best of his life. They were proud of him—he knew that. And he loved them both. It was one of the reasons he'd lasted as long as he had with Kayla's quest. He couldn't imagine losing them both and in such a horrible way. If he'd had a brother, maybe he couldn't believe he could kill two loving people like that either.

He knew not all parents were as good as his—his were living proof of the old joke about how the older you got, the smarter your parents seemed to get—but Kayla's, from what he remembered, hadn't been bad, although he'd thought they favored their son a bit too much.

Which made what Chad was accused of doing make even less sense.

Hot water streamed over him, and he felt a bit more awake. He finished quickly; he had an online meeting today with an app developer in Nevada who wanted a video for an upcoming trade show.

He was just pulling on his socks when his phone rang

again. His pulse kicked up, but a quick glance showed the smiling picture of his mother, one he'd taken a couple of years ago at their thirtieth wedding anniversary. Odd how that happened sometimes—he'd think about them and then they'd call, or he'd call and his mom or dad would say they'd just been thinking about him.

He reached for the phone, thankful he hadn't told his folks about his decision to leave Kayla so now he didn't have to explain why he was back. His mother had been telling him, gently and with love, that perhaps he should find someone more willing to focus on him than the past. She cared for Kayla, but she loved her son and wanted him to find the kind of happiness she had with his father.

His answer had always been that he was happy. He loved Kayla and admired her loyalty to her brother. But in some part of his mind he was agreeing. He wanted someone who wasn't caught up by the past, who was focused on a future with him.

Problem was, he wanted that person to be Kayla, and he hadn't been ready to give up on that.

Until two weeks ago.

And now?

What happened now, he thought as he prepped himself to sound cheerful to his mother, depended on Kayla.

And Quinn Foxworth and his crew.

Chapter 9

Dane tapped his fingers idly on the restaurant table as he waited for Kayla.

She was trying. Truly making an effort. Dane could see that. Whenever she wasn't working, she was pushing for them to be together. She called him regularly, texted him and told him she loved him so often that the ache inside started to ease up. This was the way he'd always wanted it to be. He should be happy. He was happy. He'd be delirious if it wasn't for the nagging question of how long this would last.

She rarely mentioned Chad or even the Foxworth Foundation. He knew she was likely in regular contact with Quinn and Hayley, but she said nothing. Had there been no developments, or was she just not telling him?

He nearly laughed aloud at himself.

You can't have it both ways, he told himself. You either want her to talk about it, or you don't want to hear it. That's a conflict you can't resolve by updating drivers or getting new hardware.

That sort of humming awareness he had whenever she was around suddenly kicked into high gear. Oddly, he thought of Cutter and how the dog not only knew someone was coming, but also who. Maybe the dog really was more human than canine.

Or maybe you're more dog, he thought wryly.

Whichever, his instincts were right because a moment

later he saw her coming down the aisle of the restaurant toward him.

There wasn't a trace of the gawky, skinny girl from the tree branch in the lovely, graceful woman approaching. Her hair, cut in that way that made it sweep forward in a smooth curve just at her jawline, made him want to see it tousled from his hands and a night of passion again. The gray silk blouse tucked into black slacks emphasized the curves he knew so well. Need cramped his body, and he had to consciously suck in a breath to get any air at all. He barely managed to stand as she came to a stop beside the table.

"I'm not late, am I?"

She sounded anxious, and he shook his head, still unable to speak for a moment. She slid her bag—he'd always thought that huge thing she carried too large to be called merely a purse—off her shoulder and settled into the chair he held for her.

He was breathing again, albeit a bit deeply.

"How was work?" he asked, taking refuge in small talk.

"Sad."

He barely managed not to say, "Isn't it always?"

Kayla's grief counseling service for crime victims and their friends and families was thorough, coordinating and running group meetings of survivors, arranging appointments with therapists and often personally contacting people she thought could benefit from their services. It was the brainchild of Kayla herself and a wealthy private benefactor who had been in need years ago but there had been nothing of the kind available, nothing with this kind of specific focus. So the woman had channeled the money left to her by her murdered husband into this idea and hired Kayla to run it.

And Kayla was great at it—he knew that, just as he knew it was work that was much needed.

He was also convinced that it was part of the reason she

had never been able to move on from her own tragedy. He didn't doubt that, as she told him, it helped her to help others who lived with the same kind of grief, but it also meant she was immersed in it every day. He would never ask her to quit—and if he did she'd probably have been the one to walk away—but he wished she could find a little more balance. But it didn't appear she saw the irony of someone who'd never quite gotten over her own grief counseling others.

"A new arrival?"

"No. I didn't mean sad like that. Sad because Mr. Egland is leaving."

He quickly placed the name. "That's the older guy whose wife died in the arson fire?"

She nodded. "He's going back home to Texas."

"I thought you talked him out of that."

"We talked him out of making the decision when he was so torn up with grief he wasn't thinking straight. Now he's calmer, more rational, and we all agreed it was the best thing for him to be close to the rest of his family."

He caught the undertone in her voice. "But you'll miss him."

"Yes. He's a very sweet man."

"You get so involved with them, Kayla." They'd had this discussion before, but he couldn't seem to help himself. "And then it hurts you when they move on."

"But it makes me proud, too. Proud of what we do."

"You should be," he agreed. "I just wish it wasn't so consuming."

"Actually," she said, her voice a tad too casual, "I've been thinking of cutting back a little."

"What, to ten-hour days instead of twelve?"

"Look who's talking, mister I'll-just-work-a-little-more-on-that-project-tonight-even-though-it's-midnight."

Dane lowered his gaze. She knew him too well. One of the

reasons they had ended up living at her place was because he had this habit of coming up with the perfect solution to a problem right around that midnight hour. At his place, all he needed to do to go back to work was walk down the hall to the den. And then he would be sucked in for hours.

It was a habit he'd slipped back into in the two weeks they'd been apart, if for no other reason than it was the only way he could avoid the pain for a little while.

"What if we both cut back?" he suggested, figuring because she was trying so hard not to make everything about this new search for Chad, he could at least make an effort, too.

"And give the time to us? I like that idea," she said, so heartfelt his doubts receded. And when she reached across the table to take his hand, he felt as if all the pain and sadness of the past two weeks—hell, of the past two years—fell away.

"We're so damn good together, Kayla," he said softly.

"Yes. We always have been. And I took that for granted. I'm sorry."

And with that quiet, heartfelt apology, Dane felt a flood of renewed love and hope. They would make it, he thought. Foxworth would find what they found, or they would not find anything, but it didn't matter.

They would make it.

"Tonight was wonderful," Kayla said, meaning it with all her heart.

"It was. The salmon was great."

"I didn't mean the food."

"I know."

She realized then that he felt as awkward as she did, standing on her doorstep—what had been *their* doorstep—and feeling unsure about what would happen next.

She knew what she wanted to happen. She just didn't know how to go about getting it. She was afraid to assume he was ready to pick up where they'd left off, no matter how much she wanted exactly that.

She looked up at him, and he met her gaze steadily. With that knowledge borne of years of loving this man, she knew that although the decision was his, the asking must come from her. For a moment she wrestled with how to say it, then finally remembered this was Dane, and with Dane the best way was always upfront and honest.

"Will you stay?"

The simple question hung in the air for a moment, and Kayla would have sworn her heart had stopped beating in the silence. Was it that hard a decision for him? Had she lost him after all?

Then he let out a long breath.

And smiled. That lovely Dane smile she so loved.

They were going to be all right.

It wasn't like nothing had changed because things had. The bedroom was the same, but they weren't. She was a little thinner—eating had been the last thing on her mind when he was gone. The fact that he was too heartened her somehow; she'd had a vision in her mind of him going on happily, glad to be relieved of the burden of her baggage.

But it was more than that. It was the way he carefully, slowly undressed her, caressing each inch of skin revealed as if he'd never seen it before. She understood because every bit of him, broad shoulders, powerful arms, the cords of his neck, was newly precious to her. He'd even stopped her after she'd pulled off his shirt, when her fingers would have gone to the top button of his jeans.

He was handling her as if they'd never been together. As if it was that first night, when she'd turned twenty-one.

She had thought she would want to hurry. She'd been aching for him every moment since he'd walked out. She'd imagined, if this ever happened again, that they would be wildly hungry from the time apart. But now—

As she put her hands on his shoulders to try to pull him closer, he released her bra and gently, almost reverently cupped her breasts. Her breath caught. For a moment that seem liked forever he simply held her, as if he were savoring the feel of soft flesh rounding into his hands.

That halted breath escaped in a low moan as, at last, he brushed his thumbs over her nipples. Her hands slid helplessly downward, gripping the solid muscle of his upper arms as she swayed. Still he moved slowly, so slowly, and finally she understood.

He was seducing her all over again, not because she was unwilling, but in case she had forgotten how unutterably good they were together.

His presence, she realized as at last he let her work down his zipper as he did the same with hers, wasn't the only thing she'd taken for granted. She'd taken this for granted, this hot, physical connection. It had been this way since the beginning and hadn't faded at all in five years. He could still make her shiver from across a room, and she knew, with a quiet, feminine sort of pride, that she did the same to him.

"This is forever, Kayla," he'd said that first night. "No turning back. Are you sure?"

"Is that why you made us wait?" she'd asked.

"You needed to be old enough to know for sure what you want."

"I've known since I was fourteen," she'd told him.

It had been nothing less than the truth. She'd loved him since the day, instead of insisting on helping her out of that tree, he'd climbed up to join her. And instead of helping her get down, he'd inspected possible routes, told her which one he himself would use, and then let her do it herself.

Now, she owed him this, she thought as they at last went

down to the bed in a tangle. No more protests or pleas for him to move faster, to satiate the hunger that had been building. She gave herself up to his hands, his mouth. This would be at his pace, but all the while she knew his goal was to drive her mad with need, and in the end her pleasure would be as great if not greater than his. Because this was Dane, and he knew her, knew how to touch her, to kiss her, to take her exactly as she wanted to be taken.

And the next time, because now she was sure there would be one, she would return the favor, calling up everything she'd learned of him, of what he liked, to make sure he would be the one driven mad. She would show him she understood, that she knew what they'd nearly lost, how rare and special it was.

And then he was easing into her, hot and hard, slow and taunting, and rational thought fled. Her body arched in eager anticipation as he slid home bit by bit, and the low groan that broke from him, the first sign he wasn't as completely in control as he'd seemed, made her every muscle clench.

He lifted his head, looked straight into her eyes. "Don't throw this away, Kayla."

She tightened her arms around him. "No more taking for granted," she said.

Her words were apparently what he'd needed to hear because he abandoned all efforts at teasing slowness and began to move with an urgency that was no less compelling. Kayla gave herself up to the driving stroke of his body, let slip all restraint and reveled in the sweet, delicious fact that he was hers again.

For now.

Chapter 10

This time Kayla smiled when she saw the dog racing out to greet them. He seemed delighted to see his new friends. In fact, when he skidded to a stop in front of them and looked from her to Dane and back again, he seemed delighted not just to see them, but to see them together.

"Cutter, you are a very different dog," Dane said, reaching down to scratch his ear.

"Isn't he?" Kayla said, glad she wasn't the only one who saw it. "Hayley says sometimes she thinks he's more human than dog. But smarter."

Dane laughed. It was a good sound, one that gave her hope.

They headed toward the building. Quinn had called Kayla and asked her to meet him here. She had called Dane, who insisted on coming with her, as she knew he would. He'd made a promise that he would see this through with her, and Dane always kept his promises.

They started to turn on the gravel path that led to the main door of the building, but the dog cut them off. Then he trotted a few steps to their right, away from the door and along the path that led to the warehouse. He stopped and looked over his shoulder at them.

"I've been here before," Kayla said. "That's what started this."

"What?"

She realized she hadn't really told Dane what had happened that morning. It had sounded so silly, the idea that the dog had purposely snatched Chad's note and carried it off to the very people who were helping her now. She'd been afraid he'd dismiss the whole thing out of hand; Dane was a very practical and sometimes literally minded guy. And in retrospect, it sounded silly even to her.

"He...sort of led me to them," she said. "I thought he was just playing, but now I'm not so sure."

Cutter gave a short bark, walked a few more steps, stopped and looked back at them once more.

"Led you like this, you mean?" Dane asked.

"Yes." She sighed. If she couldn't tell him the truth, what hope was there for them anyway? "I'd thrown away Chad's note. He took it right out of the trash can and did this until I followed him to Quinn."

She expected him to say something about her being silly or fantasizing, expected him maybe even to tease her for thinking the dog had humanlike intelligence. He did neither.

"You threw it away?"

She knew him well enough to understand. And after last night, she knew he needed, deserved, to hear it. "I did. I wadded it up and tossed it. It wasn't worth what it had cost me."

He let out a long, compressed sigh.

At that moment, Cutter apparently lost patience with their lack of attention. Or their stupidity, Kayla thought. The dog trotted back and circled behind them. He didn't quite nip at their heels, but he nudged them both pointedly.

"I guess we'd better cooperate," Dane said.

His voice sounded strange, and she couldn't tell if he was sorry the conversation had been interrupted or if he was relieved. He wasn't like other guys she knew of from her friends, often dodging anything that could be described as serious discussion of the relationship. Those friends envied her the way she and Dane were always able to talk. But despite last night, things weren't usual between them now and hadn't been for a long time.

"I love you."

It burst from her as her mind seized on the declaration as the one most important thing to say right now.

"I love you, too," he said. "Enough to give us this one last chance."

The finality in his voice told her he meant what he said. Last night had been a reminder of what she was risking. For all his easygoing nature and his tremendous patience, there was a line Dane would not be pushed past, and she had reached it. She had made promises she intended to keep, but she'd be the first to admit that if they found Chad—

Dane stopped dead in the open doorway of the warehouse, where Cutter had led them.

"Whoa."

The man who had been tinkering with something on the sleek, black helicopter inside spun around, his right hand whipping to his side. For an instant Kayla's breath caught; he'd moved like he was used to having a gun there. But then he noticed Cutter and went from alert and primed to relaxed and smiling.

"A little warning would be good, buddy," he said to the dog who trotted toward him. The dog made a strange noise that sounded oddly like a snort of disgust. "Yeah, yeah, they're friendlies. I get it."

He walked toward them then. "Hi. You must be Kayla and Dane. I'm Teague Johnson."

He held out a hand. Kayla took it, noticing that while he didn't have a crushing grip, he didn't treat her like she was some delicate flower who would crumple at a solid clasp, either. Still, she noticed when he then shook Dane's hand, it was firmer. A guy thing, she thought.

And he was definitely a guy. From his buzz-cut sandy-brown hair to his battered leather jacket to his jeans with a hole in one knee, he was a guy. There was something about him, in the way he stood, the way he carried himself, that made her wonder, as she had with Quinn, if he'd been in the military. If so, it had to have been recently; he looked young.

"Nice," Dane said, gesturing at the helicopter. There was an undertone of awed appreciation in his voice.

"That it is," Teague agreed with a crooked grin that made Kayla smile in turn. "Quinn's newest toy. He got tired of trying to arrange transport when we needed to move in a hurry."

"And he can afford that?" Dane asked.

Teague laughed, apparently not hearing, or at least not reacting to, the faintly suspicious note in Dane's voice. But Kayla wasn't sure anyone who didn't know him as she did would notice.

"Thanks to Charlie, our resident financial genius, the Foxworth Foundation can afford a lot. What we do isn't always cheap."

"So you work for Quinn?"

"I'm part of his team, yes," Teague said. "Lately he's been letting me fly this baby."

"That's nice," Kayla said as she looked at the aircraft. She supposed it was nice, to him. "They make me a little nervous. I've never flown in one, and I hope to keep it that way."

"Well, if you don't like this, we have a pretty little blue and white airplane out at the airstrip," Teague said.

"Charlie must be really good," Dane said dryly.

Cutter gave a low sound and darted away, drawing their attention for a moment.

"Quinn," Teague said.

"What?"

"That was his Quinn sound. He must be back."

"You're saying he has different sounds for different people?"

"For Quinn and Hayley he does. Hayley's is a happy bark. Quinn's is that rumble. Me and the guys, we have to share one. Except Rafe. For some reason he gets his own." The crooked grin flashed again. "I swear, that dog isn't really a dog. I'm not sure what he is, except he's part of the team."

Kayla liked that. Liked that the dog was apparently accepted and welcomed by all. It made her feel better about them somehow.

"What happened there?" she asked, pointing to what looked like a patch of some kind that marred the sleek black surface.

"Same thing that happened there," Teague said cheerfully, indicating an odd, ragged hole farther back that she hadn't noticed yet.

"That looks like a bullet hole," Dane said.

"It is. That one doesn't affect anything, so Quinn wanted to keep it. Sort of a souvenir."

Kayla stared incredulously. "A souvenir? A bullet hole as a souvenir?"

"It's from the mission where he met Hayley," Teague explained.

That bit of information startled her and, oddly, warmed her a little. It was a strange feeling.

"Did she shoot at you?" Kayla asked.

Teague laughed. "She would have if she'd been armed, I think. We did sort of kidnap her."

Kayla gasped. Dane, perversely, laughed. "Now that's a story I'd like to hear."

"Some other time."

Quinn's voice came from behind them, and they turned to see him entering the warehouse, Cutter trotting at his side.

"Right now," he went on as he and the dog came to a halt beside them, "we need to talk about a possible lead."

Kayla's breath caught. "To Chad?" she said, then felt silly; what else?

"It may amount to nothing, and I warn you, it's not fresh, but it's the first thing we've turned up."

Kayla felt the old, eternal hope rise within her. And as they walked back toward the main building, she reached down to scratch behind Cutter's right ear in silent thanks. The dog made a soft, yowling little noise that sounded for all the world like encouragement.

Kayla shook her head in wonder. Maybe Teague was right, and he wasn't really just a dog.

She didn't know how or why this had happened, but she felt heartened about her brother for the first time in a long time, and for that she had to thank this furry conspirator.

Chapter 11

Dane stared down at the image on the paper on the table before him.

"Wow."

Kayla seemed beyond words, and looking at the computer-generated picture of Chad at his current age, he understood why.

"We tried doing this a couple of years ago for the social network pages she set up," Dane said, "but it didn't come out anywhere near this good."

"It's a special talent. Our tech guru, Tyler Hewitt, is a genius," Quinn said. "We do a lot of missing person cases. He took some standard image-aging software and tweaked it a bit, and the results have been amazing."

"He looks different," Dane said, "yet I'd recognize him in a minute."

"Is this what you wanted me to see?" Kayla asked. "Is this for flyers or posting or—"

"Someone thinks they saw him."

Kayla jumped. "Easy," Dane said. "He said it's not fresh."

"But it's more than I've had in so long," she said almost breathlessly. "Where?"

"A small town in Northern California. Not impossibly far from the note you got from Redding."

"That was three months ago." Kayla said it evenly, but Dane suspected she was trying to keep disappointment out of her voice, remembering she'd been warned the lead wasn't fresh.

"Yes. But it's a starting place."

"Who recognized him?"

Quinn shook his head. "It wasn't that definite. Just that the picture looked like somebody they'd seen. In a video game store."

Kayla's head came up sharply. "A video game store? That was one of Chad's passions."

Quinn nodded. "That's why we took this one seriously."

"How'd you manage this?" Dane asked. He didn't want to burst Kayla's bubble, but this seemed a bit much after only a few days. "This is hundreds of miles away and a little town, but you just happen to come across the one person who thinks he saw him?"

"We didn't. Not in the sense you mean."

Quinn leaned back in his chair. To Dane's surprise, the look he gave him seemed almost approving.

"You know we don't charge money for what we do," he said.

Dane instantly registered the key word in that statement. "Money," he said.

"What we've done instead," Quinn said, "is build a network. Of ordinary people across the country, people who don't stand out, who don't make people clam up like the police sometimes do, people who can watch, notice, without being noticed much themselves."

Dane's gaze narrowed. "You're saying...that's what you charge for your help?"

Quinn nodded. "Help in turn, at some later date. Most of our people are happy to do it. They never forget what it was like to be the one backed into a corner, the one at the end of their rope, the victim of injustice."

"Like you were," Kayla said softly.

Quinn's gaze shifted to her, but he said nothing.

"Your parents." If Quinn was upset, it didn't show, except maybe in a slight lowering of his brows. "Hayley told me. I think she thought I needed to know you really did understand," Kayla continued, apparently feeling the need to explain or to defend Hayley.

"Then I trust her judgment," Quinn said. Briskly, he went on. "We'll be leaving for California first thing in the morning."

"Taking that little toy in the warehouse?" Dane asked.

Quinn grinned suddenly, like a guy with the coolest car in town. "It is sweet, isn't it? But no. We'll take the plane. The Siskiyous are mountains I take seriously, and I'd rather be way above them."

"Okay," Kayla said.

There was undeniable excitement in her voice, and Dane supposed he couldn't blame her. And he realized that if this turned out to be just another disappointment for her, he wasn't going to be very happy with Quinn and company.

"I'll let you know as soon as we speak to our person there if it seems there's anything to this."

Kayla shook her head. "You won't have to. I'm going with you."

Dane went still. Quinn's gaze narrowed. "I don't think that would be the best idea," Quinn said. "And it's not necessary. We'll check it out, and if there's anything to it then you can—"

"No. I want to go now. I need to. I need to *do* something. Something besides sit at home and wonder."

"You've already logged more frequent flyer miles than any pilot, searching for Chad," Dane pointed out.

"Don't you see? This is the first chance in months, the first real possibility somebody may have seen him!"

Dane thought she was building this up too much, and obviously so did Quinn. But Dane knew that when Kayla focused on something, there was no stopping her. It took a considerable effort for him to quash the reaction that had become nearly automatic over the past couple of years. He'd promised her he would give this a full, honest shot. One last time.

Then it would be over, one way or another.

"All right," he said. "We'll both go." He glanced at Quinn. "Assuming there's room in this plane of yours."

"There's room," Quinn said. "But it's still not a good idea. It could well be a wasted trip."

"Won't be the first," Dane said. He saw Kayla wince, and he sighed. "Sorry. I meant what I said. This gets every chance to work."

So if I have to walk away, I can walk away clean, knowing I gave it as much as I could.

He hated that those were the words that formed in his mind, but he couldn't deny them. It was the truth. For all the sweetness rediscovered last night, it hadn't really changed anything. If Kayla couldn't or wouldn't give this up, or at least relegate it to second place in her life, then he would have to walk away again. No matter that it would nearly kill him to do it.

He was tired of being that second place holder himself.

It simmered in him as they headed back to her place to pack a small bag in case what needed to be done couldn't be done in a single day. He'd brought his own things back inside; they'd never made it out of his car anyway.

By the time they got there he was at a near boil. He wanted her to be crystal clear on what she was risking, what she was on the verge of throwing away. Last night's slow, sweet reunion had been one thing, but he was in no mood for slow and sweet now. He was fighting for his life, for their life together, and the kid gloves were off.

He grabbed her the moment they stepped inside. He kissed her fiercely, demanding her full attention. After a moment of startled surprise she gave in, kissing him back as if she understood.

But then this was Kayla, and she always understood.

As if that kiss had been the spark to tinder, the fire they'd always shared leaped to life. But he wasn't satisfied with that; he threw fuel on the flames, tearing at her clothes, needing, demanding, until she was with him, yanking at his shirt, his jeans.

They went down to the floor right there, no niceties this time. In seconds he was inside her. He felt her nails dig into his back at the sudden invasion, but it wasn't enough. He wanted her clawing at him, wanted her as mad, as desperate as he was, wanted to stamp himself on her so completely she would never, ever be able to forget this moment. He wanted her tied to him forever, and he used his body to tell her in the only way he could express it right now.

He clenched his jaw and held back, even as she began to go wild beneath him. She locked herself around him, as if she knew exactly what he wanted and that made it what she wanted, too. He rolled to his back, taking her with him, giving control over to her now, wanting her to show him she was as hot as he was. He needed to see it, to feel it, and somehow all the fear and frustration that had been growing in him for so long seemed wrapped up in that need.

As if she knew, she rode him with an eager ferocity that nearly drove him out of his mind, and in the last seconds, when he knew he couldn't wait any longer, he rolled them back and drove deep, heard her cry out, felt the first clenching of her body around him, then let himself go as her name ripped from his throat.

Inside the small airplane, Kayla sensed Dane's tension, knew the effort he was making to keep his promise to her. It made her feel better and worse at the same time; better because he was keeping to his word, and worse because it was clearly an effort. She realized with a sinking feeling that he thought this was going to be as fruitless as every other trip she'd made and that he was only coming with her because he'd promised her this one last chance.

She looked around the interior of the plane again, hoping for distraction. She and Dane had once taken a flight to Victoria, B.C., on a seaplane that had been even smaller than this, and she'd loved it. Much better than the helicopter that Dane had seemed so enamored of.

The young man who had been working on that helicopter was at the controls of the plane now, with Quinn in the copilot's seat. Somewhat to her surprise, Hayley had come with them.

"I'm the unofficial flight attendant," she said with a grin, handing out sodas.

There was no separate cockpit, so she was able to turn and hand a can to Quinn and offer one to Teague, who declined. Hayley's seat and the empty one next to her backed up to the pilot's, whereas Kayla's and Dane's faced forward. The cabin was finished nicely, with leather seating and large, rectangular windows, and there was plenty of room for Dane's long legs to stretch out.

"Nice," Dane said.

"Quinn's other toy," Hayley said with a smile. "He wanted a small jet, but Charlie slapped the purse strings shut on that."

Dane had been looking back at the cabin, but now he leaned forward to study what he could see of the instrument panels. It looked horrifyingly complicated to Kayla, although not much different than the big-screen gaming system his friend and partner Serge had. Dane had such an affinity for things electronic she wouldn't be surprised if he could figure most of them out simply by watching them long enough.

"It's pressurized?" Dane asked after a minute or two studying one section of the controls.

Hayley nodded. "Quinn was able to justify to Charlie the need for a pressurized cabin with all the mountains around us."

"I thought only jets were pressurized."

"This is the single exception in small planes. And that," Hayley said with a laugh, "is the sum total of my knowledge, I'm afraid." She gestured toward the front. "You want more, you'll have to ask them."

Dane smiled. "I will."

"Maybe on the way back you can sit up front."

"That," Dane said, his eyes alight, "would be exceptionally cool."

His excitement made Kayla smile. For a moment she wondered if he'd come along as much for the plane ride as for the search for Chad. And why not? she asked herself. She was glad he was enjoying the flight—it made her feel less guilty.

"Who takes care of Cutter when you have to leave?" Kayla asked.

"Usually our neighbor, who adores him. Or he stays with Rafe, another of our team, when he insists."

"The guy or the dog?" Dane joked.

"The dog," Hayley answered, sounding dead serious. "I think he knows Rafe's in a rough patch right now because he's been spending more time with him. Plus, the man has never had a dog, so Cutter's determined to introduce him to the joys."

Both Dane and Kayla blinked.

"I know, I know," Hayley said with a laugh. "But believe me, hang around Cutter long enough, and you'll start thinking that way, too."

The plane bounced slightly, as Quinn had warned them it might as they went over the mountains. Kayla shifted in her seat to look out the window. The movement, and a physical awareness that stopped just short of soreness, reminded her in a very personal way of what had happened between her and Dane the moment they'd set foot in her house last night. It wasn't that they hadn't had wild, hungry sex before, but nothing quite like that. From the beginning Dane's intent had been clear, he'd wanted to drive her crazy and he'd succeeded.

Admirably.

She felt her cheeks heat at the memory and was glad her face was turned away at the moment. Only the sure knowledge that, in the end, he'd been as wild as he'd made her let her regain some composure.

When they reached the small airport, the plane set down with a gentle thump that Kayla barely felt. She glanced toward Teague.

"He's good," Hayley said. "And almost as good with the helicopter. Quinn's been teaching him."

"I always wanted to learn to fly," Dane said, startling Kayla.

"You never told me that," she said.

He glanced at her. "I have. You just weren't hearing much at the time."

His tone was gentle, not accusing, but she felt stung nevertheless. Not by him, but inwardly; if he had indeed told her that, and she had completely missed it, what else had she missed? What else had been lost in the fog of grief and confusion?

She'd always thought she remembered everything about him, that she knew him better than anyone, that if someone asked her what his hopes, his dreams, his innermost thoughts were, she could tell them.

Now that confidence was shaken, and she didn't know how to feel about that.

It was still nagging at her as the five of them piled into the rental car Hayley had arranged the day before. Teague, as the shortest of the three men at a mere five-eleven, was relegated to the back seat while Quinn drove and Dane took the passenger seat. Hayley teased him gently about it, but Teague's crooked grin never faltered.

"Hey, I'm back here with two beautiful ladies—seems like I'm the lucky one," he said.

"Just remember who signs your paycheck," Quinn said in clearly mock warning.

"Yep," the irrepressible Teague retorted, "Charlie."

Hayley laughed, and the easy camaraderie lightened even Kayla's mood.

The town was close by, and it only took a few minutes to reach their destination. Kayla felt her pulse begin to pick up the moment she saw the sign for the game store. It looked like just the sort of place Chad would hang out. And when they stepped into the interior, with rows of the latest in games and equipment, and even a section for fan gear, it felt even more so.

The man behind the counter glanced at them, then put down the game controller he'd been inspecting. Light gleamed on a smooth, bald scalp fringed by silver hair. So much for the stereotype of gamers all being geeky fan boys, Kayla thought.

"Help you?"

"I'm Quinn Foxworth," Quinn said, holding out a hand. Somewhat to Kayla's surprise, the man reached out and grasped it without hesitation, and the handshake was welcoming and hearty.

"I'm Colin Brown. You're the folks who helped Henry Shigeta," the man said. "He told me you'd be coming."

"Yes."

"What you did, that did my heart good," the man said. "They'd been fighting that bastard Inskip for a long time. Always thought he was crooked as the day is long."

"And you were right," Quinn said.

"Damn straight. Taking bribes, letting his 'friends' build whatever they wanted wherever, but keeping good people like Henry and his wife from building the home they'd planned their whole lives on their own property. Not sure three years in jail is enough, though."

"I was more concerned that he never have power over people again," Quinn said. "And I think we took care of that."

The man smiled widely. "That you did. Now," he said briskly, "you're here about that picture Henry showed me?"

"Yes."

"I've been studying it, and the more I looked the more familiar he looked. So I went around and talked to Dustin." He glanced at their little group. "He's a kid who's always hanging out here. He knows all the regulars, so when a stranger comes in, he notices. So I showed him the picture."

"Did he know him?" Hayley asked.

Colin nodded. "He recognized him right off. 'That's that Chad guy,' he said."

Kayla's heart took a little jump in her chest and her knees went a little wobbly. In the same instant she felt Dane's arm around her, supporting her.

That's that Chad guy.

If Dane hadn't been holding her, she might well have sunk to her knees on the floor.

Chad.

At last.

Chapter 12

"It was still three months ago," Hayley said.

Dane watched as Kayla nodded. She hadn't said much since they'd left the game store. They were sitting now in a booth in the town's only restaurant, a small place built to resemble a railroad dining car. It looked old, but Dane noticed a small alcove at one end that appeared to be an internet set-up with a single computer, and he'd seen a sign in the window indicating free Wi-Fi. They were the only people here now, and he wondered if the place got busier later on or in the evenings.

Quinn and Teague had left them here while they went on what Teague called a recon. They would get the lay of the land, Quinn had said, then they'd all decide what to do.

"But it fits," Hayley was saying now. "The time frame is about right, given when he mailed the note from Redding, which is only thirty miles from here."

Dane realized then that Hayley was probably here to babysit them while Quinn went and did…whatever it was he did in cases like this. If Kayla had taken Quinn's advice and stayed home, it probably would have been just Quinn and Teague making this trip, or maybe even just Quinn himself. In this small town where everybody seemed to know everyone and everyone's business, Dane was guessing Quinn would have little trouble getting people to cooperate. After what they'd done for the Shigetas, he wasn't surprised that the Foxworth reputation obviously preceded the man with the name.

Dane had been a little surprised that Foxworth had become involved in such a small, relatively insignificant local case as the Shigeta's fight with the county government. That they had only improved his opinion of them.

They were, he thought, genuine champions of lost causes, just as they said. He liked that.

He just wasn't sure he liked what had just happened. If Mr. Brown and the kid he'd spoken to were right, and Dane had no reason to think they weren't, the lead was still three months old. Yet Kayla was as wound up and excited as if they'd walked into the game shop five minutes after Chad had walked out.

"It's just the closest I've been," Kayla said, fiddling with the salt shaker on the table, spinning it with restless fingers. He'd never seen her completely still for long while awake—it just wasn't her nature.

"I understand," Hayley said. "I just don't want you to get your hopes up too high, when we don't know if this will really lead to anything. It could—"

She broke off, and Dane knew before she looked that Quinn must be approaching; he could see it in the look in Hayley's eyes. Did he look like that when he saw Kayla after even a short time apart? He was willing to bet he did.

And then Quinn was there, sliding onto the booth bench beside Hayley, kissing her cheek before he turned to face them.

"He was hitchhiking," Quinn said without preamble.

Dane heard Kayla's breath catch.

"How'd you find that out?" Dane asked.

"Guy at the hardware store said I should catch up with the postal carrier. Said she'd been on this route for fifteen years and knew damn near everything about everyone. And that if there'd been a stranger around, chances are she'd know more about him than anyone."

"I gather you found her?" Dane asked.

"Yeah." Quinn's gaze shifted to Kayla. "She recognized Chad."

Dane felt her tense beside him. But she said only "And?"

"He was out on the highway. She said it was raining, and he looked pretty wet and miserable, but she's prohibited from picking up hitchhikers."

"But he was all right?"

Kayla's voice was so full of worry that Dane felt a jab of guilt. She loved her brother and he was the only immediate family she had left, and if he really was innocent as she believed, then he was a victim second only to their parents. He shouldn't have made it so hard on her.

"She thought so. He wasn't hurt or anything."

Kayla let out a relieved sigh as the waitress, a young, bored-looking woman who refilled their coffee, added a mug for Quinn, then vanished anew into the back, probably thinking they weren't worth her time because they weren't ordering lunch.

After she left, Quinn continued.

"She said he was only a few blocks from the senior center, so she sent him there. Said she knew they'd take him in, dry him off and feed him."

"We should go there," Kayla said, making as if to rise immediately.

"Teague's already there. He was on that side of town, so I called him and gave him the info. He should be here soon with whatever he finds."

"Oh." She sank back down. "Thank you."

"We'll find what's here to be found," Quinn assured her, then, in an almost warning tone, added, "But as I said from the beginning, I can't promise you'll like it."

"I have to know," Kayla said. "But I hate just sitting here. I feel like I should be doing something. Anything."

"You have been," Dane said quietly. "For ten years you have been."

She turned to look at him. "But I've never been this close," she said, eagerness building in her voice. "Surely you see that now. This is real, this is a chance finally to really find my brother and bring him home!"

Several things hit Dane at once. First was the fact that, until now, he'd never really thought she'd find him, so he'd never considered what would happen if she did. Bring him home? He could only imagine what that would be like. And he didn't like the feel of it at all.

Kayla's expression changed as she watched him. "Aren't you even a little happy about it?"

No. No, I'm not.

He didn't speak it because he was afraid if he did he'd sound like a spoiled child who'd just been told another baby was on the way. It didn't matter; she read him anyway.

"Fine," she snapped. "Why did you even come if that's how you feel?"

That the usually private Kayla was dragging this out in front of Quinn and Hayley told Dane volumes. He looked at her, at the set of her mouth, the rekindled resolve in her expression.

She was as determined as ever. And he felt a slow, creeping chill overtake him as he finally admitted to himself she would keep this up to the ends of the Earth if she had to.

She was lost to him.

Even as he thought it she turned away. "What do we do next?" she asked eagerly.

"We wait and see what Teague found out," Quinn said with a nod toward the window. Dane looked and saw the pilot headed for them at a brisk pace. He looked like a man who had something to say.

He could feel the renewed energy fairly radiating from Kayla as Teague joined them.

"What did you find?" she asked before he'd even sat down.

Teague glanced at Quinn. Something seemed to be communicated between the two men in the moment before Quinn nodded.

"She wants to know it all," he said.

Teague nodded, but his usual friendly smile was missing when he spoke. "They remember him, all right."

Kayla leaned forward eagerly. "They do? Did he say where he was going?"

Teague hesitated for about three seconds, and Dane got the sense he was trying to find a better way to say what he had to say. And he found himself, despite it all, waiting uneasily for what was coming.

"They remember him," Teague said at last, "because he cleaned them out when he left."

Quinn leaned back. Hayley sighed. Kayla frowned. "What?" she asked, clearly puzzled.

"He emptied the Bingo box." Teague's tone was remarkably level, but his sentiments on the action were still obvious. "Two hundred and fifty dollars. Stole every last penny."

Chapter 13

"Are they sure it was him?"

Kayla sounded doubtful, and it dug at the raw spot inside Dane that knew they were over for good. The knowledge hadn't reached his heart and gut yet, but his intellect knew in that cold, dispassionate way that was the beginning of the human mind learning to accept the unacceptable.

"Oh, please," Dane said, unable to hold back. "Don't defend him. Why would a guy who stole the money his eight-year-old sister saved up for a bike feel a qualm about stealing from senior citizens?"

Color flared in Kayla's cheeks. "I wasn't defending him. I was just asking if they were sure."

"They were," Teague said, his voice more sympathetic now, as if, although he despised what her brother had done, he felt sorry for Kayla. Whether it was for having to deal with this news, or for just having a jerk of a brother, Dane wasn't sure.

Hell, he wasn't sure of anything anymore. The brief interlude when it had seemed they might make it, when she'd been ready and willing to put all this on the shelf where it belonged and go on with their lives, had apparently been only that, an interlude. A precious, beautiful, intimate interlude, destined to end.

Chad Tucker had stolen something much more valuable than the contents of that money box from him and left him with only the sad remnants, memories of the life he'd thought was going to be forever. He'd always assumed they'd get married, had even figured her twenty-fifth birthday would be the day he'd formally ask her. He wanted her to have a chance to live enough to be sure, although he'd been sure for years. But by the time that birthday had rolled around, he'd been so tired of all things Chad, he hadn't proposed after all.

"There was a witness who saw him take it and run for the back door," Teague was saying. "By the time the local sheriff got there, he was long gone."

"Did you talk to the sheriff's office?"

"Yes. They looked up the report for me. Nothing much there except the usual conflicting eyewitness descriptions. But I talked to several people who were there that day. They all agreed the guy in our image was him, but there was nothing that helps figure out where he is now."

"Anything else?" Quinn asked.

Teague's mouth quirked. "I felt kind of bad, bringing it up again. Apparently there's an ongoing disagreement between the folks who wanted him hunted down and arrested before he spent it all on drugs, and the ones who thought if he needed the money that badly they should have just given it to him. It was getting kind of heated when I left."

Dane winced inwardly. That sounded a little too close to the arguments he and Kayla had had over her brother. Maybe there really was no middle ground, anywhere.

To her credit, Kayla didn't try to defend Chad once she'd heard Teague's story. She sat silently, looking troubled. His instinct was to comfort, as it always had been with her, but he quashed the urge. It was going to be a long, hard battle to kill the habits of more than a decade, and he wasn't looking forward to it.

But he was starting to accept that it was going to be necessary.

"It's your call, Kayla," Quinn said. "Do we keep going?"

"I…" She hesitated, flicked a glance at Dane. He said nothing. He already knew what she was going to say.

It's not your business anymore, he told himself. And that alone jabbed at him sharply. Disengaging was going to be a painful process.

"I can't quit now, not this close."

And there it was, Dane thought.

"Kayla," Hayley began.

"I know," Kayla said. "It could come to nothing, but it's still the most definite information I've had in all this time. Every other time, nobody remembered him, not even at the post office where he mailed the notes."

"This all would have been easier if he'd used email to contact you," Quinn said. "We could have tracked that, found an IP, and Tyler would have had it nailed down in a hurry."

"He could have. He obviously looked at her support group's website to get the P.O. Box, and the email address is right there. But he didn't," Dane said, beyond caring now that he sounded as bleak as he felt. "Because he doesn't want to be found. Not even by Kayla. Maybe especially not by her."

"What's that supposed to mean?" she asked, clearly stung.

He told himself it didn't matter. That he didn't care anymore. And while even as he thought it he knew the latter wasn't true, he was afraid the former was.

"He's been toying with you for ten years," he said, letting out some of his frustration. "Just when you start to get past it, another one of those damn notes comes. Never enough for you to find him, just enough to remind you he's out there. To make sure you never forget."

"I don't want to forget!"

"You think he doesn't know that?"

Dane was aware that Hayley was staring out the window, clearly trying to ignore them. Quinn, however, was listening to every word, not in the manner of someone who enjoyed hearing other people's disputes but more like someone who wanted every tiny bit of data in case it might help.

Dane wondered what Quinn would get out of this exchange. And it was a measure of the devastation he was feeling inside that he didn't really care.

"What do you want me to do?" Kayla demanded. "Just pretend he's not out there? Maybe stay home, spend his half of the insurance money? Maybe you'd like that, is that it?"

Under normal circumstances, Dane would have laughed that ridiculous accusation off, but nothing was normal about how he was feeling right now.

"What if you did find him?" he asked. Now that it had occurred to him, he wondered if she had ever thought beyond the immediate goal herself. "You talked about bringing him home. Did you ever think what that would mean? That the first people waiting to welcome him would be the police?"

Kayla's eyes widened, and the color drained from her cheeks. She was too smart for it not to have occurred to her, but her expression told him she'd put this in the "deal with it when it happens" category.

"Did you think that because they didn't have the manpower and resources to go on an out-of-state manhunt that they'd just forget about him?"

Kayla turned to look at Quinn. "But…you'll help me prove he didn't do it, right?"

"We'll help you find the truth," Quinn said gently but firmly. "I warned you from the beginning you might not like what we find."

Kayla lowered her eyes to her coffee mug, as if the last bit of dark liquid held the answers she wanted to hear.

"And you agreed to accept what they found," Dane reminded her.

"I know that." There was a snap in her voice.

"But you won't, will you?" Dane said wearily. "You'll just

go on and on, throwing your life away, throwing our lives away."

Her head came up sharply. "That's not true."

"How long are you going to live in complete denial, Kayla?"

"I'm not in denial. You think I don't know we may never find him, may never be able to prove he's innocent?"

"No. I think you'll never face the real truth." Dane knew he was headed into no-return territory, that if he continued he'd be looking at nothing but ashes. But wasn't he anyway?

"And what truth might that be?" Quinn's voice came from across the table, sounding calm and merely interested. Dane never took his eyes off Kayla. She was glaring at him, and in that moment he let go of the last, tiny shred of hope.

"That Chad did it," he said flatly.

Chapter 14

Kayla was still shaking. She tried to tell herself it was anger that was causing the tremors that gripped her, but deep down she knew better. Oh, there was anger, but it was dwarfed by a rush of other emotions she couldn't even begin to sort out, not yet.

Dane thought Chad was guilty.

Had he always? If so, how had she not known that?

She'd known he had never believed in the hunt for Chad the way she did, but he'd supported her, at least until recently. She'd even admitted he had a right to feel the way he did; when the tenth anniversary of her parents' murders and Chad's disappearance had rolled around, she'd been a little stunned herself to realize how long it had been and how relatively little she'd accomplished in those years.

And she had meant everything she'd said. She'd meant her promise that she would accept whatever Foxworth found or didn't find and move on. She'd been so relieved when Dane had agreed to give them another chance and had spent the past few days beyond grateful that he had come back. Nothing meant more to her than Dane and what they'd built between them.

Except that it had apparently all been built on a lie.

She hadn't said a word since Dane's flat declaration. Nor had he. At least not to her.

He had spoken to Quinn privately. The man had taken Dane aside, no doubt to quiz him on his accusation. She'd watched, still a little in shock. She could only imagine what Dane was telling him.

Meanwhile Hayley had gently reassured her that this changed nothing, that Foxworth would continue as long as she wanted them to, while Teague made an awkward escape as soon as he could, looking uncomfortable with the sudden flare of emotion. She couldn't blame him. She'd like to escape herself.

When the little town was dry of information, including the tiny clue Teague had gleaned from one of the seniors that Chad had talked about Seattle before he'd absconded with the money, they headed back to the small airstrip.

It was no less awkward there when Dane jumped at the chance to sit up front with Teague. She reminded herself that the suggestion he do so had come on the flight down here, before any of this had happened, but somehow that didn't make it seem any less a pointed display of the new, seemingly unbridgeable distance between them.

They'd been in the air for half an hour when Hayley, who had been talking quietly with Quinn in the back-facing seats, got up and crossed the small cabin to sit beside her.

"He's just tired of it," she said. "It's been ten years."

"He promised," Kayla said, aware she sounded a bit like a thwarted child but unable to help it at the moment. "He said he'd see this through with me."

"Apparently he thinks he has. And he does have a point."

She didn't want to hear any defense just now, but she didn't want to antagonize the only people left on her side either.

"This lead may be more detailed than you've ever had before, but it's still three months cold. We know more, and that will help, but I'm not sure how much closer we really are."

Kayla winced. Maybe they weren't on her side either. Maybe she really was alone in this.

"Quinn said we'd keep going as long as you wanted us

to. He meant it. It's only been a week, so we've really only just begun."

Soothed slightly, Kayla tried to pull herself out of the emotional murk. "What's the longest you've spent looking for someone?"

"Well, I don't know all the Foxworth history yet. I do know there are some cases that have gone for more than a year. And two that are still open after longer than that."

She glanced over at Quinn, who was reading through his own notes taken during the hours spent canvassing the small town.

"Those are the ones that eat at him. He hates not being able to at least give people the kind of closure he never got."

"He's a remarkable man," Kayla said, meaning it.

"Yes, he is," Hayley agreed, her voice soft, full of love and admiration and respect. All the things she herself had always felt for Dane.

Until now.

"I won't say he didn't mean it," Hayley said, obviously seeing Kayla's gaze flick up front to Dane and then quickly away. "I can't read his mind. But I'm guessing he feels like he's been putting his life—your lives—on hold for ten years, and now he's thinking it's never going to end."

"I think he pretty much ended it today."

"Doesn't have to be that way," Hayley said. "You can get past this."

"Get past him believing my brother is guilty?"

Hayley gave a half shrug. "I got past Quinn kidnapping me."

Kayla seized on the diversion. "Teague said something about that. It was really true?"

Hayley nodded. "In the middle of the night, Cutter and I both, in that blessed black helicopter of his."

"And those were really bullet holes?"

"Yes." Hayley's expression changed; whatever memory had just struck her, she didn't like it much. "And I'd be happy to tell you the whole, annoyingly heroic, self-sacrificing story, but right now I think you need to focus on one thing."

"Finding Chad," Kayla said with a nod.

"I was thinking more along the lines of deciding how high a price you're willing to pay."

This time it was Hayley who glanced forward to the copilot's seat where Dane sat, giving every appearance of being engrossed in Teague's explanations of what was going on, and no doubt asking very intelligent questions about the "slick, new avionics" Teague had been so eager to show off.

"He's a good man, Kayla. They don't come along every day."

Don't lose a good man chasing after a bad one.

Someone had told her that once. Crystal's mother, she thought. Although she obviously hadn't meant it to refer to Chad. Or maybe she had; Crystal had always had a bit of a crush on him.

Kayla felt the old ache and tried to quash it. Crystal had been her best friend. Or at least she'd thought she was her best friend; the girl, and the friendship, had vanished after that bloody night. In adult retrospect she was sure Crystal just hadn't known how to deal with such trauma, hadn't wanted to be around it. It was a dose of harsh, grim reality delivered years before a young mind knew how to cope. Kayla didn't blame her, not anymore, but it still hurt to have been abandoned that way.

Only one person had stayed, only one person had been there through it all, supporting her, helping her on every step of the awful path she'd had to walk.

And he was sitting a few feet away, yet at the moment as far away as the moon.

Don't lose a good man chasing after a bad one.

Dane was definitely a good man. She could never deny that, no matter what happened between them.

She just couldn't accept that her brother was a bad one.

Chapter 15

Teague had gone into such detail that by the time they landed, Dane felt as if he should be able to fly the darn plane himself. But he'd given all the information less than his full attention. Because it was hard to concentrate when your whole life had just fallen apart.

He wished he hadn't said it, but at the same time he was glad it was out. He'd been thinking it for a long time.

Do you really think he did it, or are you convicting him in your mind because he's ruining your life without even being here?

Quinn Foxworth's words echoed in his head. And Dane wasn't really sure of the answer.

"I've been where she is," Quinn had said. "And I wanted the person who murdered my parents dead as much as she wants to find Chad."

"And you got that, eventually." Even as he'd said it, Dane knew it wasn't a good analogy; Quinn, he suspected, was the kind of man who would want to do the job himself.

"After he got to spend three years at home with his family, three years that we and the families of the other victims never got, I'll never get over that."

"But look how you channeled that," Dane had countered. "Into something really good."

"Kayla's work is something good."

He was still chewing on it as they piled into the car they'd come to the airstrip in early that morning. Funny how different things had been then. If he could have imagined how it would go, he never would have gotten on that plane.

He couldn't deny Quinn's words. She was doing good work, and she had credibility with grief-stricken fellow travelers that couldn't be denied. It made her very effective.

It also drained her. In fact, he thought now as they went about the business of deplaning, the real problems had started about then. At first he'd been glad, no, delighted that she'd found something to do other than search for her brother. But the work did take a lot out of her, and he suspected there simply wasn't enough energy for all three: the work, her obsession with Chad, and him.

He'd just never thought it would be him who would lose. He'd always thought she'd get past it, get over it, that it would gradually fade.

He told himself to snap out of it as they reached the Foxworth buildings. It hadn't faded, and it was time to accept it never would.

He and Kayla had come in his car, so there would be an uncomfortable trip back to her place. And then he would, once more, gather up what things he had there—only this time they wouldn't be going back.

They got out of the big SUV. Dane heard a bark, and Cutter came dashing toward them, he wasn't sure from where. The dog greeted Hayley and Quinn joyously and gave Teague a nudge that seemed almost teasing. Then he turned to Dane and stopped. The animal looked from him to Kayla, who was standing a careful three feet away. Cutter came forward, stood between them for a moment, then sat.

A sound escaped from the dog, something so much like an exasperated, weary, human sigh that Dane blinked.

"Did I mention," Hayley said casually, "that Cutter has very good instincts about people who belong together?"

Kayla let out a harsh, compressed breath. Dane made himself not look at her.

"How is he with insurmountable obstacles?" he asked sourly.

"I don't think the word insurmountable is in his vocabulary," Quinn said dryly. "Which is, by the way, huge. For a dog."

"Not so huge for whatever he really is," Hayley quipped.

The awkward moment passed, although Cutter was still looking at them both as if he were contemplating drastic action.

"—stolen money would have bought him a ticket if he was really headed back north." Dane tuned into Quinn as he spoke to Kayla. "We'll start working that angle."

Dane tuned back out again, telling himself it no longer concerned him. He separated himself, walked over toward his car, hitting the button on the fob to unlock it.

To his surprise, Cutter followed him. And positioned himself between Dane and the driver's door.

"What? I didn't pet you hello, so I can't leave?"

He reached down and scratched behind the dog's ears, but it had no effect. Cutter never even reacted, and his steady, intense gaze was unnerving.

"What do you want me to do?" Dane asked; clearly the dog wanted something.

For the first time Cutter's gaze shifted, to Kayla, now twenty feet away. Then the dog's eyes were back on him, steady, intense, commanding.

Dane gave a sharp shake of his head. He was giving this animal far too much credit. He was, after all, just a dog.

When Kayla finally came over to the car, she came nowhere near him, nor did she say a word as she opened the passenger door. Cutter didn't pull the same stunt with her, so apparently in the dog's view, he was the one who was supposed to bend. Again.

"Sorry, buddy," he said to the dog, "I can't. Not this time."

For an instant something flickered in the animal's eyes, something oddly like understanding. Acknowledgment. Something.

And he was losing his mind, giving human attributes and intelligence to a dog, however remarkable he might be.

He got into the driver's seat. Cutter trotted around the car to the passenger side, where Kayla had now slid into the seat. He poked his nose at her, then rested his chin on her knee. She bent over the dog, petting him, crooning something he couldn't hear into those alert ears. Maybe that's what she needed, Dane thought. A dog. A companion who would never question what she was doing, never begrudge her her obsession, who would go along with her every desperate effort unconditionally.

The light was fading as he started the car and headed back to the little house he'd thought of as home for nearly four years now. They didn't speak, and the atmosphere between them grew stiffer, chillier, with every mile.

When they got there, he pulled into the driveway but not the garage. Kayla glanced at him, and he knew she had seen this simple action—or lack of action—for the sign it was. He wasn't staying.

He got out, slamming the car door shut with more force than was necessary. He regretted it when he realized her neighbor, Mr. Reyes, was outside working on his pickup, and the noise had made him look their way. But after a friendly wave he stuck his head back under the hood. At least it wasn't the man's wife, who would have come over to say hello and put them through ten minutes of agony as she chattered on.

Kayla just sat for a moment, then got out of the car, moving gingerly, as if every motion hurt. He had to stop himself from going to her.

"Let me grab my stuff, and you'll be rid of me," he said, hating the way he sounded but not able to stop the bitterness that was welling up in him from seeping into his voice.

"Fine."

Short, sharp, to the point. Not a word of protest, not a single request to reconsider.

"Kayla—"

"Just hurry and get out," she snapped. "Get it over with."

It was done. The rupture was complete and final. She'd made her choice, and it wasn't him.

He was so focused on that choice that he was unprepared for the flood of memories that hit him the moment they walked into the house. The past few days, when they'd made love hungrily, everywhere, whenever the need took them, every sweet touch flavored with gratitude that they hadn't lost this singular passion.

He couldn't deal with this. He grabbed up things and threw them in the duffel bag he'd stuffed into a corner of the closet. Clothes, shoes, razor, toothbrush, books, his tablet, they all went haphazardly into the bag and he zipped it hastily shut; he'd sort it all out later.

He intended to just leave. To walk out the door without a word because there was nothing left to say. But as he passed the bookshelf in the living room, something stopped him. He looked at the row of framed photographs she had there. Her parents, them all as a family, and at the other end one of him she'd taken last year, and Chad's high school portrait.

He reached out and moved Chad's picture in front of his own. It was childish, he knew it, but he did it anyway. Then he turned around to look at her.

"You've made your choice, Kayla. I hope you're happy with it when you're a lonely old woman still chasing a phantom."

"What makes you think I'll be lonely?" she retorted. "Do you think you're the only man in the world?"

He knew it had been a mistake; he should have just walked out as he'd intended. "No," he said quietly. "But no other man will love you like I do."

It wasn't until he was back in his car, sitting in the darkness, trying to will himself to turn the key, that he realized he'd used the present tense.

With a realization of just what was ahead of him, just how long and hard learning to live without her was going to be, he started the car and drove into the night.

Chapter 16

Kayla awoke from the dream with a gasp. For a moment everything seemed strange. Nothing looked right. Disoriented, she jerked upright. Once she had, the familiar outlines reassured her; she wasn't in the bedroom, but the living room.

But nothing could reassure her after that dream.

The peaceful quiet of the night surrounded her; this had always been a quiet neighborhood. It was one of the reasons she'd chosen it. Deciding to move had been instantaneous; she knew there was no way she could stay in the house that her parents had died in. She'd sold it to the first person who'd been willing to buy, taking a loss and not caring.

Dane had tried to slow her down to no avail. Hayley understood, she thought. Her mother had died of natural causes, she'd told her, otherwise she never would have been able to stay in her home—which wasn't far from Kayla's—either.

But whether or not he agreed with the move, Dane had helped. As usual. In fact, he'd been the one who'd found this house in the first place, although she'd fallen in love with it the moment she'd seen it.

As usual, he'd known exactly what she'd needed, just how much space, the big trees providing a sense of privacy and the small garden that was glorious in the spring and summer, tempting her outside. The little house had nestled in that setting like a fairy tale cottage, and she'd nearly giggled in appreciation.

Dane had helped her change the inside slightly, opening

up the kitchen to the living room so it didn't seem so small and closed in and then adding the big windows to look out on that garden, which in turn inspired her to keep working on it.

She'd been happier here than she'd thought she could ever be again. And yet now it seemed like a hollow, echoing place she wanted to escape.

She'd given up on sleep after two restless hours in her empty bed. Dane's absence hammered at her, no matter how she tried to pretend, going about her routine as if nothing had changed, hoping the ritual of washing her face, brushing her teeth, checking her alarm, would soothe her troubled mind and allow her to sleep. She had to work tomorrow, and there was no way she could miss the scheduled sessions—there were new people just starting on the long, sad path, and she needed to be there to help.

None of it worked.

Finally conceding there was no way she was going to sleep, she'd gotten up and moved to the living room. Curled up on her couch, she'd turned on the television, then turned it back off, picked up a book then put it down, finally grabbed her phone and played a mindless game until her eyes couldn't bear it anymore.

Just before two she'd finally dozed off, only to have her weary brain take Dane's words and tweak them into a too-real scenario; she'd been putting the photographs he'd moved back the way they'd been when she'd caught a glimpse of her own reflection in the glass of the framed portrait of Chad. A reflection of a wrinkled, gray-haired woman who looked a bit mad.

Needing to move, she uncurled her legs and stood up. She didn't turn on the lamp on the table beside her, didn't want the light to emphasize the emptiness of what had once been her beloved little home. In the dark, she could pretend it wasn't empty, pretend Dane was just in the other room, as always.

She could be in denial.

How long are you going to live in complete denial, Kayla?

"I'm not," she said aloud to the quiet room.

Denying she was living in denial.

She let out a disgusted sigh, angry at herself, at Dane, at the world in a way she hadn't been for a long time.

Defiantly, she walked over to the shelf of photos. She picked up the one of Chad Dane had moved and put it back, telling herself she wasn't glad she couldn't see any reflections in the dark.

She admitted she was glad she couldn't see Dane's, the pain was too raw, too fresh. But then, she didn't have to look to see the images in her mind. She knew them as well as she knew her own image. The picture of her whole family, the last taken while it had still existed, the shot of her parents at their twentieth—and last—anniversary. Then Chad with Troy, working on the motorcycle they had later crashed into the sound, which had then resulted in the joyriding incident; a guy couldn't be without wheels, Chad had said, laughing it off.

And then Dane. She had many more of him, some in other places in the house, but the one here was her favorite. It captured the essence of him, quiet yet energetic, thoughtful yet not brooding, serious but with a grin just about to break loose and light up his eyes.

And everything else within a hundred miles, she thought.

The ache welled up inside her until she nearly cried out at the pain of it. And there in the dark, she moved the pictures once more. Held Chad's for a moment, thinking the words that had kept her going for so long; she had to do this. She had to care about Chad because no one else did. She was all he had. But the old mantra wasn't working tonight.

She put the photos back exactly as Dane had moved them, with Chad's portrait blocking him.

Because he'd been right.

She did cry then, unable to stop it. She felt the despair building, knew she was on the verge of a meltdown the likes of which she hadn't had in a long time. Before she'd always had the mysterious, unknown killer to blame for the destruction of life as she'd known it.

Now she was very afraid she had no one to blame but herself. She—

An explosion of sound so loud she felt it as much as heard it was followed instantly by a simultaneous flare of yellow light and a shock wave that knocked her into the bookshelves.

She staggered, too stunned to even grab at anything for support. She went to her knees. She heard an odd, crackling sound. Struggled to her feet. And then she smelled smoke. Only a little, then suddenly it billowed out of the back of the house, harsh and thick. She coughed.

Fire. The house was on fire. Smoke was filling the room, making her cough harder and harder, and she realized flames could soon follow. But it was the smoke, wasn't it? Wasn't that the real danger? Didn't more people die of smoke inhalation than actually burned?

Stop thinking, start doing, she ordered herself, while you can still breathe at all.

She dropped to her knees and found some clearer air. She began to crawl, not really thinking of anything except getting away, getting outside. She headed for the front door, or at least where she thought it was; had she gotten turned around in the chaos?

It was getting harder and harder to focus, to breathe; her body was slipping out of her control as it coughed forcefully, trying to rid itself of the smothering smoke.

She heard a yell from outside, over the sound of the fire licking away at her home.

Dane?

No, Dane was gone. He'd left her; she'd thrown him away.

Dizzy with fear now, she tried to reach for the doorknob. She couldn't find it as the smoke spread, lowered.

Was it gone?

Everything else was.

Dane was gone.

Chad was gone.

Her parents were gone.

Why not join the parade?

The last thing she remembered was a rush of cool, night air, and the fleeting thought that maybe death wasn't so bad after all.

Chapter 17

Sirens.

Quinn came awake sharply. Immediately alert, he was assessing before Hayley even stirred beside him. He raised up on one elbow. The noise continued, and he turned his head slightly. North to south, he thought. And far enough away that he began to relax a little. A few blocks over and pulling away, he thought. And out here a block was a significant distance.

The sirens stopped. The only sound was the drip of rain from the eaves; the summer shower had started just after one. He knew that because Hayley, who loved the sound, had gotten up to open the window. Naked. Which had inspired him to welcome her back to bed in a way that had made him think very fondly of the Northwest's ever possible rain.

"Quinn?"

Hayley's soft voice came out of the dark. Just the sound of her saying his name was enough to tangle him up inside; sometimes he still had trouble believing this incredible woman was his.

"Can you tell where it was?"

"It's all right. It's not too close. Go back to sleep."

He dropped back down, rolling to his side to pull her into the curve of his body. She was soft and warm and sleek and smooth and he wanted her all over again despite the fact that they'd made love well into the night last night, as if they'd needed to reassure themselves that they were fine after seeing Dane and Kayla's love start to crumble before their eyes.

He heard another sound that distracted him from the decision of whether to let her sleep or pursue the urge that was building in him. This one was from inside, the sound of a dog's quiet footfalls. Cutter.

The sirens must have unsettled him, Quinn thought. Probably even hurt those super-sensitive ears of his that seemed to hear at incredible distances even for a dog.

And then Cutter was there, his head up to see into the bed, looking at them. Even in the dark Quinn knew it because he could see the faint gleam of the dog's eyes reflecting what light there was. He had a vague memory of reading that dogs could see better than people at night. It had been in the spate of dog research he'd done after the drug cartel case. The case that had brought Hayley—and the uncanny, sometimes too clever Cutter—into his life, changing it forever, in ways he would have never dared hope for.

"Hey, furry one," Hayley said to the dog, reaching out a slender arm to stroke the dog's head. "We're okay."

As if that had been all he needed—to know his people were okay—the dog gave Hayley's fingers a quick swipe with his tongue and turned away.

"That dog is…." Words failed him.

"Yes, he is," Hayley said, and he could hear the smile in her voice. "Lucky me, I have two of the most amazing males on the planet right here with me."

Well, if that was how she was feeling, that made his decision easier. He leaned over her and nibbled lightly on her ear and felt with satisfaction the tiny shiver that went through her. He pulled her closer, ready to—

Cutter was back.

This time he nudged Hayley slightly with his nose. His cold nose, Hayley indicated.

"Settle down, Cutter," she told him. "It was just sirens,

and they weren't that close. Somebody's having trouble, but not us."

But the dog began to pace, then pace and whine, from the bed to the bedroom door and back again.

"Is he usually like that?" Quinn asked. He'd seen a lot of unique behavior from Cutter in the past few months, but not this. "After he hears sirens, I mean?"

"No," Hayley said. "They're rare out here, and they wake him, of course, but he settles back down quickly. And he never whines like that. This is…odd."

Odd. Used in conjunction with Cutter, that was never something to ignore. Quinn sighed. Shelving his erotic plans, he sat up. Hayley sat up beside him. Quinn reached for the lamp on his side of the bed.

Light flooded the room. The room that, thanks to Hayley's gentle understanding, was as much his as hers. She'd told him she wanted to make changes anyway, once she'd decided to stay here after her mother's death, but she'd been putting it off. So she'd insisted they move everything out of the house, put back only what he liked, and make mutual decisions on adding new things. "That way it's new for both of us," she had said. "I don't want you to feel like a guest in someone else's house."

Because he'd practically been living in the Foxworth office, in a room at the back downstairs that he'd converted to a functional bedroom, he wasn't about to complain, but he appreciated the gesture more than he'd ever expected he would. In return he decided not to rebuild on the property Foxworth owned next door, although he'd had the ruins of the house there removed. Now Cutter had lots of room to run and explore without ever leaving home turf.

The dog had stopped his pacing when the light came on and had spun around to look toward them. After a moment, when they didn't move, he sat in the middle of the floor and began to howl. Loudly.

"What the...?" Quinn exclaimed.

"I don't know," Hayley said. "He's never done that."

She got up and went to the obviously distressed dog, kneeling beside him. "Cutter, sweetie, it's all right."

Quinn watched as she hugged the dog reassuringly. Cutter accepted the gesture with another swipe of his tongue, this time over her chin, but the ear-splitting howling resumed.

Only now, in between howls, the dog seemed to be focusing on Quinn. And when Cutter was focused on you, Quinn had quickly learned, it was good to pay attention.

Feeling a bit like the sheep these Belgian breeds were known to herd, he got out of bed himself.

"Okay, dog," he muttered as he joined Hayley crouching beside the animal, "you got us both up, now what?"

The howling stopped. Cutter darted away, disappearing for a moment into the small walk-in closet off the master bathroom.

He came back with a shoe.

Hayley drew back, startled, as the dog dropped one of her lug-soled slip-ons in front of her, then raced back to the closet.

He came back again, this time with one of Quinn's battered, lace-up military boots, which he dropped very nearly on Quinn's bare foot.

Then Cutter spun on his hindquarters and darted to the bedroom door, where he sat, looking over his shoulder at them with every evidence of impatience, as if he were waiting for his not-too-bright humans to get the message.

Quinn looked at Hayley, whose expression told him she was as bewildered as he was.

But if there was anything he'd come to know since these two had made his life something full of joy and wonder instead of the steady slog of determination it had once been, it was that you ignored this dog at your peril.

Hayley sighed.

Quinn echoed it.

"I guess we're going…somewhere," he said. "In the middle of the night. In the rain," he added with a wry grimace at the dog.

"Yes. And given this started with the sirens," Hayley began.

"We start by finding where they went," Quinn finished.

Dane hadn't been asleep—in fact, he had just made himself stop pacing the floor again when the knock on the door startled him. Considering the hour, it had been more of a pounding than a knock. His brows furrowed. Probably woke the neighbors in both apartments beside him. He picked up his phone and tapped it to see that it was after 2:00 a.m.

"Dane Burdette, Redwood Cove police, open up."

For a moment he thought it was Jarrod, the cop from downstairs, making a lousy joke. But the guy didn't seem the type. A million scenarios cascaded through his mind as he crossed the living room. Maybe they'd finally found Chad. But why would they be here? Wouldn't they go to Kayla?

Fear spiked through him. If his long suppressed suspicion was true, if Chad really had murdered their parents, then what would stop him from coming back for his sister? It sounded crazy; she'd been his sole defender for so long, but then, Dane didn't get how somebody could kill their parents in the first place.

His brain raced through all those chaotic thoughts in the time it took him to get to the front door. He shifted his phone to his left hand and grabbed the doorknob just as another hammering came.

"Okay, okay," he was saying as he pulled it open.

Two uniformed officers stood there. One about his own age, one older. They both looked stern. No, beyond that. They looked grim. And wary. Watchful. It was a small department, and he wondered what was so important they sent this percentage of it to his door and at this hour.

"What's wrong?" he asked.

"We need to talk to you, Mr. Burdette."

Puzzled, and still fighting the chaos of his thoughts, he stood aside to let them in. The older man's name tag said R. Carpenter, the younger D. Harvey.

"Is this about Chad? Did he come back?"

The two men exchanged glances. "Chad?"

"Chad Tucker. He— Never mind. If this was about him, you'd know the name, right?"

"Tucker. Related to Kayla Tucker?"

A stab of foreboding shot through him, and Dane's stomach knotted. "Her brother. Is she all right?"

"Interesting that you're worried about that."

It took everything he had not to let his rapidly building panic show. "Her brother," he said slowly, "likely murdered their parents ten years ago. Then vanished. If he's back—"

"I remember a little about that case," the older officer said. "It was pretty ugly."

"Then you should know why I'm worried. Is Kayla all right?"

"How do you know about that case?"

"I lived next door at the time. I was the first one there, when Kayla started screaming."

"Were you?" the older man said, in an odd tone.

"She was just a kid. Sixteen. If you'd heard what she sounded like, you would have come running, too."

"And you were how old?" It seemed the older officer was taking charge of things, and the younger one was staying silent. Dane wondered if he was a trainee or something. He looked young enough.

"Eighteen," he answered.

"The same age as the primary suspect," Carpenter said.

Apparently he remembered more than just a little about the case, Dane thought.

"I think you'd better come with us, Mr. Burdette."

"I'm not moving a step until you tell me if this has to do with Kayla, if she's all right."

"From what a witness tells us, you had a fight with Ms. Tucker earlier tonight."

"A fight? What the…."

Mr. Reyes. He supposed the little scene in the driveway could be interpreted that way.

"We've been…disagreeing. About her brother. She insists he's innocent, I think he's not."

"Where have you been since that time?"

"Here. I came straight here."

The younger officer looked him up and down. The older officer walked around him, looking at him even more intently. Looking for what? Dane wondered.

"You're still dressed."

"I knew I wasn't going to sleep so I didn't bother trying."

"Hmm. Convenient."

Dane didn't like the way this was going. And he still didn't have an answer about Kayla.

"What the hell is going on?"

"What have you been doing all night?"

"I had an online chat session with a company in Dublin we're prepping a video for." He added, "It was 1:00 a.m. here, but nine in the morning there."

"They can verify that?"

"Sure."

"I'd like to take a look around your apartment, Mr. Burdette. Do I have your permission?"

"You tell me if Kayla's all right, you can look all you want." He was starting to feel desperate now.

The older officer moved to face him head-on. Dane got the distinct feeling he was being studied, assessed. Why? He was just forming some vague idea that the man wanted to see how he'd react to what he was about to say when the words came and blasted any further thoughts out of his mind.

"Ms. Tucker's home was firebombed tonight."

A sensation Dane hadn't felt since the night he'd heard Kayla's screams from next door flooded him. He staggered slightly as an enervating chill sapped strength from his muscles and put his brain in a fog. He heard a sound and vaguely realized he'd dropped his cell phone.

Kayla.

"Is she…?"

He couldn't say it. He just couldn't. The officer just looked at him, waiting, for what Dane didn't know.

The phone he'd dropped rang. Feeling as if he were moving underwater he looked at it. Hoping against hope Kayla's familiar photo would be showing.

There was no photo at all. Just a name, the most recent one he'd added to his contact list.

Foxworth.

Slowly, still feeling that numbing paralysis, he bent to pick up the phone.

The officer beat him to it. He glanced at the screen. "Foxworth again," he muttered.

"I need to answer it," Dane said, a little amazed he could still talk at all. But Foxworth, either Quinn or Hayley, might know something, and at least they'd tell him. Unlike these guys, who seemed to be playing some kind of game he didn't know the rules to.

"Put it on speaker," the officer said.

"Speaker?" Didn't they have to have a warrant to listen to somebody's calls? he wondered.

"You were the last one to see Ms. Tucker. And we haven't had a chance to check out these Foxworth people yet. If you've got nothing to hide, put it on speaker."

Nothing to hide. And it wasn't a suggestion or even a request. It was an order. And Dane suddenly, belatedly realized that these deputies weren't here to deliver bad news.

They weren't here to tell him the woman he'd loved for years was dead.

They were here because he was a suspect.

Chapter 18

"You won't believe this, but Cutter sent us."

Kayla wiggled her nose in irritation at the oxygen cannula the E.R. staff insisted she keep on. She felt much better now, and she wished they'd take it off. But when she spoke, or tried to, her voice was just raspy enough that she thought maybe they were right about it.

"He did?"

Hayley nodded. "We heard the sirens—you're not that far from us—but when it quieted down we didn't think much more about it. But Cutter wouldn't let us go back to sleep. He started pacing the bedroom, whining, coming over to us, then walking to the door, back and forth."

Kayla thought of her initial encounter with the dog and then the way he'd led them to Teague in the warehouse. That part wasn't surprising.

"Finally he sat in the middle of the room and started howling, like a wolf looking at a full moon. We had to get up before he'd shut up."

"But then he did?"

Hayley laughed. "Yes. He was too busy dragging our shoes over to us. We got the clue at that point."

"Are you sure he's just a dog?"

"Sometimes, I'm not sure at all."

Kayla shifted, winced as the three stitches in the back of her left shoulder pulled slightly. She knew she'd gotten off lucky with some cuts and what would be a colorful array of bruises. The smoke had been the worst, but Mr. Reyes, bless him, had gotten there and broken the window in the front door to open it in time.

"Where is Quinn?" she asked.

"He's talking to the investigators." Hayley smiled. "There's always a bit of lag time while they check us out."

"Like Dane did," Kayla said, that stubborn inner ache rising, making her outward injuries pale in comparison.

"He was pretty thorough," Hayley agreed. "He was worried about you."

"He's not anymore," Kayla muttered.

"Don't be so sure. I've seen you two together. You don't turn feelings like that off so quickly."

"It wasn't quick. It took ten years." She sounded as bleak as she felt. She knew she had driven him to this.

"Don't give up yet," Hayley said gently. Then, "The investigators will be here momentarily, I'm sure. Is there anything you want to tell me before they arrive?"

"I don't know who it was," she said. "I didn't hear anything. I couldn't sleep so I was in the living room."

"That probably saved your life," Hayley said.

"The house," Kayla began.

Hayley shook her head. "I don't know. The fire department was still all over it when the paramedics loaded you up. I wanted to stay with you, so I didn't really see how bad it was."

"Thank you," Kayla said. "I would have felt…really alone if you hadn't."

Hayley smiled. "You're not alone. But think, Kayla. Was there anyone around? Did you hear any cars, any noises in the yard?"

Kayla tried, replaying the awful night in her mind, but nothing surfaced. "I don't remember anything, but I was pretty upset, so I'm not sure I would have noticed."

But the process of trying to remember if she'd heard or

seen anything unusual kick-started Kayla's brain. Things tumbled into place, and with a little shock she realized that someone had tried to kill her tonight.

And that made her realize she'd been so focused on finding Chad and proving he hadn't killed their parents that she hadn't spent a whole lot of time thinking about who actually had.

"Do you think this is connected? To my parents, I mean?"

"It does seem odd that shortly after we start looking into things you get attacked."

Kayla didn't know whether to hope this was all connected or hope it wasn't.

"Maybe my work, maybe somebody from the counseling group? One of them had a son murdered a month ago."

"We're looking into it," Hayley agreed.

"Definitely." Quinn's voice came from over Hayley's shoulder as he parted the curtains and stepped into the E.R. alcove. "How are you?"

"Okay. I think."

Quinn nodded. "A detective and the arson investigator are right on my heels. Anything I need to know?"

"She doesn't remember anything out of the ordinary," Hayley said.

"Not surprising. Maybe later. How bad was your fight with Dane?"

"Fight?"

"In the driveway."

Kayla frowned, then remembered Mr. Reyes had been in his own driveway at the time. Given the man had saved her life, she found it hard to be upset with him.

"It wasn't a fight. We were a little tense, snapped at each other, but that's all."

"Any threats?"

Kayla blinked. "What?"

"Did he make any threats. 'You'll be sorry,' 'I'll make you pay,' anything like that?"

Bewildered, Kayla stared at him. "Dane?" She sounded as incredulous as she felt. "Of course not. Dane would never say—"

She broke off, suddenly realizing the import behind his question.

"No! No, no, no. Not Dane. Never in a million years."

"You sound awfully sure about a guy who just walked out on you," Quinn said, his gaze never leaving her.

"He had every right to do that," Kayla said miserably. "But it doesn't change who he is inside."

"You're interfering in an investigation, Mr. Foxworth."

The warning came from behind them in a voice that held the ring of command.

"Ms. Tucker is a client, Detective Dunbar," Quinn said without missing a beat. A dark-haired man in civilian clothes, but with an air about him that matched the voice, pushed aside the curtains. Even Kayla could have guessed he was a cop. He was tall and rangy and looked fit and tough. A touch of grey at his temples suggested he might be older than Quinn, although he didn't really look it otherwise.

"Is Dane Burdette a client, too?"

Quinn hesitated, which already Kayla knew was unlike him. She took advantage even as she wondered if he'd done it purposefully, to give her this chance.

"Yes," she said quickly. "And he did *not* do this. He would never, ever do anything remotely like this."

"I've heard the same from the family and friends of everything from terrorists to serial killers."

He didn't say it coldly or cruelly; in fact, if anything his tone was sad as he looked at her.

"He didn't do it," Kayla insisted. And it struck her suddenly that she was once more in the position of protesting the innocence of someone the police seemed to have already decided was guilty.

"He has no alibi. He can't prove he wasn't there," Dunbar said.

"But that's not the question, is it?" Quinn said. "The question is can you prove he was?"

"Where is he now?" Kayla demanded.

"You seem very concerned," Detective Dunbar said. "Didn't you two just break up yesterday?"

"I've loved him since I was fourteen," Kayla said, "and I still do. You're not listening." She shook her head, then wished she hadn't as the room spun a little. She closed her eyes. "God, do the police never listen?" she whispered.

"I'm listening," Dunbar said, sounding different now, but Kayla felt too drained at the moment to answer. As if he sensed that, although Kayla wasn't yet ready to cede that much sensitivity to him, he changed tack and began to question her instead on what exactly had happened.

She opened her eyes and went through it all again but remembered nothing new to add to the account.

"So you say you heard nothing, saw nothing, until the actual explosion itself," the detective said. He didn't say it in an accusing tone, but to Kayla it sounded that way anyway.

"I wasn't even in that room," she explained again. "I was in the front of the house."

"Still, a broken window makes a lot of noise."

"Is that how it was done?" Hayley asked.

The detective didn't look at her as he nodded; he kept his gaze on Kayla's face.

"I'm not the arson people, but it looked to me like there was a small explosion in addition to a pretty standard Molotov cocktail, with the ignition point at the foot of the bed, although it spread fast enough and was hot enough that I'm thinking there might have been more than just gasoline involved. Probably trying to destroy any evidence."

Kayla smothered a shiver. She hadn't realized until this moment just how narrow her escape had been. If she had stayed in bed, she might well be dead.

As if he thought he'd put her off guard, Dunbar went back to his questioning.

"And you were upset," the detective said. "Distracted, by the fight you had earlier."

"It was not a fight," she insisted, pushing back another shiver of reaction. Right now it was more important to convince this man. "And I was upset by Dane's absence, not a couple of sharp words."

She closed her eyes again, feeling battered now.

"It was Dane's choice," she heard Hayley say.

Kayla's eyes snapped open. It didn't seem like Hayley to rub it in.

"Exactly," Quinn agreed, looking at the detective. "He's the one who walked away—she didn't leave him—so why would he turn around and try to kill her?"

"Maybe he's angry over why he had to walk away," Dunbar said. Kayla thought she heard doubt in his voice, as if he'd wondered that himself. Then again, maybe it was wishful thinking.

"When Dane gets angry, which isn't often, he goes out and rides his bike twenty miles," Kayla said. "If he's really mad, he does half of it uphill. *That's* how he deals with anger. Not blowing things up or…"

Her voice trailed off. The very idea of Dane trying to kill anyone, let alone her, was beyond absurd, too absurd to deserve being put into words.

The detective's cell phone rang. Kayla supposed the no phone rule in emergency rooms didn't apply to police. He walked a few feet away and answered quietly.

Moments later he was back. His gaze was fastened on Quinn.

"You're that Foxworth? The one who helped take down that cop-killer over in Seattle?"

"We played a small part, yes," Quinn said.

"Word I got was it was more than a small part. He shot you."

Kayla's eyes widened, and she saw Hayley's gaze snap to Quinn.

"Not well," Quinn answered dryly. "He left me standing."

"So that scar's from some 'stupid accident'?" Hayley said, her voice tight.

A glance at the woman's face confirmed this information was news to Hayley, too. Hayley's expression told Kayla there would be a discussion about this later. She didn't envy Quinn; the woman did not look pleased.

"It was stupid. But the bullet ended up being the final nail in his incarceration coffin," Quinn added.

The detective smiled then. Which made his next words as he turned back to her even more ominous.

"Burdette's in custody."

Chapter 19

"He wouldn't. He didn't," Kayla said fiercely, staring at Quinn and Hayley as if she could will them to believe.

"You must feel like you've spent half your life saying that," Hayley said, reaching out to take Kayla's hand.

"But with Chad it's just faith. With Dane it's rock-solid fact. He simply would never do such a thing. To anyone."

Quinn studied her silently. Detective Dunbar had left them, with an admonition to Kayla that he'd want to speak to her again later. It wasn't quite "Don't leave town," but it was close enough.

And now, she thought, he was off to grill Dane. Already assuming he was guilty, just as the police then had assumed Chad was guilty. History repeating itself. She stifled a moan, barely.

"We'll get it straightened out," Quinn promised.

"You believe me? That he wouldn't do this?" Kayla pleaded.

"He doesn't seem the type," Quinn said. "Not a sneak attack like this."

Kayla felt a little less pressure in her chest. "He's not. At all."

"Who is?"

"What?"

"Who would be the type? If it's not Dane, it's somebody else. Who?"

Kayla blinked. "I have no idea." Her earlier thought ran

through her mind, that she'd been so focused on proving Chad hadn't killed their parents that she hadn't thought enough about who had. Now she was looking at that same kind of question again, with the intended victim clearly she herself.

Belatedly, something about his question occurred to her.

"Wait, you think this is someone I know?"

"It's someone who obviously knows you. Or at least enough about you and your home to place that bomb in the most likely place. So it's a possibility."

That made it all even worse.

Kayla shook her head, wishing she could think more clearly. This time, at least, the room didn't spin.

"So now you think this isn't connected to my parents' murders?"

"I think it's far too early to take any options off the table," Quinn said.

"I wish the police had thought that way ten years ago," Kayla said, not caring about the bitter note that had come into her voice.

"I think," Quinn said, "you might find Detective Dunbar a different type."

"Type?"

"He's ex-LAPD. I get the feeling he takes things a bit personally. It may be why he left. That kind of cop takes a real beating in places with frequent serious crimes."

"Personally?" Hayley asked.

Quinn nodded. "The kind who takes the work home with him. Good for victims, not so good on the cop."

"He didn't seem to be on my side," Kayla said.

Quinn smiled. "Don't mistake me. He's still a good, thorough cop, I think. What he did here was pretty standard. He has to ask those questions, look for holes in your story. It's his job."

"What kind of holes?"

Quinn shrugged. "They have to consider all the possibilities. Insurance on the house, for instance."

With her fuzzy head, it took her a moment to get there. "You mean…I might have done this myself to get the insurance money?"

"It's been done. And you were safely out of the room."

"She needed stitches and oxygen. Your interpretation of the word 'safely' and mine obviously don't match," Hayley said, and there was such a "We're going to talk about this later" tone in her voice that Kayla nearly smiled despite her turmoil. Quinn had some explaining to do about that getting shot business, obviously.

"I love…loved my house. I would never—"

She broke off. It all seemed like too much; she wanted nothing more than to lie down and sleep for a week. Tears brimmed and she dashed them away angrily. She would not be one of those weepy women who fell apart. She'd done that once, gone completely to pieces, and while Chad's fate was apparently being sealed she'd done little to head it off. She'd only made it through at all because of Dane's unwavering support.

And now he was in trouble.

With an effort she sat up.

"I want out of here."

"Whoa," Hayley said. "Take it easy."

"I've been x-rayed and hooked up to machines for hours. I'm fine, and I want out of here." She yanked the oxygen tube over her head and pulled the clip-like monitor off her finger.

"You're fine now," Quinn said. "Smoke inhalation can be tricky. Sometimes you seem fine at first, but a day later your lungs—"

"I'll deal with that a day later then," she said.

Quinn grimaced slightly, then said, "I'll find the doctor."

After he'd gone, Kayla looked at Hayley. "I have to help Dane. He didn't do this."

"I know."

For a moment Kayla just looked at her. Was she merely placating her? Trying to keep her calm?

"He wouldn't do this. He felt he had to make a choice and he did, but he would never try to hurt you."

Just hearing those words from someone else was a salve to Kayla's battered emotions. Tears escaped this time, and before she could wipe them away Hayley was handing her a tissue.

"We'll help him," Hayley assured her. "Whether this is connected to Chad or not."

After a study of the improving trend of her oxygen saturation levels since she'd been here and securing a promise she would return for a follow-up comparison chest X-ray, and after Hayley had assured her Kayla wouldn't be left alone for the next couple of days, the doctor agreed to release her.

"The coughing resumes, or she starts sounding more hoarse, I want her back here."

"If I have to carry her," Quinn said, and Kayla wasn't quite sure if that was a promise or a threat.

"I want to see Dane. Even if he doesn't want to see me."

"He's still being questioned, I'm sure," Quinn said. "For now let's get you cleaned up and some clothes that don't smell of smoke."

"Clothes," Kayla said, almost numbly. "I probably don't have any, do I?"

"We'll deal with all that," Hayley said as they got into Quinn's SUV.

Kayla paused before sliding into the backseat. "My car."

It wasn't a question, but Quinn answered as if it had been. "The garage looked fine from what I could see. The fire fighters did a good job keeping it from spreading. The fire itself was confined mostly to the bedroom. The rest of the house seemed okay, except for smoke damage. Definitely reparable."

She didn't answer, although she appreciated the information. It was too much to think about just now.

"If you ever wanted a bigger bedroom, now's your chance," Quinn said.

"Is that your version of looking on the bright side?" Hayley asked.

"My version of the bright side is that she's not dead," Quinn said.

A moment passed before Hayley said, "Point taken," with a smile.

They were, Kayla realized, talking to each other so she wouldn't feel pressured to join in. And not for the first time tonight—well, it was nearly morning now—she was thankful for this remarkable couple who had come into her life.

Or been dragged into it, she thought, remembering the determined dog who had brought all this about.

Hayley turned in her seat to look at Kayla. "I'm a bit taller than you, but we're close enough in size I think we can find you something to wear. Then you need to get some sleep."

"But—"

"I'll check on Dane's status," Quinn said, correctly interpreting her protest.

It occurred to her finally to wonder where they were going. Had the smoke affected her brain, her thought process? The doctor had said it could but that she didn't think she'd breathed enough to do damage, and surely if that were the case she wouldn't have released her. She must just be tired. She had, after all, been up all night.

"Where are we going?" she asked.

"You're coming home with us," Hayley said.

That sounded surprisingly comforting. The only pang it gave her was the realization that if things were as they should

be, it would be Dane taking care of her and they'd be headed
to his apartment.

What turned out, oddly, to be most comforting about it
all was the greeting she got when they arrived at the house
tucked into the trees. She heard the bark first, looked up and
in the growing light of dawn saw Cutter racing toward them.
The moment she opened the car door, the dog was there, by-
passing his own people, as if he could see they were fine but
he wasn't so sure about her. He nudged her with his inquisitive nose and licked at her hands and then her face when she
bent to greet him.

"Hello, Cutter," she said formally. "I guess I have you to
thank for sending the cavalry."

The dog whined, his tail wagging madly. As if satisfied
now she was truly all right, he danced over to greet Hayley,
who had exited the car also. The dog then looked into the
vehicle at Quinn.

"I'll go do another round with Detective Dunbar," he said,
and Kayla had the oddest feeling he was explaining to the
dog as much as anyone.

Somehow, it wouldn't surprise her.

Chapter 20

Dane paced the small, windowless interview room. Two and a half strides one way, three the other. Definitely small.

He'd been here for hours now, and every minute of it had been spent worrying about Kayla more than himself. He'd managed to find out she was alive, but they would not tell him her condition. She might yet die, as far as he knew. It was killing him not to be able to go to her, and he tried to focus on something else.

A firebomb.

It seemed too bizarre, too impossible to be real. Who the hell would toss an incendiary device into Kayla's house? Why? She'd never done anything to hurt anyone—only tried to help people who were dealing with a grief she knew all too much about.

His logical mind warned him against making assumptions based on too little information, but he couldn't help thinking this somehow had to be connected to her parents' murders. And maybe that was logical; what were the odds that an average citizen would twice in their lives be a direct casualty of violent crime?

But after ten years?

His mind tried to spiral toward grim images of a smoking, burning ruin of what had been Kayla's—and his—home once more, and he yanked it back.

The door opened. The same detective who had questioned him before stepped in. Dunbar. In another life, he might have liked the guy, Dane thought. He kind of reminded him of his father—not now, he wasn't old enough, but back when his father had been the same age, mid-thirties, maybe forty.

"Did you see Kayla?" he asked as the man shut the door behind him; he'd heard him tell one of the officers he was heading to the hospital when he'd left a couple of hours ago.

The man didn't answer. He crossed the room and tossed a folder on the small table in the center of the room.

"Sit down."

"Did you see her? Is she all right? Tell me, damn it, and I'll sit all you want."

Dunbar studied him for a moment. "You're not in the strongest bargaining position here."

"I want one simple answer to one simple question. You want answers to many. Sounds like you'd be getting the best of the deal."

Dane thought he saw the man's mouth twitch at one corner. "Can't say I don't admire your logic," he said. Then, coldly, "You should be thankful she's alive. Murder by arson is a death penalty special circumstance."

"Yeah, I heard," Dane said. The officer now standing outside the door had almost gleefully pointed that out.

"That'll land you in Walla Walla waiting for the needle or the noose." He'd said it as if it were the chorus of a song, Dane had thought. Not that it mattered. He wouldn't care, not if Kayla was dead.

But she wasn't. He clung to that.

"Sit down," Dunbar said, "and I promise you before I leave, you'll have your answer."

"Is this your carrot on a stick approach? Forget it. I want to know how Kayla is. Now."

"You don't trust me?"

Dane had to think about that one. "I was raised to trust the police," he finally said. "To believe you're the good guys.

And I do. If it was anything else, if it was anyone but Kayla, I'd be in that chair telling you whatever you want to know."

"But you broke up with her."

"You don't turn off a decade of loving somebody overnight."

Something flickered in the detective's eyes, something dark and shadowy. As if a vision from a nightmare of his own had just shot through his mind.

"No," he agreed softly, "you don't."

"Please," Dane said, just as softly, "just tell me if she's all right."

Dunbar studied him for a long, silent moment. And at last, as if he'd reached some sort of inner conclusion, he spoke.

"She's all right. Minor smoke inhalation, a couple of stitches was the worst of it."

A wave of relief swamped Dane. He sat, not in response to the answer and the agreement so much as because he wasn't sure he could keep standing.

Kayla was all right.

"She reacted pretty quickly, considering," Dunbar was saying. "She got down on the floor and I'm guessing got to the door before the smoke did much damage. And her neighbor got her outside right away."

"Bless Mr. Reyes," Dane said, still feeling a bit wobbly.

Dunbar pulled out the chair across the table and sat down himself. "Lucky for her he was still up and awake, and he ran over."

"He's a night owl. Thank God."

"He said you were a…good kid, I think is how he put it. Said you helped him fix his garage door once."

Dane blinked. "Yeah. Couple of years ago. He had the old style, with the big springs, and one of them broke."

"And the lady on the other side said you saved her cat."

Dane was completely puzzled now. What the hell was all

this about? "I… No. The cat could have gotten down from the roof by himself, and would have, but I was afraid Mrs. Kramer would have a heart attack over it first."

"If you didn't do this, who do you think did?"

The abrupt change back to the grim business of the night threw him. As, he thought, it was probably intended to.

"I've been trying to figure that out," he said. "It just makes no sense to me that it's not…connected to what happened ten years ago. Nobody could want to hurt Kayla. She spends her life trying to help people who are going through what she went through."

"But she deals mostly with crime victims. Which puts her on the radar of criminals."

Dane frowned; he'd not thought of it quite like that. "You mean you think this is related to her work?"

"I'm leaving all options on the table at this point."

Dane had the sudden thought that if this man had been the one investigating Kayla's parents' murders, perhaps things might have turned out differently.

"I can't help you with that. What happens in those sessions is confidential, and Kayla never talks about it."

"Never?"

"I mean, she'll tell me someone new joined and why they're there, but what they say in those sessions is sacred to her. She'd never reveal it, so I don't know anything. Not even names."

"Sounds like an AA meeting."

"It is like one in that people have to trust her to open up. She'd never betray that trust."

"Then who else would want her dead?"

Dane winced at the bald statement. Maybe it was the shock, but he was still having trouble wrapping his mind around the idea that anyone would want to kill Kayla.

"My first thought was Chad," he admitted. "That maybe he was back."

"And you think he'd try to kill her? His own sister?"

"If he killed their parents, why would that be a stretch?"

"According to Ms. Tucker, that's a very big if."

"I know. She's never believed he did it."

"But you did?"

"Not in the beginning. I stood by her and helped her search for him, thinking he had just panicked and run. But the more time passed and he didn't come back but kept sending those notes…"

Dane's voice trailed off, and he shrugged.

"You changed your view."

"He just wasn't acting like somebody who was innocent."

"So you think he's back? And tried to kill his sister?"

Dane sighed. "I don't know. None of this makes any sense. If Chad's back, why would he try to kill her? Wouldn't he at least talk to her first, find out if she was still insisting on his innocence? Why would he kill the one person who'd stood by him the whole time?"

"You're assuming he knows that."

Dane's brows furrowed. "I… Yes, I guess I am." Another thought hit him. "Are you thinking maybe Chad feels she's a threat?"

"There's never been any direct contact, right? If I were a guy who murdered my own parents, I might be thinking my stubborn little sister would never give up looking for the killer."

"You mean he thinks she's looking for the killer, which would be him, rather than what she's really been doing, which is trying to find him to prove him innocent?"

Dane turned the idea over in his mind. It made sense.

"But then why would he keep sending those notes?" he asked. "Why wouldn't he just cut off all contact?"

"That's the kink in that theory," Dunbar admitted. "Which brings us back to the other big question. If it isn't connected to the murder of her parents and it isn't her brother, who else would want her dead?"

Something in the way the man was looking at him told Dane what he was thinking.

"Look, I know you have to look at me, I know there's some hideous statistic about how often murders are committed by someone the victim knows. Hell, I've even used those stats, trying to get Kayla to admit the possibility Chad killed their folks. But I didn't do this, and the more time you waste with me, the less time you're spending looking for the guy who did."

"Funny thing about my job," Dunbar said, leaning back in his chair. "I get to decide what's a waste of time and what's not."

Dane sighed. "What do you want from me? I've told you where I was, everything that happened. What else is there?"

"Let's say, just for the sake of this discussion, I believe you."

Hope surged in him, and Dane was almost taken in by Dunbar's casual tone. He had to remind himself this was no normal discussion—this was an interrogation.

And I'll bet he's good at it, Dane thought.

"Give me some alternatives," Dunbar said. "Her brother, I got that, but as far as we know he's not around."

Dane shook his head in frustration. "I told you, there's nobody. This is Kayla, for God's sake. She's…she's…"

He stopped. None of the words that came to mind were going to help him. Because they all stemmed from the pain of having to walk away from her and the life he'd always thought they'd have.

"No angry clients, ex-boyfriends?"

"She's been mine since we were kids," Dane said. "Everybody knew that. Chad used to rag on her about us—'two nerds in love,' he used to say. When she turned sixteen she... blossomed, I guess. People noticed."

"Guys noticed."

Dane nodded. "Guys who never noticed her before. I mean, Chad's friend Troy always used to ask her to leave me for him, but she thought he was just teasing his best friend's little sister. But then other guys started asking her out."

"And?"

"She always said no. In case you hadn't noticed, Kayla's loyal to the core." His mouth twisted wryly. "Which is why we're in this mess."

"So you're sure she never cheated on you?"

Dane laughed, short and sharp. "She doesn't have it in her. That's just not who she is."

"Thought you had her under control, did you?" Again Dunbar's voice seemed a hair too mild.

Dane laughed again at the very thought. "Nobody 'controls' a woman as smart as Kayla. I'm saying if she wanted out she'd say so."

"Hmm."

Nice and noncommittal, Dane thought. And the silence that spun out afterward invited him to fill it with anything to relieve the tension. Yes, Dunbar was good, he thought. He said nothing more.

A rap on the door disrupted the silence. Dunbar rose and went to talk with the officer outside. The door closed, leaving Dane to wonder what was going on now.

There was no clock in the room, he supposed intentionally; you couldn't complain about how long you'd been in here if you didn't know how long it had been. He couldn't even look at his phone for the time because they'd taken it when they'd brought him here and were probably going through it call by call, contact by contact.

At first he hadn't been worried, other than that they might screw something up, settings or something. There was nothing in that phone that shouldn't be—no incriminating pictures or texts or mysterious phone numbers. Nothing in the least suspicious, unless you found a game of Drone Hunt suspicious.

But now he was wondering. Who knows what might seem suspicious to the police?

Sitting there, alone after Dunbar's interrogation and with the immediate dread about Kayla relieved, the reality of his situation finally began to sink in. And no amount of knowing that that was probably exactly how they wanted him to feel helped alleviate it.

And perversely, ironically, he found himself wondering if he'd been wrong, if maybe Chad was innocent after all.

It could happen. He was sitting here a prime suspect, wasn't he?

And for the first time, it occurred to him to wonder if he was a prime suspect to Kayla, too.

Chapter 21

When the interview room door opened again, Dane was surprised to see Quinn Foxworth come in alone.

Dane glanced at the door, then back to Quinn.

"Aren't they afraid I'll try to strangle you or something?" he asked wearily.

"I think they're assuming I could defend myself," Quinn said.

Dane didn't doubt that. Quinn Foxworth was a tough guy in a very literal sense.

"And I told them they could wait until your lawyer arrived, or let me talk to you now and avoid the burden of attorney-client privilege," Quinn said.

"I don't have a lawyer," Dane said, puzzled.

"You will if it turns out you need one. We have a couple on call. Frankly, I don't think it will come to that."

"You're more confident than I am."

Quinn smiled easily. "That's part of the game. They keep you worried and off balance so you'll make a mistake, say something you shouldn't, to give yourself away."

"But there's nothing to give away."

"So I've been told. Rather vehemently, I might add."

Quinn's expression told him by who. "Kayla," he said, relief softening his voice. "She's really all right?"

"Yes. Cuts and bruises mostly."

Dane finally let himself believe it. Quinn saw his reaction. "They told you that, didn't they?"

"Eventually," Dane said, remembering the battle of wills with Dunbar. "But I wasn't sure they weren't just saying she was okay to get me to talk."

"Good thinking. And if Dunbar had really thought you were guilty, a good tactic."

"You think he doesn't? I mean, I practically lived in that house. It's not like there's not evidence of that."

"I think if he really thought you were guilty, he wouldn't have let me in here no matter what I said."

Dane looked around the room. "Are they listening?"

"Probably," Quinn said cheerfully. "Not a problem."

"Kayla believes I didn't do this?"

"Her defense of you was what they call 'spirited.'"

Dane felt the pressure that had been building in him since he'd wondered if she, too, suspected him, ease a little.

Apparently Quinn found his expression easy to read. "After ten years of her believing in her brother, why would you think she'd abandon you so quickly?"

"Because I said I thought he was guilty. It's the only part of her life where she's not…reasonable."

"Do you really think he did it?"

"I did," Dane admitted. He glanced around at his surroundings and added, "Then."

"Easier to see how the wheels of the system grind when you're in the middle of it, isn't it?"

"I've always believed the cops were the good guys."

"They are," Quinn said. "And I get the feeling Dunbar is a particularly good one. But they're human, contrary to what some think. And when you're fighting a constant, never-ending battle like they do, there are going to be mistakes made."

"Like arresting the wrong guy?"

"They haven't arrested you yet," Quinn pointed out. "There are cases, yes. But remarkably few, considering. More often the courts—or politicians—have a tendency to let the wrong guy walk."

Because Kayla had told him Quinn's history, of how and why the Foxworth Foundation had come to be, Dane was amazed he could speak so calmly about it.

"I didn't do this," Dane said, already weary of protesting his innocence and feeling again that perverse twinge of empathy for Chad.

"I believe you. You didn't do this."

He hesitated. This man had no reason, no long history with him to draw on to reach that conclusion. "You do?"

Quinn nodded. "And I promised Kayla you'd get all the help you need to prove it."

Relief swamped him. And he realized what he felt had to be somewhat like what Kayla had felt when she'd realized she had effective, resourceful help in her search for her brother.

"I'm beginning to realize I've been…not as understanding as I thought I was," Dane said with a grimace.

"A dose of walking in another's shoes does tend to promote understanding," Quinn said.

Quinn's cell chirped the arrival of a text message. He pulled it out and read what appeared to be rather lengthy text.

"I'll be right back," he said and left the room. Dane didn't start pacing again; he wasn't sure he could even get up. He was suddenly tired, almost shaky, as if the adrenaline that had been coursing through him from the moment he'd heard about what had happened had finally ebbed, leaving him enervated.

The door opened again, and Dunbar was back. This time he had Dane's cell phone and handed it over to him. It was turned on with a familiar screen glowing.

"I like the game," the detective said. "You do that?"

"My partner," Dane said. "He does a little designing on the side."

"Cute. He should market it."

"He may," Dane answered, puzzled by the change in attitude.

"Let me know. You'll be able to because you won't be leaving town."

"I hadn't planned to," Dane said, but the last word was spoken to the detective's back as he walked away.

And then Quinn was back.

"Let's get you out of here."

"Out?" Dane was almost afraid to believe it. "I can go?"

"Yes." Quinn nodded his head toward the door.

"What—"

"Let's go," Quinn said, leading him out.

Dane took the hint and stayed quiet. Unlike his arrival, his exit was through the front door. He followed Quinn out the double glass doors into a brilliantly sunny morning.

"It cleared out," he said, blinking at the brightness. The sun rose early this time of year, and even now, at 5:30 a.m., it was well clear of the Cascade Mountains.

"Good thing it rained last night," Quinn said.

"Because of the fire."

Quinn shook his head. "Because that's probably the main reason you're walking out of here."

Dane's brows lowered. "What do you mean?"

Quinn unlocked the doors of the blue SUV and they got in.

"So be thankful for the rain," Quinn went on, "and the cop that lives downstairs from you."

"Jarrod? What's he got to do with it?"

"His parking space is next to yours."

"I know, but—"

"He worked a split shift on DUI patrol last night. Got home about 3:00 a.m. His car was wet. Yours was dry. He noticed."

"Damn," Dane said, half to himself. "Thank you, Jarrod. I'll wash your car for you next time."

"It's not enough to clear you completely—you could have used another method to get there—but it got you out for now."

"I'll quit complaining when he parks crooked."

Quinn grinned as he started the engine. "He wasn't real happy when Teague woke him up two hours after he got to bed, but he cooperated. Called Detective Dunbar right away."

They pulled out of the parking lot. Dane wondered where they'd be going but was more curious about what had just happened.

"That was the text?"

"Part of it." Quinn shrugged. "The officers talked to most of your neighbors, but they knew your neighbor had worked that late shift, that he'd been on the street at the time of the explosion, so they let him slide, figuring they'd check with him later. We weren't so considerate, I'm afraid."

"Thanks for that," Dane said fervently. "What was the other part of the text?"

"It was word from our tech-head, that he'd pulled your on-line messaging session with the company in Dublin from your system. Under the circumstances, I didn't think you'd mind."

Dane drew back. "He hacked me? How'd he do that? I've got some pretty tight security in place."

"So he told me. But he's good," Quinn said.

"He must be really, really good."

"He is."

"Now they might say anybody could have been pretending to be you," Quinn said.

Dane shook his head. "I've got a log of that discussion. It's pretty detailed, with stuff only I would know."

"Good."

Quinn made a right turn, away from Kayla's place and his apartment building.

"We're not going to Kayla's?"

"No. I think you'd best stay away for a while. Later maybe."

"Afraid I'll get upset? It was practically my home, too."

"No. It's the returning to the scene of the crime thing. Arsonists have a tendency to do that. Don't want to make Dunbar change his mind."

Dane sighed. "Not sure I want to see it anyway."

"Actually, from the front, it doesn't look like anything happened. It was just the back. The bedroom."

Dane suppressed a shudder. "God. She could have been killed."

"If she'd been in there, yes."

"Why wasn't she?"

Quinn glanced at him. "Same reason you weren't sleeping at two in the morning, I imagine."

He couldn't deny that so Dane fell silent, wrestling with the one question that now seemed paramount. He hadn't bombed Kayla's house, so who had?

"Who the hell would have done it?" he muttered.

"That's the real question, isn't it?" Quinn said. "If we take you out of the picture, then the most likely possibilities are it's connected to what happened ten years ago or to Kayla's work now."

"But why would anybody try to hurt somebody who's just helping people? And if it's connected to her folks, why now, after all this time?"

"If we knew those answers we'd have the answer," Quinn said as he made another turn that told Dane they were headed out to Foxworth.

"Dunbar said all options were still on the table."

"I said he's a good cop."

"So you think he's considering the other possibilities?"

"I know he is. I'm guessing the speculation is that somebody in her counseling group is a threat. They're all the victims of crimes, which means there are perpetrators. Maybe one that's still on the loose is afraid Kayla will discover something from one of them."

"But then why not go after the person? Why go after her?"

"Exactly the problem with that theory."

"Then it has to be related to her folks, even if it was ten years ago."

"That's a long time to stay dormant," Quinn said.

"But something's changed," Dane said. "She has you looking into it now. It's not just her trying on her own anymore."

"Yes."

"Foxworth has a high level of success. If the killer found out you were involved…"

"It could be that our presence has stirred up something," Quinn said, "whoever the killer is. And the bottom line is always that there's no statute of limitations on murder."

Dane absorbed all the implications. "That means…he's back."

"Assuming he ever really left, yes."

Quinn's calm tone told Dane the man had already realized that. He was beginning to doubt Quinn was ever really surprised by anything.

"What now?"

"Now? We turn up the heat."

Chapter 22

Dane heard the trumpeting bark and saw Cutter already racing through the open warehouse door the moment the SUV cleared the trees.

"He doesn't miss much, does he?"

Quinn laughed. "I don't think he misses anything."

There was a bright red smaller SUV Dane hadn't seen before parked near the office building door.

"That's Hayley's," Quinn said. "They're here."

They. "You don't mean just Hayley and Cutter, do you?"

"I doubt Hayley—or Cutter for that matter—would let Kayla out of their sight just now."

The dog was at the passenger door of the car, waiting with ill-concealed impatience for Dane to exit. Puzzled, Dane glanced at Quinn.

"Why isn't he over there waiting for you?"

"He knows I'm all right. You, not so much. He always knows who needs checking on."

Dane opened the door and stepped out. Cutter moved to him, sniffing, looking, nudging. Finally he sat, apparently satisfied that Dane had come to no harm while out of his care.

"You," Dane said, rubbing a hand over the dog's dark head, "are something else, dog."

Cutter made a sound that Dane could only call satisfied. Whether it was that he was all right, or that he had finally realized the uniqueness of this animal, Dane wasn't sure.

Cutter's head turned just slightly, back toward the warehouse. Seconds later a man came out, someone Dane hadn't seen before. Tall and rangy, he walked with a barely perceptible limp on his left side. He was wiping his hands on a shop rag; he'd clearly been working on something mechanical.

"Rafe Crawford, Dane Burdette," Quinn said.

Rafe nodded, indicating with the greasy rag why he wasn't offering a hand to shake. "Checking out the backup generator."

Dane nodded at the man. Without the distraction of a handshake, it was the man's eyes he noticed; they reminded him of Kayla's, not in color but in a certain quality of having seen too much, of reflecting too much pain lived through.

Opposites, he thought, the two Foxworth men they'd met. Teague, with his easy, crooked grin and jokes, and now this man, unsmiling in face or eyes. That interested him—as much as anything outside his own current dilemma did just now.

"Is it working all right?" Quinn asked the newcomer.

Rafe nodded. "Not that it's as crucial, now that you're living…elsewhere."

Quinn's smile, quick and contented, was the only answer he gave to that.

"You got things settled in Boise?" he asked.

Rafe nodded again. "Everybody arrived. Happy reunion."

"Good. Why don't you take some time? That was a tough one."

"I'm good."

"Didn't say you weren't."

Rafe glanced at Dane. "Thought you might need another body on this one."

"Interested?"

"Cold case," Rafe said with a shrug.

"All right then," Quinn said. "Meet us inside."

"I'll go clean up."

"What was that all about?" Dane asked. It was obvious

the two men were old friends; they'd spoken in the kind of shorthand that showed long familiarity.

"Rafe's got a thing for cold cases," Quinn said. "And he never gives up on them."

"He and Kayla should relate then," Dane said. There was none of the recent sourness at the thought in his voice or his mind; nearly losing her had wiped all that away, at least for now.

But it hadn't really changed anything. It hadn't caused some great revelation about how much he loved her—he'd already known that. He'd always known that.

Just like he knew he always would love her.

Even if he had to go on without her.

Hayley met them at the door.

"You're here early," Quinn said.

"She just couldn't bear to stay still any longer, so we came here."

"How is Kayla?" Dane asked, unable to hold back the question long enough to offer a hello.

Hayley didn't seem offended by the lack of a greeting. "She's steadier now. She'll be sore tomorrow, I'm guessing, but for now she's all right. As soon as we're done going over everything, I'm going to run over to her place and see what I can salvage in the way of immediate needs."

"They'll let you in?" Dane asked.

She smiled. "I checked just now, and the arson investigator has pulled all his evidence. Besides, the fire chief was a friend of my father's. I'll get in."

"Do they know what it was yet?"

"They're still reconstructing. But I'll pester them until we know."

Quinn snorted. "You, a pest? Nah."

She smiled sweetly at him. "If I wasn't, we probably wouldn't be here now."

Quinn's voice went soft. "And I wouldn't trade that for anything."

"Nor would I."

Dane shifted as pain jabbed through him. He and Kayla had once sounded like that. Teasing in the most loving way possible. Hayley flicked a glance at Dane, and he knew something must have shown in his face because she went on briskly.

"Kayla wanted to come, too, but I don't think that's wise. And she doesn't need to see the damage yet."

"Agreed," Quinn said. "I think they should both stay away until we find out who was really behind this."

"Teague's working on that, by the way. He called while you were at the police station, said he had an idea he was going to check out."

"That's why I hired the boy," Quinn said with a grin. "Let's get started."

The moment she heard footsteps on the stairs Kayla knew, with that sort of sixth sense that always told her when Dane was nearby, before they even got close to the door. Hayley had been in and out a couple of times, and the tall, lean, intimidating man she'd introduced as Rafe Crawford had come through that door once, but this time it was Dane. She could feel it.

She drew in a deep breath and tried to steady herself. She'd rehearsed it all in her mind from the moment Hayley had told her Quinn had gotten Dane out and they were on their way. She would greet him like a normal person. It would be awkward, sure, as it always was between former lovers, she supposed. She didn't actually know; Dane was the only lover she'd ever had.

The only lover she'd ever wanted.

She would greet him no differently than, say, she would

greet Quinn when he came in. Pleasantly but as a man who didn't belong to her.

It hit her again, as it had so many times last night before her world had exploded. He didn't belong to her anymore.

Which meant he was free to belong to someone else.

Images shot through her mind, of Dane with some unknown, carefree, unhaunted woman who could give him the kind of love he deserved, free of baggage. She could see him smiling with her, laughing with her, making love to her. It hurt so badly she would swear she was bleeding inside.

Quinn and Hayley had been there for her last night, she couldn't deny that. But it wasn't the same, not by a long shot. Nothing could replace the comfort and knowledge of a shared history. She'd always had Dane to turn to for comfort. Had always counted on him to be there. And then he was gone, and she felt more lost than she had since the night she'd come home to find her parents lying dead in their blood-spattered den.

Was it worth it? Was this endless pursuit really worth it? Trying to find someone who clearly didn't want to be found even, or as Dane had said, maybe especially not by her?

She'd thought before about quitting, but she hadn't. She'd even sort of prided herself on not giving up. But was it truly all worth it if it cost her the one person who had always been her rock?

She felt the sudden urge to call it all off, to finally give it up, except that now it had gotten even more complicated.

Now someone had tried to kill her.

The door opened. Quinn came through first.

And then there was Dane, looking tired and almost as haggard as she felt.

All her good intentions vanished and she ran to him. She couldn't help herself—he looked so weary. She may have had the worst of it physically, but to see Dane, strong, steady Dane, look like this was more than she could bear.

She threw her arms around him. After a split-second delay perhaps only she would notice, his arms came up and wrapped around her. For a long moment they simply stood there, as if either of them would fall without the support of the other.

Don't talk, she ordered herself. Don't say anything because then you'll have to face reality, that this is only temporary, that it's only because of what happened, that he's holding you because you were hurt, that he would do it for anyone who needed it because he was the kind of man who helped.

He spoke first.

"You're really all right?"

She nodded against his chest.

"Stitches?"

She nodded again, this time hunching her left shoulder to indicate where.

"Your hair smells different."

She sighed at the simple yet intimate statement. And gave in.

"Yes. I borrowed some of Hayley's shampoo."

She felt him move then, lifting his head to look at Hayley and Quinn, who were quietly ignoring them.

"Thank you for taking care of her," he said.

"Of course," Hayley said. "Do you want some more time? We could go—"

"No."

The flat statement dug into that painful place inside Kayla. She heard Dane draw in a deep breath.

"I'll take care of her now. I'm not leaving her alone again until this is over."

Hope, battered, bloody, yet ever-ready to rise again, stirred from that painful place. As if he'd sensed it—of course he did, Dane always knew—he quickly smashed it into oblivion.

"Nothing's changed," he said to her. "I just want to walk away by my choice—not have that choice made by someone else, leaving me to grieve your death."

Kayla shuddered, then straightened and stopped leaning on him. Just as she was going to have to learn to do the rest of her life.

Chapter 23

"Thanks, Chief Byers," Hayley said into her cell phone, then pushed the button to disconnect.

They had all fallen silent when the call from the fire chief had come in. They were seated around the same table where they'd begun this barely a week ago. So much had happened in that short time, Kayla thought as Hayley listened carefully.

"He got the reports just now," Hayley said as she set the phone down.

"Good of him to call so quickly," Quinn said.

"He and my dad were close. When I was little he was like my uncle. And he helped when my mother was ill and was there for me when she died."

"That puts him on the 'come running if he calls' list for me then," Quinn said.

To Kayla's surprise, Hayley blushed. It reminded her that, relatively speaking, their relationship was fairly new. Of course, relative to her and Dane, and at their ages, most were.

She glanced at him surreptitiously. He'd taken a seat across the table from her this time, making an obvious, physical point about the new distance between them. She should have expected this, she'd thought when he'd done it. Dane was not a man to make a decision and then crumble at the first difficulty. The strength that had always been hers to borrow when needed was now arrayed against her, and he was as distant as if that table was miles wide.

She was distracted slightly when Cutter showed his displeasure with the new arrangement. He walked from Dane to her and back again, nudging them and whining quietly.

"Not now, sweetie," Hayley said softly to the dog, who sighed audibly and plopped down on the floor. Kayla felt the weight on her right foot and looked down to see his head resting on her toe. Coincidentally—or perhaps not because this was Cutter—his tail appeared to be wrapped around Dane's left ankle, as if the dog would maintain contact between them even if they wouldn't.

She scratched the dog's ear, straightened and looked at Dane. He didn't react. His expression was stony, emotionless. If he'd noticed the flash of warmth, of tenderness between Hayley and Quinn, or the oddly touching action of their dog, he wasn't reacting.

She had put that expression on his face, she thought sadly. She had never meant to do that.

Kayla tuned back into what Hayley was saying about the device used to start the fire.

"—the explosion was apparently some type of homemade grenade. The fire starter was a rather amateurish Molotov cocktail, he said. The bottle he used was too heavy to shatter, so it only broke into a couple of big pieces, which contained things a little."

"That doesn't help narrow it down much," Quinn said. "It could still go either way unless Chad had a fascination with fire. Did he?"

This was clearly directed at her, Kayla realized. "No," she said. "Never."

"Never interested in blowing up toy buildings or cherry bombs in mailboxes or the like?"

"No," she said again. "Firecrackers as a kid, but we all did that. I don't think he'd even know how to build something like this, even it if was simple."

"Too much like chemistry," Dane said. "Which is too much like work."

"That's—"

"True," Dane said, cutting her off. "Did you think I really believed that chem homework you asked for help with was your friend Crystal's?"

"A moot point," Quinn said rather quickly, as if he thought another kind of explosion was imminent. "He's obviously had enough time to have learned."

"And he didn't have to learn well. Good thing he never did, isn't it?" Dane asked.

Kayla opened her mouth to protest, a reaction she hadn't realized until now had become so automatic. She stopped herself and remained silent. Something about Dane's tone was…different.

"But it was effective enough," Hayley said. "If Kayla had been in that room, the outcome would probably have been very different. If there's a next time—"

"If there is she won't be alone," Dane said.

The words should have heartened her, and they would have if Kayla hadn't just realized why he sounded so odd, why his voice was so different. Gone was the trace of irritation, impatience. He was speaking in a dispassionate voice. Like a man not personally involved.

He was speaking as if he were some kind of bodyguard who had never met her before, as if he were simply doing a job he felt obligated to do.

This is what it would be like, she thought, if Dane really didn't care. Fear grew in her until she could hardly breathe. With an effort almost as great as it had taken to get to the front door last night, she reined in her rampaging thoughts and made herself pay attention.

"—he thinks Foxworth would quit and go away, even if

he'd been successful, he's very, very wrong," Quinn was saying. "We don't give up."

Kayla remembered Hayley telling her something about a leak, possibly a mole, who had threatened the operation that had thrown her and Quinn together. And that Quinn would never, ever stop until he found who it was. It eased Kayla's mind a little, that idea, that even if something happened to her, there were people now who would carry on.

"What about Rod Warren?" Dane asked. "If he was into burning small creatures…."

"Good point," Quinn said.

"And torturing animals is frequently a warning sign of sociopathic behavior," Hayley said.

"Why don't you call Detective Dunbar and plant that idea," Quinn said. "He liked you."

Hayley let out a muffled, embarrassed sound. "Please."

"Trust me on this. I know when a man's looking at my fiancée that way." Hayley blushed then. "Fortunately, I also know he's the kind of man who'd never poach."

Hayley glanced at Kayla as if for female support. "Don't you just love it when they go all guy on you?"

"Yes." With an effort, Kayla didn't look at Dane. "As a matter of fact I do."

Dane said nothing, and Kayla wished she'd kept her mouth shut.

"Do we have that list of the crime victim group members?" Quinn asked quickly, as if he'd sensed the tension.

"I have it," Hayley said, pulling a sheet out of the file. Then she turned to the laptop computer that sat on the table beside her. "And here's the background we've turned up on them. I finished entering it all from Teague's notes while we were waiting for you to get here."

Quinn smiled at her. Kayla remembered Hayley telling her about how she'd begun actually working with Foxworth, after meeting—and falling for—Quinn. How she'd been rather rudderless after her mother's death, and finding this work that so appealed to her had been the second-best thing, after finding Quinn, that had ever happened to her.

Obviously she'd gotten into it wholeheartedly and efficiently. She envied them the obvious solidity of their lives together. She was sure they would make it. While she and Dane might not.

She clung to that "might" with a fierceness that she knew was foolish even as she did it. One look across at Dane's face told her that.

"Here's the one that had caught my eye," Hayley said as the screen went live and an image flashed up on the screen.

"Art Solis?" Kayla asked, startled.

"He's working for a building contractor now, but he used to work for the Department of Transportation. Road construction. Assigned to a mountain district."

"They occasionally use explosives," Dane said, as if he were contemplating a merely interesting puzzle.

"No!" Kayla shook her head. "Art would never hurt anyone. He's a sweet, nice man. He was devastated by his daughter's death. In fact, he's still in the processing stage, practically nonfunctional."

Hayley patted Kayla's hand. "I said he *had* caught my eye. But the call from Chief Byers changes that."

Quinn nodded. "Not dealing with a pro here. And if he's in the state Kayla describes, not likely. But then again, if he's in that state, he might have been sloppier than he would have if he were thinking straight."

"But why would he?" Kayla asked. "Samantha was killed when her car was broadsided by an escaping bank robber. Why would that make me a target? In fact, why would I become a target to any of them?"

"Maybe none of them are thinking straight," Dane said.

"He's right," Hayley said gently when Kayla tightened her jaw to keep from reacting. "You know better than most that grief can deeply affect your thinking."

"Reasons are something we may have to figure out later," Quinn said. "Right now we just need to know if there are any others with the potential."

They began to go through the list. Kayla watched uncomfortably as the familiar names flashed by on the screen. She knew the painful stories behind every name, and she didn't like that they were being paraded like this. She hadn't betrayed any confidences, had only given names that weren't confidential anyway, but Foxworth clearly had an efficient and far-reaching research capability.

She simply couldn't believe that any of them would be involved. Why would a victim who knew the pain they had experienced do something that could cause someone else the same kind of pain? She knew there were people out there who were simply wired wrong, sociopaths, even psychopaths, but none of her people fit that description. She just couldn't wrap her mind around the idea—

Quinn's cell phone rang, and Kayla was thankful for the interruption.

"They wouldn't," she insisted quietly as Quinn turned slightly away to listen to whoever had called. "They've been through too much pain themselves to want to cause it for others."

"Sometimes grief can send people over the edge," Dane said. It was in that same, uninvolved tone, yet Kayla couldn't help wondering if it had been aimed at her. She heard Quinn speaking to whoever had called but so quietly she couldn't understand what he was saying. She focused on Dane's assertion.

"Those are the people who don't come looking for help

in the first place," she said, keeping her voice even with an effort.

Dane didn't look at her when she spoke, but he did look thoughtful. "Fair point," he said.

Fair. Oh, yes, Dane was fair. He always had been. Sometimes it had annoyed her, when she was running hot over something and he insisted on pointing out the validity of some aspect on the other side. But now it just hurt. Because when it had come down to something that hurt her, personally, he'd ever and always tossed that out and stood with her. He'd always had her back, whether he agreed completely or not.

Until now.

Quinn stood up, and all three still seated at the table looked at him. He slipped his phone back into his pocket. For a moment he said nothing, and Kayla felt apprehension building inside her. When his gaze shifted, and settled on her, it spiked into fear.

"That was Teague," he finally said. "He's been out covering old ground to see if anyone saw or heard anything that might tie into the firebombing."

"And?" Dane asked when Kayla didn't, couldn't speak.

"He didn't find anything new there. But he did learn something else."

When Quinn didn't go on immediately, Kayla found her voice. "What?" she demanded because it was clear that whatever it was, Quinn wasn't happy about having to tell her.

"He found someone who saw your brother."

Kayla's heart leaped. "Where? When? Who saw him? Are they sure?"

The questions tumbled from her excitedly. She'd hoped Foxworth could really help, that they were as good as they said, but to get this close in such a short time? They were miracle workers.

Dane leaned back in his chair, and she got the impression

he was mentally and physically backing away. But her excitement over the news made her put that on hold for the moment.

"Where?" she repeated, wondering why Quinn wouldn't just tell her.

And then he did, in a voice that held no pleasure or triumph.

"Here."

Kayla's breath caught. "Here? In Redwood Cove? But that's crazy. Why would he come back and not contact me?"

"Maybe he did, in his own, charming way," Dane said, and there was something dark and harsh in his tone.

She made the jump quickly. He thought Chad had done this. With no proof at all, even less than had been at the scene of the murders ten years ago.

She glared at him, wanting suddenly to prod him into saying it, even as she realized it was with the hope he would make her angry enough to start getting over him.

"What's that supposed to mean?" she asked him, her voice sharp.

"Depends on the answer to 'when,'" Dane said with a glance at Quinn.

Quinn sighed. Kayla turned back to him.

In a voice so gentle she knew the words were going to hold pain, in his view anyway, Quinn finally answered her.

"Last night. Just after 2:00 a.m. Near your house."

Chapter 24

Kayla felt like a suddenly punctured balloon. Deflated, limp. Pressure had been building up inside her until she'd felt as if she would come apart, and then, in less than ten words, Quinn Foxworth had burst the bubble she'd been living in.

Chad. Here.

Without contacting her.

Last night.

Near her home.

At about the time of the explosion.

"Who saw him?" It was Dane, speaking calmly, as if the world hadn't just collapsed.

Because it's only your world now. Not his.

"Troy Reid," Quinn said.

Kayla's head came up. "Troy saw him?"

This destroyed her tiny, lingering hope that it had been a mistake, that someone had only thought they'd seen Chad or had seen someone who looked like him. Troy had known Chad too well—he wouldn't make a mistake like that.

"Yes. And," Quinn added, "Teague said he was pretty upset when he told Troy what had happened. He wanted to know if you were all right, if you needed anything. He'll probably call you later."

"Where is my brother now?"

"We don't know," Quinn answered.

She frowned. "Troy didn't know? They were always best friends."

"He says he has no idea. Teague says he said he was completely surprised when he saw him—a little shocked even that Chad hadn't let him know he was back."

"The great Troy Reid caught off guard," Dane muttered. "I would have liked to have seen that."

There was a whiff of the old rivalry in his voice, and Kayla didn't know whether to be angry or secretly pleased about it. Maybe Dane hadn't shut things off as completely as it seemed.

"Now what?" she asked.

"We keep looking. You get some rest."

"But I—"

Dane cut her off. "You've been up all night, and you've been hurt, shocked and through hell. You need sleep."

She would have been happier about his interruption if he'd sounded more concerned and less like that impartial bodyguard she'd thought of earlier. But the thought of collapsing into bed was suddenly so appealing she thought if she closed her eyes she might doze off right here.

And then it struck her.

She didn't have a bed. Not anymore.

"Where?" She wished she hadn't sounded quite so forlorn.

"My place," Dane said.

"Or ours," Hayley put in.

"Neither," Quinn said, relieving her of that decision. "Until we're sure who's behind this, you should stay clear of anyplace you'd be expected to go."

Thankful that there was at least some doubt, somewhere, that Chad had done this, Kayla nodded.

"Where then?" she asked.

"We're a little short on safe houses in the area at the moment," he said.

"Speaking of things that have been blown up," Hayley said. There was a lighthearted note in her voice that seemed at odds with the words, and she and Quinn exchanged a glance that made Kayla smile despite her own turmoil, knowing the story of how they had met.

"There's an old motel over by Freedom Bay," Dane said.

"And Mrs. Clark's B and B," Kayla said. "Although I wouldn't want to cause her any problems."

"The motel, I think," Quinn said. "And you should take one of our cars, just in case."

He picked up his cell phone and pushed a single button.

"Rafe? We need a car. An anonymous one. Can we borrow yours?" A pause, then, "Okay, thanks."

He disconnected and looked at Kayla with a smile. "It looks like it couldn't get out of its own way, but looks are deceiving. More important, it blends."

"I'll be careful with it," Kayla said.

"I'll drive."

Her head snapped around to stare at Dane.

"I told you, I'm not leaving you alone until this is over." He looked at Quinn. "You have any problem with that?"

"None. I assumed," Quinn said easily. "We'll get you both some clothes and whatever else you need at the moment."

And just like that, she was dispensed with. Her next move decided by the men. She would have argued if she wasn't so tired. Too tired to even think.

Which told her, she supposed, that she shouldn't be arguing at all. Maybe it wasn't a male thing. Maybe it was the awake deciding for the half-asleep. And just as well.

Quinn hadn't been kidding, Dane thought. The slightly battered, decade-old silver coupe didn't look like much, but it purred like a big cat and shifted like silk, and when he put his foot in it from a stop sign he discovered it had some big dog tendencies, too—quick and powerful enough to bark the tires.

But most welcome for him was the fact that he didn't have to make an adjustment for his long legs. He and Rafe were about the same height, and he always felt a little cramped in most cars. Not this one, despite the fact that it seemed no bigger than any other average car on the road.

"A wolf in sheep's clothing," he murmured as they left the city limits and headed down the narrower part of the road through thicker trees and dappled sunlight.

"Sort of like its owner," Kayla said, the first time she'd spoken since they'd left Foxworth. "A little beat up on the outside but lethally effective."

Dane glanced at her, curious enough about what she'd said to set aside his determination to speak to her as little as possible. "Lethally?"

"Hayley told me he's the team sniper."

Team *sniper?*

Dane's perception of Foxworth as a do-gooder, strictly investigative-type organization shifted suddenly. They had—needed—a sniper?

"Teague wasn't kidding when he said Quinn kidnapped her. That really is how they met."

Dane knew her well enough to recognize she was feeling the urge to talk, to pretend things were normal between them simply because they were not. She kept going with the story, and he hoped she wasn't harboring the hope that pretending long enough could make it real. Yet he found it a relief himself; the strain of being with her was already beginning to wear at the edges of his control.

"Explosions, sieges, literal fly-by-night escapes and a sniper?" Dane said when she had finished the tale, shaking his head. "There's obviously a hell of a lot more to the Foxworth Foundation than I realized."

"Hayley said they do occasionally get involved in nasty situations. That this witness they helped knew of them because they'd rescued an American girl from a drug cartel. Took her right out from under the nose of some big drug lord."

"Sounds like something we have government people for," Dane said.

"But they didn't do anything. Bogged down in diplomacy and political haggling, Hayley said, and the girl nearly died. Would have, if they hadn't gone in and gotten her."

"Bet that made them unpopular in some quarters."

"Hayley said that's the best part. They're independent, not connected to any agency, and have extensive resources. They don't need anyone's approval to act."

"What about fallout afterward?"

"I guess some of those resources go to some really good attorneys," Kayla said.

"So they're not beholden to anyone, but there are many, many people beholden to them," Dane said.

"That's how it works."

"Sort of gives a new definition to balance of power, doesn't it?" he mused aloud.

"Exactly," Kayla said with a small laugh.

And Dane realized that somehow things had slipped back into normal. As if her pretending really had made it real.

He was going to have to be on guard, he thought. It would be very, very easy to let it happen, to let it all slide away like a patch of debris floating in a stream, forgotten once it was out of sight and replaced by clear, fresh water.

The motel, with a small café attached, appeared on the right, tucked back into the trees. The nearest other buildings had been left behind at least a mile back. Dane wasn't sure if that was good or bad, but Quinn had seemed happy enough with the choice, and with his new awareness of some of the unexpected skills of the whole Foxworth organization, he decided that was good enough.

He'd have to stay alert and aware, though. And right now, after the long, rough night, he was feeling a bit ragged. But it was Kayla who had been hurt, who needed rest; he was just going to have to manage.

He ordered Kayla to stay in the car with the doors locked while he went into the office. He found that the ever-efficient Hayley had called ahead for them, and he was back in moments with a key in his pocket. An old-fashioned key dangling from a ring that also held a heavy brass tag in the shape of an orca, that icon of the Northwest.

Then he walked to the café and ordered two of the largest coffees they had and a couple of sandwiches for later. Once they were in, he didn't want to come back out unless he had to.

The room was at the far end of a row of six, and Dane guessed it had been chosen specifically for that location; there were no vending machines, no laundry facility, nothing was beyond that last door, so no one had reason to be there except the occupants. He wouldn't be surprised if Quinn knew that already. Or had been able to find it out in the time it had taken them to get here; the Foxworth research capabilities were very impressive.

He parked the car near the opposite end of the building, as Quinn had suggested. He wasn't sure it would help if Chad— or whoever—came after them, but it might slow him down enough for them to realize he was there and give them time to escape.

He just had to be awake to realize it.

"We're down here," he said when Kayla gave him a puzzled look as he started to walk back along the row of doors. She looked more than just puzzled by his actions, but he wanted her inside and safe before he explained about the slight diversion of parking the car in front of a different room.

It wasn't until he had the door open and they'd stepped inside that she turned to look at him, then at the single room key, and asked the simple question that had apparently really been behind the deeper intensity of her expression.

"We?"

He steeled himself. "One room. Two beds."

She looked around, saw the two queen-size beds, and color crept up into her cheeks.

Two beds, he told himself. No problem. Sure.

Dane closed the door behind them, refusing to think about the hell he'd let himself in for.

Maybe he'd have no problem staying awake after all.

Chapter 25

"Do your folks ever fight?"

Dane blinked at the seeming non sequitur and at the oddity of it in itself; she knew his parents, they—

Damn.

It hit him abruptly. He was going to have to tell them. And his mother would be…maybe not pleased but relieved. And that would smart. It would probably be best to just let her think he'd finally seen the light, that he'd finally taken her advice after all these years.

"Do they?"

"No. They've been married thirty years."

"Are you saying they don't have anything to fight about anymore, or that they never did?"

He frowned. Was she really trying to make some sort of comparison between what was happening between them and a marital spat?

"Of course they did. When I was a kid they'd argue now and then, just not much anymore. They've learned how to deal. What's that got to do with anything?"

"They love each other more than any couple I've ever known. I just wondered if it was always smooth sailing."

Just like that she took the wind out of his sails. And reminded him of something he'd once learned that he'd shoved so far back into the "don't want to think about it" part of his mind that he indeed rarely did.

When he was nineteen, home from college for a visit, he'd

learned his parents had actually separated for a while. His uncle Alex, who his mother had always said needed a governor on his mouth, had let slip one day that Dane's father had once spent several weeks sleeping in his attic room. To this day he didn't know the full story of what had happened with them at the time relative newlyweds; neither of them would discuss it.

"Newlywed problems. We worked it out," was all his mother would say, "and because it was before you were born, it's not your concern."

"Working it out is *why* you were born," his father had quipped, earning him a simultaneous glare and blush from his wife. And that had embarrassed the still teenaged Dane enough that he dropped the subject forever.

He'd never told Kayla that, he realized. That was at the time when his long absences away at school, and the unrelenting peer pressure over loving someone younger at that stage of life, had stretched their relationship to its thinnest. Until now.

Only Kayla's unswerving loyalty had kept them going back then. The same unswerving loyalty she had to her brother. Could he really hold that against her when he had reaped the benefits? And hadn't she been just as loyal to him, even when he'd been the prime suspect in the attack on her?

And there it was, he thought. Just what he'd been afraid of. An hour alone with her in a motel room, and he was looking for reasons to backtrack, to change his mind, to go back to what they'd had, that loving, deep, and then passionate relationship that had been his foundation for so long.

"I'm going to go out and look around. Quinn said to make sure I knew what normal looked like here so I could spot anything different."

"Makes sense," she said, not calling him on the abrupt change of subject.

"I need you to promise me to stay here."

"I'll go with—"

"No."

It came out more sharply than he'd meant it to. She jerked back as if he'd raised a hand to her, and that hurt as much as if she'd actually slapped him.

"You're the target," he said. "The last thing we need is you outside advertising where you are."

She couldn't argue with that, he told himself.

"And you want to be alone," she said. "Away. From me."

No, she didn't argue, but she didn't leave it at that, either. She knew him too well.

"Yes," he said, not seeing the point in denying it. His brain knew the truth; they were over. His heart, gut and especially his body were taking a lot longer to get the message.

"I'll rap on the window first when I come back."

She didn't answer. He supposed there was nothing more to say. He set the lock, closed the door behind him, shoved the key into his pocket and just stood there for a moment.

In the short time they'd been inside clouds had rolled in, turning what had been a sunny day into the typical grayness. "January" in the Northwest, he thought. Normally it didn't bother him; this time of year the sun rose at 4:30 a.m. and it didn't really get dark until nearly ten, so there was more than enough daylight. At 4:30 a.m., it seemed too much.

But that was in Kayla's house, where her bedroom windows faced—had faced—east. He wondered what was left of it now.

She'd wanted to go by, wanted to see just how bad it was, but he'd followed Quinn's advice to get her under wraps right away. It had been only advice, but something about the man, some air of knowledge, of command, made it hard to do anything else.

Dane knew he was ex-military, and he suspected that both

Teague and Rafe were also. He'd asked once if all Foxworth people were, and got, "Many, but not all," as his answer.

He wondered what a nonmilitary person had to do or be to make it into the Foxworth fold, what criteria they had. From what he'd seen of Quinn, it was probably very particular.

Dane walked around the building, trying to untangle his chaotic thoughts. He was usually more organized in his thinking, and this tumbling from one subject to the next, like a billiard ball bouncing off the sides of the table, was disconcerting. He knew it was all to keep from thinking about the one thing that was unbearable, but he couldn't seem to find anything strong enough to put it out of his mind.

He finished his circuit, trying to set the details in his mind. The faded red sedan parked behind the office was likely the clerk's, and he guessed whoever worked the next shift would park in the same place. The trees had been cleared enough to give a good fifteen feet of grass around the back of the building, and the parking area was a clear field of view out to the street.

He supposed it would be possible to come in through the trees and not be seen. It appeared to be open forest behind them, and fences weren't the norm out here. So if he assumed any approach would be from the rear, the only weakness he could see was the bathroom window. It was the only window in the room that opened to the back. It was high, but not impossible to reach. And it was small, but an adult could get through if they had time to squirm or were particularly athletic. The frosted glass prevented anyone from seeing inside but also declared exactly what room it was.

Once he had it set in his mind, he headed back. Kayla had opened the curtains in the front window, but thankfully she wasn't in sight. He tapped the window with his knuckles as he went by to let her know it was him.

When he unlocked the door and stepped inside, he saw

that she had pulled one of the two upholstered chairs off to one side, to where she could see through the opened curtains but not be seen except by someone right at the window or at an extreme angle. So she was, at least, taking this seriously. That relieved some of the pressure that had been building.

She was sitting in that chair and talking on her phone. She glanced up when he came in.

"You're not telling anyone where you are?"

The look she gave him was both answer and opinion.

"Sorry," he muttered as he locked the door behind him, stifling the urge to close the curtains; she was taking care and he didn't want to upset her more than she already was.

He walked back to the bathroom and checked the window that had caught his attention. There was a latch on the lower sash, but it was a bit flimsy and old, and he imagined it wouldn't take a lot to overpower or break it, even from the outside.

Warning was the best he could do, so he took the paper-wrapped glasses that were next to the ice-bucket on the dresser, unwrapped them and lined them up on upper edge of the lower sash of the window. There was just enough room for them to balance a bit precariously. He might not be able to stop somebody from trying to open that window, but at least he could make it a noisy proposition. He'd have to warn Kayla; it wouldn't take much to knock those off.

When he came back into the main room, Kayla was off the phone.

"Hayley is coming over. She's bringing clothes and tooth-brushes and stuff."

He tensed. "Clothes? She's not going to your place, is she?"

Kayla looked at him rather oddly. "No, she bought things. My stuff will need to be cleaned. If there's anything left," she ended sadly. "I gave her your sizes and preferences earlier."

"Oh." He tried to ignore the implied intimacy of that last

bit. She was still giving him that quizzical look, and he felt compelled to add, "I just didn't want her coming from there straight here. Quinn said arsonists like to revisit."

"And you thought he might follow her? When did you become Mr. Super Spy?"

"The moment somebody tried to kill you," he said.

She stared at him for a moment, then lowered her gaze. He saw the faint tinge of color appear in her cheeks. He knew her too well not to guess accurately what she was thinking.

"I don't want it to end that way," he repeated bluntly. "We'll see this through, and then we can both walk away clean."

Her head came up. "If we see this through," she said, "then the reason you're leaving will be resolved."

He'd thought of that. Repeatedly. But right now he was hurting too much to see hope there. "Unless it's not Chad. Then you'll go on and on searching until you've wasted your life on it."

"I promised you I'd accept what Foxworth found."

"What they've found is evidence your brother tried to kill you."

"Evidence someone did," she said, her defense of Chad immediate and automatic.

"I believe we've just arrived back at what they call square one."

For a long moment they stood there silently, the impasse almost tangible between them. He saw the pain in her eyes and guessed it was probably echoed in his. He would never have believed it would come to this, nor could he keep going. He would see this through, make sure she was safe. This would end—they would end—on his terms. And then he would start learning to live a life without her.

Somehow.

Chapter 26

The slamming of a car door and a bark sounded from outside almost simultaneously. Hayley, Kayla thought. And Cutter, apparently.

She walked to the window and saw that Hayley had also parked farther down the row of rooms on the other side of their borrowed car. She doubted anybody could have found them this quickly, but she supposed the precaution was wise.

A quick glance at Dane told her he approved. He seemed so different now, she thought with a growing qualm. He wasn't her laid-back, easygoing Dane anymore. He was edgy, sharp and…distant. As if it were already over, as if he were already pulling back, treating her as if she were merely someone he knew, not someone he'd spent ten years of his life with, not someone who had been his passionate and only lover for the last five of those.

She heard another bark and looked out the window in time to see Cutter jump from the back of Hayley's small red SUV to the ground. He raced ahead, coming to a stop at their door. How he knew which room they were in was beyond her.

"He must have picked up our scent or something," Dane said.

Kayla smothered the instant pang; they had always been so in tune they answered each other's unspoken thoughts.

The sound of scratching came at the door, then the doorknob rattled.

"I swear, if you gave him a key, he'd figure out how to

use it," Kayla said as she walked over to the door. She was grateful for the distraction; she simply couldn't bear thinking about a life without Dane. Especially because she'd done it herself, with her inability to let go of her faith in her brother.

For a long time it had seemed to her an unfair pressure. How could he expect her to give up her quest to find Chad? But now, faced with the price of that quest, she wasn't at all sure anymore that it was worth it. Chad was her brother and she loved him, but Dane was her entire future.

Or at least, he had been.

She turned the knob, but didn't have to pull the door open; Cutter took care of that. He pushed it back and came in as if he belonged. He greeted them both with nudges and licks and then sat before them, looking from one to the other. And as if he'd read the tension between them, he let out an audible sigh that sounded exasperated. If he was human, Kayla thought, he'd be shaking his head in disgust at them.

"That dog," Dane muttered.

And then Hayley was there, four shopping bags in hand. She stepped in, and Kayla closed the door behind her.

"Nice enough," Hayley said as she scanned the room.

"It's clean," Kayla said.

"Always my priority," Hayley said with a laugh. "I can put up with old and worn if it's clean."

"Especially the bathroom," Kayla said, forcing a smile in response.

"Speaking of which, careful around the window in there," Dane said, then explained what he'd done with the glasses.

"Good idea," Hayley said.

"It's the only vulnerable spot on that side."

"He's turned into quite the operative," Kayla said, trying to keep her tone even. "Quinn must have taught him a lot in a short time."

"Or he's just thinking of everything. When someone you love is in danger, it happens that way."

Kayla stopped herself from saying he didn't love her, not anymore. She didn't want to hear it, not aloud, not in her own voice, because that would make it too real. Besides, it wasn't true, not really. He couldn't turn it off just like that—it wasn't humanly possible. Dane might be the strongest man she'd ever known, in his own quiet way, but he wasn't a robot who could turn his emotions off at will. His love might be dying, but it wasn't dead yet. She wasn't sure that gave her much hope, but she clung to what flicker there was.

"His and her clothes," Hayley said, holding up two of the bags and tossing them on one of the beds. "Jeans and T-shirts, underwear, socks and shoes for you, Kayla, because yours are pretty messed up. Toothbrushes and toothpaste, razors, all that are in there too."

"Thank you," she answered.

Dane merely nodded; if he found anything uncomfortable about Hayley buying him underwear, it didn't show. Odd; if it had been reversed and Quinn had done the shopping, she would have been beyond embarrassed at the sight of the silky bra and panties she found in the bag.

Guys, she thought.

"He does still love you, you know," Hayley said quietly when Dane had gone to put the toiletries in the bathroom. "Look how he came running when you needed him."

"You don't understand," Kayla said tiredly. "That's just Dane. It's who he is."

She reached down and petted Cutter's silky head. There was something amazingly soothing about the action, as she'd learned after the explosion when she'd spent a long, quiet time huddled on the couch in Hayley and Quinn's living room, with the dog half in her lap. She'd finally gone to sleep, a surprisingly dreamless, peaceful sleep she'd never expected to manage.

Hayley held up the third bag. "Some books and magazines if you get bored."

"Thank you," she repeated. "When you said you'd help find Chad, I never thought it would come to this kind of thing."

Hayley laughed. "If there's one thing I've learned since going to work at Foxworth, it's that things rarely go how you think they will."

"Want to make fate laugh, make plans," Dane said as he came back.

Was that aimed at her? Kayla wondered. Was there an undertone of bitterness in the words? There was certainly a harsh note that wasn't like him. But then, nothing was normal anymore. Not in a world where they, of all couples, could be torn apart.

"Exactly," Hayley said. "Now, you should be okay here at least for a while. Quinn's working on a better location, but that takes a little time."

"How long do you think I'm going to have to hide?" Kayla asked, more than a little alarmed at the idea it might be more than a day or two.

"Until we find who did this," Hayley said, serious now. She might have been putting on a cheerful front, but she didn't make light of the situation.

"You really think I'm still in danger?"

"That's what we're trying to avoid. And to that end, I'm leaving you our portable burglar alarm."

Kayla blinked, looking around for some bag or package she hadn't seen. Then Cutter yipped, sounding very pleased with himself.

Or his assignment, Kayla realized.

"Cutter?" Dane said, sounding startled now.

"Cutter," Hayley confirmed. "He's better than any mechanical alarm system. And this way you both can get some sleep."

With an effort Kayla didn't look at Dane. And she was grateful when Hayley went on, giving instructions on how it would work.

"Walk him around and show him how things are now, so he'll know. Then he'll let you know long before anybody gets close enough to be trouble. And he'll show you where they're coming from."

Kayla shifted her gaze to the dog, who was watching intently. "Seriously?"

"Seriously. I can't explain it, and neither can Quinn. He just seems to know what to do."

Dane frowned. "Is he ex-military, too?"

Hayley laughed and scratched her dog's ears. "We've wondered, but we don't know. The vet says he's young, so we don't think so, but he sure seems to act like a trained war dog sometimes."

"So you haven't had him since he was a puppy?" Dane asked.

"No." Hayley smiled, and her voice went very soft. "He just showed up on my doorstep on the day I needed him most. You'll find he does that a lot. He just seems to know that, too."

Dane's mouth quirked. "You sure he's not an alien in a dog suit?"

"No," Hayley said and laughed.

The atmosphere in the room had lightened considerably, Kayla thought. Cutter was also, it seemed, a great distraction. And, she thought, he would be a buffer, something to focus on, to think about, besides the awful tension between her and Dane. Kayla wondered if that was part of the reason Hayley had brought Cutter. She wouldn't put it past her; the woman was not only kind and understanding, she was also perceptive.

"I brought some food for him and a couple of bowls," Hayley said, at last getting to the fourth bag. "He's good about only eating what he wants, so you can leave it full. Water's more important. And he's not above the occasional people-food treat, especially if you hand feed him, but don't overdo it."

"They allow dogs here?" Kayla asked, suddenly doubtful.

"They're allowing this one," Hayley said. Kayla wondered how they'd managed that and guessed it hadn't been cheap.

"He'll let you know when he needs out," Hayley went on. "He's very polite about it. He'll get your attention, then go sit by the door. Just let him go on his own, he'll be back quickly."

Dane shook his head, as if in wonder. "I suppose his... warnings are different?"

"Yes," Hayley said. "He won't leave you any doubt. If it's someone he knows, one of us, he'll give all the usual happy-dog signals. If it's not, if it's a threat, he'll act like he's going to jump out of his fur if you don't let him get at them."

"What about animals?"

"Normally, he gets as revved up as any dog when he smells or spots critters. But when he's on guard, oddly, no. He seems to know when it's people we're guarding against."

Dane shook his head. Hayley laughed.

"We've given up trying to figure it out. Especially because every day he surprises us with something new." She grinned. "Of course, just about the time we decide he really is that alien in disguise, he does something utterly doglike, like digging up the garden or dragging home a dead tree rat, and we slide back into reality."

Kayla and Dane both laughed in turn. It seemed impossible not to.

Hayley took something out of the bag slung over her shoulder. She handed it to Dane. Kayla thought at first it was a cell phone, but it only had four numbered buttons and a couple of larger ones—one was black with the standard on/off symbol and the other red.

"This is a Foxworth walkie-talkie. It uses rotating frequencies, but the signal is always scrambled, so no one can hear you except someone with another one of these. It has a range of about five miles. If you need anything, use it. But if something happens, if Cutter signals strangers coming, you use that red button. It broadcasts to everyone, and Quinn, Rafe and Teague all have them on them now."

"But if its range is only five miles…" Dane began.

"There will be somebody within that range at all times until this is resolved."

Kayla drew back slightly. "You mean you're guarding us?"

"We're keeping an eye on this place, yes."

"Twenty-four/seven?" Dane asked.

"Yes. Quinn's nothing if not thorough."

"But what about finding Chad?"

Kayla sensed rather than saw Dane's demeanor instantly shift; the tension was back that quickly.

"We're still on it. When one is watching, the other three—and me—are working on that."

"Sleep much?" Dane asked.

"On a case? Not so much," Hayley said. "If you turn on the TV, keep it down. Muted with closed captions would be better. Nothing to interfere with your alarm system."

She crouched down beside Cutter, who had given every appearance of following the conversation intently.

"All right, my boy," she crooned, "you know what to do. You watch, all right? Watch and warn."

The dog was on his feet instantly. In that split second he went from attentive, clever dog to…something else. Kayla couldn't describe it, exactly, but there was no doubt the animal understood the command. On alert, she supposed.

And she had to admit, it made her feel safer.

Chapter 27

"We should have gotten a dog," Kayla said.

Dane looked up from one of the magazines Hayley had bought—the latest issue of a trade magazine that was actually sitting at home on his desk unread. He usually read their main articles online, but he liked to have the print version for those occasions when he didn't have a connection or when his phone wouldn't do because the article had charts or graphs or other details he needed to see full size.

Odd. He usually would have felt unsettled by now, disconnected from the world he spent so much time in. Yet he felt no desire to check email, and no urge to check his online feeds. Nothing like a good old life and death crisis to push the online world down on your priority list.

Nothing like having your real world crumble to make the online world seem trivial.

Kayla was petting Cutter, who was curled up peacefully beside her on the bed farthest from the door. She'd spoken idly, he realized; in fact, she looked almost lulled by the dog's presence. He found it unexpectedly comforting himself. He'd had dogs as a kid but never any even remotely like this one.

And they had talked about it before, after she'd moved into the little house and he'd ended up practically living there himself. It would have been cozy, them and a four-legged kid. Like this moment had been, until she'd spoken. They had always been that way, happy just being under the same roof, even if they each were occupied with their own pursuits.

The memory wasn't soothing; it jabbed at him.

"Right," he said. "Then we could have fought over custody."

He saw her wince. Cutter's head came up sharply.

"That wasn't necessary," Kayla said. "I gave you your past tense."

She had, he realized. "Should have" not "should." No wonder he'd snapped back.

He had the grace to acknowledge the unfairness of that. He couldn't make such a point of it being over between them and then get in a mood about it when she acknowledged that point. Couldn't hold that it was okay for him to use the past tense when talking about them, then get upset if she did.

"Fine," he said and pretended to go back to the magazine.

He should be grateful, shouldn't he? That she was accepting, that she wasn't making a scene or making it even harder with weeping and wailing?

But that wasn't Kayla's way. It never had been. Her dogged determination wouldn't allow such time and energy wasters. She'd wept her soul dry when her parents had been killed, but he could count the number of times he'd seen her cry in the ten years since on his fingers, maybe plus a toe or two.

And usually on Chad's birthday, he reminded himself. On the anniversary of her parents' deaths she was quietly solemn, but on Chad's birthday she wept.

That stiffened his resolve.

Cutter let out a long-suffering sigh, as if he'd understood perfectly that they were again at a contretemps.

He'd done as Hayley had instructed—taken him out and repeated his own earlier circuit of the property. The dog had paused now and then, sniffing the air, and twice had veered off on his own to point his nose toward the woods around the motel. Dane had watched as the animal seemed to scan the trees and then the parking area, as if placing things in his mind.

The mysteries of the canine brain, he had thought at the time. This one's, at least. More on a whim than anything, he had let Cutter take the lead and take his time. And oddly, the dog had stopped in the same place he had—under the bathroom window of their unit.

How did he know? Scent again?

The dog looked up at the window, then around, for all the world as if he were judging how someone would approach that window from the trees.

At that point Dane had shaken his head and picked up the pace; when you started attributing human qualities to a dog, even a very smart one, it was time for some rest.

Yet rest, or at least sleep, eluded him. It was still afternoon, and he'd never been one for going to bed during the day.

Unless it was with Kayla.

Pain slammed into his gut, at odds with parts lower, which responded fiercely to just the thought. The memories of long, lazy weekend afternoons when they'd decided nothing on any agenda was more important than what they were doing, when they'd made love, rested, laughed, eaten and then started the cycle all over again.

Cutter's sudden movement jerked him out of the painful reverie. The dog got up, jumped to the floor and raced to the front window, his ears back, head down and a low, menacing rumble coming from his throat. Just his reaction sent Dane's adrenaline surging, and he wished he had some kind of a weapon. Not that he knew the first thing about guns, but even a baseball bat would be nice. He'd have to do something about that if this went on much longer.

So he did the only thing he could, he walked over to the window and peered through the crack in the drapes. He saw the man who had checked them into the room sweeping the walkway that ran in front of all the rooms. He'd apparently worked his way down here to the end.

"What is it?" Kayla's voice was a whisper.

"The manager," he said, reaching down to reassure Cutter, although he wasn't sure the dog would take his word that this man he didn't know was safe. But the animal shifted his gaze to him, looking as if he were evaluating Dane's ability to properly assess the potential threat.

Apparently Cutter found enough to satisfy him, and he stood down. Odd that that was the phrase that popped into his head, but it was the only one that seemed to fit.

"I wonder if he'll remember the guy," Kayla said.

"If he comes around again? I wouldn't be surprised."

"Hayley seems to think he can read minds."

"I wouldn't bet against it," Dane said, still watching as the man with the broom finished and started walking back toward the office.

They settled back into quiet, Kayla returning to the bed and Dane to the chair beside the small table. Cutter seemed to hesitate between them for a moment. Dane's gaze flicked from the dog to Kayla, who needed the comforting the dog seemed to bring.

He was wondering how to indicate to the dog he should go to her when Cutter made up his own mind in that direction and returned to his earlier position beside her. Giving her the companionship and comfort Dane could no longer give her.

Well, he could, technically. But he knew too well what would happen if he lay down on that bed with her. All his determination, all his good intentions would be seared away. The passion that ignited so quickly between them had never faded, but deep down he knew that if he gave into that fierce urge now, it would make it that much harder, that much more painful to disengage all over again.

Kayla at last stretched out, put her head on a pillow and

closed her eyes. After what she'd been through, he was amazed she'd kept going as long as she had. It wasn't long before he sensed she'd gone to sleep; he knew her so well, knew when the tension of her body changed, relaxed, when her breaths became deeper, more regular.

Cutter stayed there, his head coming up occasionally as he heard something. But whatever he heard, he apparently decided it wasn't a threat and put his head back down. He didn't, however, close his eyes. Dane wondered idly if dogs ever had trouble sleeping.

Perversely, now his own restless mind declared itself willing to shut off, and his eyes were more than happy about the idea of sleep. But now was when he couldn't, if for no other reason than he had to be awake to make sure Kayla was all right. She seemed to have suffered no serious aftereffects of the smoke, but Quinn had explained how with smoke inhalation damage sometimes took time to develop as the lungs reacted to the insult.

Then, of course, there was the fact that someone had tried to kill her.

He stayed in the not terrifically comfortable chair, fighting the urge to go lie down beside her. He tried to make himself stay awake, listening to her steady and apparently unimpaired breathing. But the long night and the stress of actually being suspected of the attack on her were catching up to him, and more than once he caught himself jolting awake.

It got harder. The room was getting warmer as the summer sun was now hitting the front of the building, and he weighed the dangers of opening a window against the dangers of him falling asleep. It wasn't worth it, he thought, and regretted the lack of air-conditioning in the room, although he accepted the practicality of not retrofitting this older place with it when simply doing just that, opening a window, would provide all the cool air necessary most of the year in this climate.

He shifted position, leaning forward and resting his elbows on his knees, so that if he dozed off he'd fall forward and wake himself up. It worked until his brain seemed to learn to balance even when asleep.

Maybe he should just get up and stay on his feet, he thought. If he kept walking, he'd have to stay awake. He'd have to be quiet or wake up Kayla, but—

A movement from the bed drew his weary gaze. Cutter was moving toward the edge of the bed, inching his way without actually getting on his feet. He slid off to the floor, as if he were being careful not to wake Kayla. He didn't seem alarmed or attuned to anything outside, so Dane waited to see if perhaps Cutter would go to the door to indicate he needed outside.

Instead, the dog came over to him and nudged his hand with his nose in apparent greeting. Then he plopped down at Dane's feet, as if he'd merely decided that now that Kayla was at last asleep, Dane was his job.

"If only you could keep me awake," Dane said to him quietly.

Cutter's head twisted to meet his gaze, and for an instant in the dog's dark eyes Dane saw something that looked amazingly like understanding. Dane nearly laughed at himself; he was getting as bad as Hayley and Quinn.

He reached down, scratching behind that right ear until the dog sighed happily. Now that was normal, he thought. Utterly doglike, as Hayley had said. He settled back in the chair, awake for the moment. He picked up the magazine but soon realized that was a mistake as his eyes began to fight to close again.

Maybe a cold shower, he thought. That might help. Might help more than just having trouble staying awake. He pondered the idea.

A tug on the leg of his jeans jerked him awake. He didn't

know how long he'd been out, but nothing had changed. The room was still too warm, the sun was still pouring around the edges of the curtains he'd closed in an attempt to foster the idea of cool darkness and Kayla was still asleep, still breathing evenly.

The only difference was the dog at his feet. The dog who had just tugged on the bottom of his jeans but now that he was awake had put his head down once more.

If only you could keep me awake...

His own words echoed in his head. And so did the memory of that moment when Cutter had given him that look that had seemed so full of an almost human understanding.

Maybe he'd been taught that, that "guard" meant someone else had to be awake, too. Could dogs learn something like that? His old Lilah had been a retriever, and she'd had her own skills that, to someone not used to them, could seem amazing in a dog. At least that was the answer he came up with. It had been in Lilah's blood, in her genes, that retriever nature.

Another memory hit him hard. The day he'd finally had to say goodbye to the dear old friend who had been there for him almost his entire life. He'd been seventeen, far too old to cry, and yet it had overwhelmed him. He'd retreated to the tree where he and Kayla had often sat, liking the feeling of being above the fuss below. She had found him there, and she, only she of everyone he knew, said and did the right thing. Which was nothing except simply taking his hand and holding it.

He'd known she would never tell, never taunt or tease him with his unmanly reaction to the loss of his childhood companion, and so he had let it out, tears and all.

And on his eighteenth birthday, she had told him that was the moment when she knew just how much she loved him. "Wait," he'd said, "I thought you said you liked how I was strong and stood up to Rod that time."

"I did."

"So do you want the strong type or the sensitive type?"

She had given him a look that seemed wise beyond her sixteen years. "Yes," she said.

He'd laughed. "Don't you think that's asking a lot?"

"Aren't I lucky I found it?"

The aches of regret and loss filled him now. Here he was, in a room alone with the woman he'd loved from that day forward. He'd experimented a little in college, as much because he felt he should as anything, but nothing had lasted. They all seemed lacking somehow.

And nothing had ever been able to erase the thought of the girl back home, who was, as she'd promised she would, growing up so that they could begin their life together.

As he watched her sleep, he drifted into memories, too tired now to fight them off. They floated through his mind, each with its own special pain attached. The first time he'd seen her, up in that tree. The day of her sixteenth birthday, when he'd stolen a minute to give Kayla her first real kiss. The day she turned eighteen and he'd driven home from college just to see her for a few hours on her special day, then turned around and drove back. The day she'd arrived at the same school herself, chosen mainly because he was there. The agony of waiting because he knew she wasn't ready, and then she turned twenty-one and had practically demanded he make love to her. And all the sweet, wonderful years since, when he'd counted himself more than lucky to have found the love of his life so early in that life.

He closed his eyes, knowing he had glossed over the horrible night that happened just days after she turned sixteen and the days of dealing with the aftermath. He didn't need to think about them again; they were etched so deeply into his mind he would never be free of them. Besides, if there was anything that could weaken his resolve, it was thinking again about what she'd been through.

He must have slipped too close to sleep because Cutter tugged on the leg of his jeans again. He snapped back to wakefulness and stared at the dog for a long moment.

"You really do get it, don't you?" he said softly, reaching out to lay his hand on the dark head.

The dog nudged his hand with his nose and swiped his fingers with his tongue. And as if satisfied he was awake and alert again, Cutter settled his chin back down on his front paws.

Dane shook his head half in wonder, half in disbelief and leaned back in the chair. His body was protesting the long stretch of sitting, but he was afraid he'd wake Kayla up if he moved around too much. Which reminded him of the careful way Cutter had slipped off the bed, as if he had the same fear but knew right now Dane needed his help more.

Damn, I'm tired. He's a dog.

But whatever the dog's intent, it worked. He was awake again. And belatedly he realized sunlight was no longer streaming around the edges of the curtains, and the room wasn't quite as warm. How long had he been lost in that reverie anyway? He reached for his cell phone to check the time, and as if the movement had triggered it, the phone vibrated on the table beside the chair; he'd turned off the ringer when Kayla had first gone to sleep. He grabbed it now before the buzz could wake her. Who was calling?

Quinn and nearly 3:00 a.m., he noted, answering both his questions at once.

He got up and walked into the bathroom before he answered.

"Everything okay?"

"Kayla's sleeping. I'm trying not to."

"Cutter can help you with that," Quinn said.

Dane's brows rose. "So he did mean to do it."

Quinn chuckled, obviously needing no further explanation. "That dog rarely does anything he doesn't mean to do."

Dane leaned against the sink, smiling wryly to himself. "I'm getting that feeling."

"Everything quiet?"

"So far."

"Good."

Dane sensed this was more than just a status check. "Something happen?"

"Somebody showed up at the house."

Dane straightened up. "At Kayla's house?"

"Yes. Teague was watching the place, just in case. Just after dark he saw somebody in a black watch cap sneaking through the side yard. He couldn't see him well enough to make an ID, but the moment Teague got out of the car he took off running back through the trees."

"You think it was Chad?"

"Don't know. Could have been a curious neighbor."

"But why would he run?"

"Good question. Teague's pretty fast, almost had him, but the guy darted down a few side yards and then out into open forest. He knew where he was going."

"So a local," Dane said.

"Seems that way."

"Or somebody who once was. Like Chad."

"Yes. And somebody also called the hospital to ask after Kayla but refused to say who he was."

Dane tensed. "To ask how she was or to find out if she was still there?"

"Both. Thankfully when he wouldn't identify himself, they didn't tell him anything. Said he got a little insistent, though. Enough so that they made a note of the number he was calling from."

He knew Foxworth and their capabilities better now, so he merely said, "And?"

"Landline listed to Franklin Warren."

"Rod's dad?"

"Any reason you can think of he'd be involved?"

"Zero. He barely knew Kayla. And he's in a wheelchair, so it surely wasn't him running away."

"What about Rod himself? Would he call?"

Dane frowned. "He's not a friend, not after that day I told you about. Kayla doesn't like him and neither do I, so I don't know why he'd call. But if he did, he'd have no reason not to say who he was. Unless he really was involved."

"All right." Quinn paused as if thinking. "All right, it's quiet now, we've got the house covered in case he comes back there and you've got Cutter inside and us outside if he gives you a warning. Why don't you try and get some sleep?"

"But Kayla—"

"She breathing all right?"

"Yes."

"Coughing?"

"Not since we got here. But they said she needed to be watched for at least twenty-four hours."

"News for you, buddy. It's been twenty-four hours and then some."

"Oh." He felt a little silly for not having put that together. "Sorry."

"Sleep deprivation will do that to you. Besides, Cutter will probably let you know if she starts having trouble. Hayley had some nightmares in the beginning, and every time she started getting restless or murmuring in her sleep, he woke her or me up."

"Someday," Dane said, "I'd like to hear that whole story."

"Someday," Quinn answered, "you might. Now get some sleep."

"Right."

Dane disconnected the call then stood there in the bathroom for a moment, pondering the likelihood of being able to follow that order thinly disguised as a suggestion. The likelihood of being able to sleep with Kayla just a few feet away.

He realized his ears were buzzing. In fact, everything above his ears seemed to be humming with that warning sound that told him he'd just about hit the wall. He'd been up nearly two nights straight; no wonder he was starting to feel wobbly.

He'd just have to hope he was tired enough.

Chapter 28

"How are they?" Hayley had stayed quiet as Quinn spoke to Dane, watching the area surrounding the motel while he was distracted with the call.

"She's been sleeping for a while. Breathing's fine, and no more coughing. I think she's probably okay."

"And Dane?"

"Hasn't slept at all. He's been too worried about her."

"That's good."

Quinn shifted to look at her. "It's good that he's so worried he hasn't slept since the day before yesterday?"

"Yes. He still loves her."

"Well, yeah, you don't turn that off by fiat," Quinn said.

"But this has been gnawing away at him for a long time. I was afraid it was too late, but now I don't think so. They can work on fixing things."

Quinn shook his head but with a smile at her. "Might be more important to find out who tried to kill her first."

Hayley shook her head. "Nothing's more important than that." She gave him a sideways look. "Which did you think was more important—getting those guys at the cabin or getting out of there alive?"

"Getting *you* out of there alive," Quinn said.

"Why?"

"Is this a trap?"

"Would I tell you if it was?"

He laughed. "You know damn well I was already half in love with you."

"Only half?" she asked sweetly.

"Yeah," he drawled, "the other half was Cutter."

Hayley grinned at him. "Oh. Well that's all right then."

"Love me, love my dog?"

"Exactly."

"Well it's a good thing I love you both then, isn't it?"

"It is," Hayley said, her voice going achingly soft. "A very, very good thing."

"Damn." Quinn sighed. "I'll be glad when Liam gets here to relieve us."

"Me, too," Hayley said. There was nothing particularly suggestive in her words, but something in her voice set him off.

"Hope he rested up on his days off," Quinn said gruffly, "because he's liable to be here the rest of the night on his own."

"And maybe longer," Hayley said, and Quinn felt his body clench with need at the promise in those words.

Quinn spent the next hour in varying states of discomfort as he made himself focus on the job at hand instead of the delectable woman beside him. And if Dane was in anywhere near the same condition inside that room, Quinn felt sorry for him.

It was going to be a long night.

Kayla's nightmare of smoke and fire took an odd turn as the splash of the firefighter's water began. Because on some level even her sleeping brain knew she hadn't been aware of that, that Mr. Reyes, bless him, had gotten her out and away before the fire trucks had actually arrived. But the watery sound was comforting nevertheless, and the nightmare shifted in the nonsensical way dreams do, and she was adrift in a boat, water lapping at the sides—

Her eyes opened.

Lapping.

The dog.

Cutter was getting a drink of water.

Reality rushed back, and there was enough of the nightmare clinging to it to make her jolt upright. She looked around the strange room, placing things in her mind as best she could in the dim light. A glance at the bedside clock told her it was just after six. She was surprised at that—she hadn't expected to sleep that long at all, not after napping through the afternoon and evening. Perhaps she'd been more stressed and traumatized than she'd been willing to admit.

She was reaching for the bedside lamp, then paused. She glanced over at the other bed. Dane was there, stretched out on his side, facing her but with his head half buried in the pillow his arm was bent back under. His other arm was in front of him, and it seemed his fist was clenched even in sleep. She sighed.

She looked around again. It was well after sunrise this time of year, but the motel faced west and the front window was still in shadow. With the blackout curtains closed, it was hard to tell what kind of day they were facing.

She nearly laughed at her own thought; she knew exactly what kind of day it was going to be. Hellish.

She sat up and swung her legs over the side of the bed. Cutter was there instantly, what light there was reflecting off his dark eyes.

"Hi," she said softly, reaching to pet that silken fur. He nudged her in turn, then tilted his head to lay it on her knee. She found it absurdly sweet and endearing.

"I'd love a dog like you," she whispered to him, "no matter what Dane says."

"I'm not sure there is another dog like him."

Dane's voice came out of the dim light from the other bed, and she felt a start of embarrassment.

"Sorry I woke you," she said stiffly.

"You didn't."

"You've been awake?"

"Since I let him out a few minutes ago. Tried not to wake you."

"You didn't," she echoed. "I think his drinking did. I started dreaming of water."

"Better than fire."

"Yes." She suppressed a shudder.

"How do you feel?"

"Fine."

"No sore throat or need to cough?"

"Throat is a bit dry and scratchy is all."

"All right."

"You didn't have to stay up—"

"Yes. I did."

She wanted to see hope in that last statement, but looking at his face all she saw was the same emotionless resolution that had sounded in his voice. She lowered her head, looking at Cutter, once more stroking his fur for the comfort as much as the communion. Silence stretched out for a long moment before he spoke again.

"Somebody was poking around your house last night."

Her head snapped up. "What?"

"They had Teague watching it. Somebody showed up a little after dark."

"Who?" She had to force out the word because she wasn't sure she really wanted the answer.

"Don't know. The instant he saw Teague he took off running. He got to the woods and vanished. He obviously knew his way around."

"So of course it must have been Chad revisiting the scene of the crime," she said, her tone creeping beyond tense into sarcasm.

"Didn't say that," he said. But to Kayla, his expression was screaming, "Who else could it be?"

That she didn't have an answer for that made her even unhappier.

"I want to see my house," she said.

"Not yet."

"You're not my boss," she snapped.

He drew back slightly, and the sharp sound of her knee-jerk answer hung in the air. She drew in a long, deep breath.

"I'm sorry," she said. "That was uncalled for."

Dane, being Dane, accepted the apology graciously. Yet in the back of her mind was the knowledge that it was easier to be gracious when you didn't really care.

"You've had a very rough couple of days. Anybody would be a bit tense," he said. "And it wasn't my idea. Quinn thinks it would be best if you stayed away until we know more."

Kayla started to answer, then realized a quick agreement with that seemed to her to carry a subtext that she wouldn't listen to him, but she would to Quinn. And it would do no good to point out that she would listen to Quinn, or Hayley, because they were impartial; Dane definitely was not. But she had no desire to add any fuel to his mood; he already felt beyond her reach and it was breaking her heart.

"And you agree," she said after a moment, carefully keeping her voice even and hoping the words were safe enough.

"Yes."

"All right," she said, giving up on the desire for now. She still wanted to see her home, start assessing the damage, figuring out what repairs were needed; she wasn't about to let whoever had done this destroy her love for her little house.

But her relationship with Dane was just as damaged, if not more, and she wasn't sure it could be repaired.

And if that were true, then the house didn't matter.

Nothing else mattered.

Cutter was suddenly on his feet, alert and looking toward the front of the room. A second later his plumed tail began to wag, and he leaped across the room to the door. He looked back over his shoulder at them with that doggy grin on his face.

All the usual happy-dog signals, Hayley had said.

A tap came on the door. Cutter yipped. Dane was already there, peering through the peephole.

"Mr. Burdette, Ms. Tucker, I'm Liam Burnett," he called through the door. Kayla thought she caught a bit of a drawl in his voice. He sounded like her college roommate, who had been from Houston. "I just relieved Quinn and Hayley. And I have coffee."

"Well, that's tempting," Dane muttered.

As if he'd guessed at their hesitation, the man outside added, "Watch Cutter. He'll verify my ID."

It sounded silly, but Kayla couldn't deny the difference in the dog now compared to how he'd reacted when the motel manager had simply come by to sweep the walk.

"Hayley did say they had one more guy who'd be joining the crew—"

Even as she said it, her cell phone dinged, announcing the arrival of a text message. She went to grab it off the nightstand.

"It's from Hayley. She says Liam Burnett is on his way with coffee." She gave a little laugh. "She says Cutter will let us know he's okay."

"Well, he did that, didn't he?" Dane said as he reached for the doorknob.

For a moment, Kayla was startled at what she saw when

the man holding two cups stepped into the room. Liam Burnett looked like an earnest Boy Scout, almost too young to be drinking the coffee he was carrying. Maybe he was, she thought, noticing he had only two of the cups from the café.

The man handed the cups in their paper sleeves to the two of them, then crouched to greet the dog.

"Hey, you ol' hound. You doing your job right?"

The swipe of a pink tongue across the young man's cheek sealed the deal for Kayla. Obviously this was a known and appreciated person in the dog's life.

"Okay, he likes you," Dane said, obviously reaching the same conclusion at the same moment. As usual. Kayla blinked at the sudden pain.

"Dogs generally do. My family's raised them for years. But this guy, he's something special."

"We've noticed," Kayla said with the best smile she could manage.

"Texas?" Dane asked.

Liam grinned. "Yes, sir. Born and bred." Then he looked at Kayla and said, with that same sort of earnestness she'd seen in his face, "I'm sorry about your trouble. But if anybody can unravel all this, it's Foxworth."

"You sound confident."

"I am. Trust them to the wall and over," he said. "Quinn turned my life around when I was headed down a wrong path."

Kayla had trouble picturing this innocent-looking guy in trouble, but she took his word for it.

"Speaking of Quinn, he'll be around later," Liam said. "He had to go talk with Rafe—you've met Rafe, haven't you?"

Dane nodded. "Interesting guy."

"If by interesting you mean downright scary sometimes, yeah, he is," Liam said with a quirky grin that spoke of both respect and liking. "He's our sniper. And he's wicked good."

"So I've heard," Kayla said. "So what's your specialty?"

"Me? I'm the tech guy mostly. And the tracker."

"Tracker?"

"I would have found that guy last night," he said. "Teague's good, and tough as the ex-marine he is, but he's a city boy. He needed me. Or Cutter."

Foxworth, Kayla thought, was a much more interesting operation than their name and website would lead you to believe.

"I keep telling him a month out in the wilds with me would fix that, but he keeps saying no. He feels bad about losing that guy in the woods like that, so I'm guessing he'll take me up on it now."

The grin had widened, and somehow Kayla felt lighter than she had in days. Something about this young man's easy charm and innocent face brightened her outlook.

No sooner did she acknowledge that welcome fact than the new arrival's cell phone rang. He answered, and within moments the easy grin and innocent expression vanished. When he hung up and looked at them, he was all business.

"What is it?" she asked.

"Rafe turned up a homeless guy who'd been squatting in an abandoned building. Said some new guy moved in, ran him off."

"So?"

Liam looked uncomfortable, but he didn't dissemble. "The description matches Chad to a T."

Kayla's breath caught in her suddenly tight throat. She sensed rather than saw Dane tense and she felt her own suddenly accelerated heartbeat. She looked at him and saw the same knowledge in his eyes.

It really was coming to a head.

And she was coming face-to-face with the distinct possibility that the end of her quest also meant the end of them.

Chapter 29

"Where?"

Kayla focused on that question so that she didn't have to face the simple fact that now that her goal might actually be within reach, she wasn't sure she wanted it. This quest had consumed her for so long she wasn't sure what would be left of her when it was finally over, one way or another.

"Out off of Breakers Road," Liam said. "Quinn's heading over there. Rafe's staying on the building because somebody will need to watch the back entrance."

Kayla wondered if she'd had too much sleep; she couldn't seem to process this.

"An abandoned building?" Chad had friends here, he had her. This made no sense. "But why would Chad—"

"I don't know," Dane said. He didn't add, "And I don't care," but Kayla heard it anyway. Apparently so did Liam because for the first time he looked uncomfortable and excused himself to go back out to his car and to his guarding of the area around them. She wondered if he'd been warned. *Watch out. They're in the middle of a breakup so things are a bit intense....*

Kayla shook off the useless speculation. She looked around automatically. Without a word Dane picked up her phone and handed it to her. That was still working fine, it seemed, that communication without words, that knowing someone so well you knew what the slightest gesture meant.

She made herself concentrate on the phone, called up the

map app they both used and entered the location. The image that popped up told her little until she backed out a click and saw the surrounding area.

"The old tag arena!" she exclaimed.

"What?"

"You know, the place that used to be a skating rink ages ago, then it was a video arcade, then a laser tag arena?"

"Out by the gravel plant? I went there a few times."

She nodded. "And Chad used to spend a lot of his free time there, with Troy and their other friends."

"They closed down years ago, didn't they? I remember my dad saying it was because the home video game systems were getting so good, and my mom saying it was more because the kids were getting out of control."

"And Chad was furious. Especially because our parents wouldn't buy him one of the home systems."

"He ever heard of a job?" Dane said.

Kayla forced herself not to defend her brother; Dane had had a part-time job from the age of sixteen and had little patience for those who expected everything to be given to them. Or made their way through life on looks and charm. Most of the time she agreed with him. Except regarding Chad.

She'd always told herself Dane just didn't understand her brother, but now she was asking herself if perhaps she shouldn't have thought more about why she always made that exception for Chad.

"I don't think it was the games so much as a place to hang out with his friends," she finally said.

"You're right about that," Dane said, his mouth twisting wryly. "Believe me."

"What do you mean?"

"I was into the games," he said. "Chad and his buddies were into harassing the younger or smaller kids who were into the games."

She stared at him. "Harassing?"

"Intimidation might be a better word. Or bullying."

"Chad wouldn't—"

"I was there. He did it to me. Personally. Would have been worse if Troy hadn't finally pulled him off me."

"You never told me that!"

"Please. You never wanted to hear a word against him."

"What did he do?"

"Picked the weakest, littlest kids and extorted their game money from them. Threatened them if they didn't hand it over. Beat me up just to demonstrate what would happen if anybody resisted."

A memory flashed through her mind of the day they'd made that promise to each other to never let others determine who they were. The day she'd sworn to make the most of what looks she had yet never deny her intelligence, and the day he'd sworn to become tough and fit and yet never give up what he loved. He'd been sporting a bruised face and skinned-up knuckles that day, but he would only tell her he'd run into a bully.

Chad.

He'd never told her it was her brother who had done it.

And it obviously wasn't open for discussion now; he had taken back his phone and was making a call. Cutter's gaze shifted to her, and she realized he'd been watching them like a human would watch a tennis match, head moving side to side as each of them spoke.

"It's Dane," he said into the phone. "Kayla knows the place Liam told us about. Chad used to hang there when it was a video arcade."

He listened for a moment. Quinn, she guessed.

"Yes," Dane said into the phone. Then "Yes," again and more listening. Kayla barely managed not to demand to know what was going on. If Chad was really this close, she wanted to know, and she wanted to know now.

What she didn't know was what she would do about it. And again she felt the uncertainty she'd never expected. How could her goal of so many years be within reach, and yet she suddenly wasn't sure she wanted it?

"All right," Dane said and ended the call. He turned to look at her, and when he spoke it was with no more emotion than a police officer making a report. "Building appears empty right now. Quinn and Rafe checked the inside and there are signs someone's living there, but they can't be sure what belongs to the homeless guy until they question him further."

"Who is he? I hadn't heard of anybody local losing their home, not lately anyway."

"Don't know who he is, but Quinn said Hayley was making arrangements for him, getting him into a shelter Foxworth helps fund."

Kayla blinked. "They're into a lot of stuff."

"Seems that way."

"So now what?"

"They're going to watch the place, see if Chad shows up."

"I should go—"

"Quinn wants us to sit tight. With watching that place, your house and here, they're spread a little thin."

"Then we should go there now, and they could stop watching this place."

"There's nobody there now. There's no point. And if there are too many people around, it could spook him and they'd lose him again."

"You're assuming it is Chad," she said.

He said nothing, but she saw his jaw tighten and knew he was holding back whatever response had come into his mind.

"All right," she said, "I admit it sounds like it is. But that's why I should be over there."

"Quinn will call if he shows up. Then we'll decide."

Reluctantly she conceded. She wasn't used to doing nothing, and they had another discussion about the possibility of taking Cutter for a walk through the woods behind the motel. Dane seemed to waver on that one. Probably, Kayla thought sourly, because he and Cutter had bonded. Then again, the dog was generally more cooperative than she had been, and she had the grace to admit that much at least.

But in the end Quinn's caution won out, and except for letting Cutter out when he needed it the door stayed shut with the "Do not disturb" sign hanging on the outside knob. And Kayla tried not to think of other times when that sign would have had an entirely different intent, times when they had hung it on the door of a room specifically to avoid interruption of a long, passionate session of enjoying how in tune their bodies and their minds were.

It was an effort to keep from pacing the room. But when she did, Cutter seemed to get wound up, and Dane, who was trying to sleep a little more, always woke up. This time the dog was curled up beside Dane on the other bed, and she noticed in sleep Dane's arm had come to rest along the dog's side. It was a picture that would have once made her smile, made the love she felt for this man bubble up inside her to overflowing.

Now it just made her hurt more.

She welcomed the distraction later when Dane woke up and, after checking the time, suggested dinner; they'd been nibbling on the snacks Hayley had brought, but a real, hot meal sounded wonderful. Dane quickly put to rest her thoughts of actually going to the restaurant by saying they'd order it to go. She didn't really quibble, although the thought of even a temporary escape was very tempting, because it didn't seem fair to leave Cutter here all alone in a strange motel room. And at this point, she wasn't sure he wouldn't figure out a way to follow them anyway.

The meal of fish and chips they ended up with wasn't the best she'd ever had, but it wasn't the worst either, and under the circumstances she figured that was enough. Mindful of Hayley's words, she gave Cutter a couple of bites of fish, which he took delicately from her fingers, while he caught the fries Dane tossed him neatly in midair.

Later, Dane amused the patient animal by taking a rolled-up sock and tossing it for him. The room was too small for the dog to run, but he seemed to enjoy the challenge of catching the makeshift ball over and over.

When darkness finally came again, Kayla didn't know what she was going to do. She didn't feel at all sleepy, and she certainly wasn't relishing another night spent in this room, with Dane so near and yet so emotionally far away. Now Dane was playing tug of war with Cutter, the worse-for-wear sock standing in for a rope. As a buffer between them, the dog was serving quite well.

"You're right," Dane said when he finally called it quits and sat down. "We should have gotten a dog."

She didn't know whether to feel gratified at the agreement or pained at the reminder of that damned past tense. And before she could decide, Dane's phone rang. At this hour, it had to be someone from Foxworth.

After he said hello, he listened for a long moment before speaking again.

"Yeah, I got some sleep. Enough, anyway. I'm good. She needed the sleep more," Dane said. Kayla's gaze shifted to the dog, who was sitting, watching Dane as if he knew who he was talking to. "And you were right—Cutter helped me stay awake."

Part of her wanted to believe he'd stayed awake to watch over her because he still loved her. But another part of her knew that was just who Dane was; if he took on a responsibility, he saw it through. And that's all she was to him now.

"No. She needs to be there." Kayla's breath caught at his words. "I know. I'll keep her back. But if it is Chad, he may only cooperate with her." Another pause, and then, "All right. We'll bring him."

He disconnected the call, slipped the phone into his pocket, leaned over and scratched Cutter's ear.

He did everything but look at her.

When he didn't speak, the words finally burst from her. "What's happening?"

"Get the sweatshirt Hayley bought you."

"I don't need a sweatshirt. I need to know what's going on."

"You will. It's cooled off outside now, and you can't take the chance of a cold when we're not sure your lungs are a hundred percent yet."

She needs to be there, he'd said. "He's there? Chad?"

"Someone is. Rafe is watching the building now, and Quinn's on his way."

She darted over to the shopping bag she'd set on the dresser and yanked out the new, zip-front sweatshirt Hayley had thoughtfully provided. She pulled it on, turned back and saw Dane watching her with a sad expression she'd seen a lot of lately. It took her a moment to work out that it was because she'd resisted his suggestion until she'd realized it had to do with Chad.

I can't play second fiddle to your fixation any longer.

For the first time she realized just how much she had made him feel that way. Now that it was too late.

His expression cleared and shifted into something painfully neutral, uncaring. "Quinn wants us to bring the dog. And then stay clear until it's safe," he said in a businesslike tone that matched the look.

He turned away then, walking to the dresser to pick up the

keys to Rafe's car. She wondered idly what Rafe was driving in the meantime and how many cars Foxworth had access to. And again she realized her mind was skittering for the safety of mundane, unimportant thoughts to avoid dealing with the biggest one of all.

"Let's go," Dane said.

Kayla shoved her hands into the pockets of the sweatshirt, mainly to hide how her hands had knotted into fists. It felt so close, so imminent. Ten years of her life, and it could all be coming together tonight.

It could all be coming apart tonight.

She said nothing as they left the room and walked to Rafe's car. Dane opened the back door and Cutter jumped in as if it were familiar territory. It probably was, from what Hayley had said. Kayla got in while Dane was doing that so that she wasn't faced with wondering if he would open the door for her as he usually did. He said nothing in turn—just walked around and got in the driver's side.

The silence continued as they drove through the night. It didn't surprise her. What was there to say now? The past ten years of her life had been aimed at this moment. She couldn't turn back now if she wanted to, despite the urge to call it all off. She'd set this in motion, and it was out of her control now.

And now she would have to live with the results.

Chapter 30

Dane hadn't been out this way in years, but not all that much had changed. The building still stood alone at the far end of what had once been a pasture of some sort. It was the size of a small barn, about a story and a half tall, with an even higher roof. The windows and doors were boarded up now, and it had the empty look of the long abandoned.

Memories stirred as he looked at it. It had been cavernous inside, a big, open space where the games had once stood in a random sort of array that had actually been carefully planned, with alcoves to give each game its own space and avoid the distraction of having a traditional pinball or shooting gallery competing with the latest alien invasion game. There had been an open, raised level across the back, about ten feet higher than the floor, where the offices were and where what security there had been often stood to overlook the space and keep order. They'd never responded quite quickly enough to stop Chad and his crew from their own form of entertainment, though.

Most of the youngest kids just quit coming. Many of the older ones, too. He himself had been too stubborn, refusing to let Chad deprive him of a favorite pastime. Although he was the same age, he'd been weaker and smaller then, the growth spurt that had taken him to over six feet yet to come. But he'd started working out, biking, running, getting strong. Oddly, he hadn't needed his new strength and confidence; they'd left him alone after that beating.

Or maybe it was that same new strength and confidence that had warned them off. He'd never really known, nor cared, as long as they stayed away.

He stopped the car about halfway down the long driveway and turned off the headlights. They were twenty yards from the building and still in the trees, where the darkness was nearly absolute. They were also at the spot where the driveway curved toward the building, and the headlights would have announced their arrival rather blatantly.

Kayla glanced at him.

"Quinn said to wait here," he said.

It was the first thing he'd said since they'd left the motel; they hadn't spoken at all on the drive. He'd been glad of it. The last thing he wanted to hear right now was her excitement at maybe seeing her brother again. He should be glad for her, he supposed, but selfishly he wasn't. Not when he thought about the price they both were paying for this obsession of hers. True, it could well be over soon, finally resolved, but too late. For them anyway.

Still, he felt compelled to warn her. "Quinn said if he's here, they'll have to call Detective Dunbar. Chad is still their prime suspect."

He wasn't sure, there in the dark, but he thought she winced. Yet she didn't speak or take her eyes off the building as they waited. Once Dane thought he saw a faint light through the upper window, as if someone had a flashlight inside, but it was quick and didn't repeat, so he wasn't certain.

Cutter was suddenly on his feet in the backseat, looking out the back window. A low rumble they'd heard before issued from his throat. If there was such a thing as a happy growl, this was it. Or maybe respectful, Dane thought.

"Quinn," Kayla said, recognizing the sound from that first day out at Foxworth just as he had.

And a moment later the big SUV pulled up beside them

and Quinn was there. And somewhat to Dane's surprise, Hayley was with him.

Dane got out and opened the car door for the anxious Cutter.

"Quiet," Hayley said to the animal as he jumped out. Obediently, the dog skipped his usual happy bark of greeting for her. But he danced at her feet until she bent down and hugged him, crooning about how much she'd missed him. Then he moved to Quinn, sitting at his feet and looking up expectantly.

"Ready to do a little work, buddy?" Quinn asked as he scratched the dog's ears.

Instantly the dog was back on his feet, tail up, ears alert, answering in the affirmative as clearly as if he could speak.

Quinn unclipped a small walkie-talkie that matched the one Hayley had given them from his belt. He keyed it and spoke.

"Rafe?"

"North side" came the laconic response.

"Cutter and I will be making the approach. Stand by, and stop anybody who leaves the building."

Instead of an answer, Dane heard a click, as if the man on the other end had simply pushed the talk button and released it. This was obviously not new to them.

"I want to go with you," Kayla said. "If Chad's in there, I need to see him."

"Not yet," Quinn said almost absently, clearly already focused on the task ahead. "Ready, boy? Let's go."

Dane understood Kayla's desire; he was feeling a bit antsy at staying here himself. But as he watched Cutter and Quinn move out across the open space between here and the building at different angles, as he saw the way Cutter raced ahead, then stopped, lifting his head into the faint breeze, sniffing, then turning his head and sniffing again, then respond to an apparent hand signal from Quinn, he realized they were a smooth-working team. And that Quinn Foxworth was far more than the executive or philanthropist he'd first thought he was.

"They've done this before, haven't they?" he asked Hayley softly.

"Yes."

"I should be there," Kayla said.

"No," Hayley said with a reassuring touch on Kayla's arm. "If you go in now, I'll go in after you, and if I go in Quinn will be mad, and trust me, you do not want to see that."

Dane couldn't help chuckling; he had no doubts that Quinn mad over Hayley putting herself at risk would be a fearsome sight.

"You've got your walkie-talkie?"

Dane nodded; he'd stuck it in his back pocket as they'd left the motel room.

"He'll call us when it's safe to come in."

Dane sensed Kayla was about to speak, but she apparently changed her mind. Just as well; if she'd insisted she'd be safe with her brother, he would have likely said something harsh. Perhaps the concept that someone had tried to kill her had finally penetrated.

Or perhaps the fact that Quinn had been armed had made her realize this wasn't necessarily going to be the joyous occasion she'd always hoped for.

For a moment he felt bad for her, so bad he almost went to comfort her, as he always had. But he kept going back to what he'd thought through yesterday as she'd slept. One of two things would happen here tonight.

One, Chad would not be there, whether it was because he never had been or because he had moved on or some other reason that didn't really matter. In which case Kayla would simply slide back into search mode, expending her time and energy and money on the endless quest.

Two, Chad would be there. And Kayla would be either delighted and lost in the happy reunion, or hurt to learn the brother she'd loved to exhaustion hadn't cared enough to keep in touch, maybe hadn't even thought about her all that much. Or worse, she'd be devastated if it turned out Chad had been guilty all along.

Whichever way it turned out, Kayla would be either continuing her search, or wrapped up one way or another in his return. And if it turned out he was back in legal trouble, if the police arrested him, she'd probably throw all that effort into defending him. Either way, the result for him would be the same.

He'd lost.

Maybe he'd never had a chance to win.

If there was anything Quinn had learned in the time since a finally generous fate had set Hayley and Cutter in his path, it was to trust them both. Right now, it was the quick, uncannily clever canine who had his full attention. He'd given up questioning how the dog seemed to always know what the mission at hand was, how he barely had to formulate a command before the dog was off and running, as if he'd already known what to do and had merely been waiting for the order.

This time was no exception. They made their entrance through a delivery door where the lock appeared to have been broken long ago judging by the weathering and rust buildup. Cutter had stopped just inside in that way he had, his head lifted, nose pumping as he processed scents, ears alert as he listened for the slightest sound with that hearing that was uncanny even for a dog. Quinn's eyes were already adjusted to the dark outside and only took a moment to change further for the deeper darkness inside the building. He kept his small, high-power LED flashlight in his pocket for the moment; he could see well enough to make out shapes in the cavernous space, and he didn't want to betray his location too soon.

In what seemed like only a few seconds, Cutter headed for the far left corner of the building with obvious purpose.

In the beginning, it had been a stretch for Quinn to trust the dog completely, to accept that he would find what they were looking for and warn of any impediments, human or otherwise. But now he knew better, and he followed without hesitation.

In the end, it seemed almost anticlimactic. Cutter signaled with a single, sharp bark that he'd found something. Quinn ran the last few feet and found Cutter at the entrance to one of the old game alcoves, one that was more walled off than the others, making it almost a private room. The dog was on his feet, his attention riveted on what—or who—was inside that space.

It was obvious the dog didn't sense a threat, but Quinn wasn't quite ready to cede full assessment of the danger to a dog. Yet. Cutter might be smart, as dogs go downright brilliant, but the concept of firearms or even knives as weapons was asking a bit much.

Now was the time for the flashlight. Quinn pulled it out and set it to spotlight mode, which was a wide, intense beam that could temporarily blind an opponent at night. With the light in his left hand and his sidearm as a precaution in his right, he made the move, leaning around the wall to look into the alcove.

The light flooded the small space like it was a stage.

Apparently Cutter had been right about the threat level. The man inside the alcove was huddled against the back wall, staring in apparent shock at the dog in front of him. He had a dark blanket pulled around him, making his pale face stand out even more. He wasn't moving, but his hands were hidden by the blanket so Quinn stayed wary, although the man seemed pinned in place more by the sight of Cutter than Quinn and the powerful flashlight. Quinn supposed the sudden appearance of a fifty-pound dog could do that, although the guy was looking at Cutter like he'd seen one too many werewolf movies.

Quinn registered all this in a split second. These were logistical details, the threat of the hidden hands, the lack of movement, the fear of the dog. Important, necessary, but not the overriding fact.

That was, simply, that they'd found him.

Because there was no doubt this man huddled in the blanket was Chad Tucker.

Chapter 31

"Guard, Cutter. Make a move and he'll tear your throat out," Quinn said pleasantly. Cutter growled for effect.

Kayla smothered a gasp at the threat. She was shaking, knowing she'd be unable to believe what she'd heard come over the small radio until she got inside and saw it for herself. Now that she was there, she wanted to rush forward those last few yards, but both Hayley and Dane were solidly between her and the goal.

And then Quinn was there, talking into his walkie-talkie.

"—pole out at the road, see if you can jury-rig some lights. Stay alert—this is a big place. Cutter hasn't triggered on anything else in here, but he's pretty focused just now."

"Copy," Rafe's voice came back.

Quinn turned to Kayla. "I've searched him for weapons, and he's clean, but I still want you to stay back far enough that he can't get his hands on you."

She started to say if it was her brother he wouldn't hurt her, but she held it back. "It's really Chad?"

"Yes."

She shivered again, her emotions a tangled mess of anticipation, excitement, apprehension and a tinge of fear. But overriding them all was the sense that it was finally done, her brother was finally home.

"Please, I need to see him."

"I know. Just don't let your emotions overrule common sense. We don't know the truth yet."

She nodded.

"He doesn't know you're here. I want to watch his reaction when he sees you. It may tell us something."

"All right."

She was aware Dane hadn't said a word, but that was better than having him make some comment that would tear her up even more inside. Still, she couldn't help glancing at him.

To her surprise, he softly said, "Go ahead. You've been living for this moment for ten years."

There was no criticism, no harshness in his tone, and for an instant he was the old Dane, solid, supportive, strong. Impulsively she reached out, took his hand and squeezed it. Then she turned and walked the last few steps to where that blessed dog who had begun all this sat.

Now that the time was here she was a shaky mess, she thought, pausing to pet the dog instead of hurrying forward. But finally she turned to face the culmination of ten years of faith, loyalty and determination. Quinn turned the bright light on him.

He was a huddled, dirty mess, with what looked to be a blanket tossed onto the floor beside him. He was unshaven, his hair scraggly and unkempt under a red baseball cap that had also seen better days. He put up a hand against the glare, blocking her view of his face. Kayla saw the hand was dirty. But it wasn't that that make her heart leap—it was the little finger on that hand, crooked and bent slightly inward, a souvenir from a long ago incident with a car door.

"Chad," she whispered, barely able to keep herself from ignoring Quinn's order to stay back.

Her first thought was that the computer-aged picture had been startlingly accurate. Her second was that good as it had been, it hadn't been able to show the haggard, haunted look in her brother's eyes. He was twenty-eight, but he looked ten years older. Ten long, hard years.

She realized that while he was lit up as if on a stage, she was still in shadow to him.

"It's me," she said.

He didn't answer, just sat with a hand still up to shade his eyes from the brightness of Quinn's powerful flashlight.

A second later a bank of lights far above came to life. Rafe, she thought, out at the power pole on the road. They only lit this corner of the spacious building, but it was enough that Quinn shut off the flashlight.

Chad dropped his hand then, and Kayla saw that although perhaps he didn't look quite as badly as he had in the flashlight's harsh beam, he still looked tired, dirty and worn.

And beaten. Broken. Smaller somehow. It was definitely Chad, although the cocky grin, the swagger, seemed gone. Even the dimple that had so charmed everyone seemed to have morphed into just a long crease in a tired face.

She wanted to go to him, wanted to throw her arms around him and hug him, but Quinn was close enough to stop her, as was Dane, and she had no doubts that they would.

She stared at her brother.

"Are you all right?"

It was, she supposed, a silly question, but it was the first thing that came to her mind.

"Is that your damned dog? Get him away from me."

For the first words she'd heard him speak in ten years, they certainly lacked something. Kayla looked at Cutter, who was sitting obediently, although he never took his eyes off Chad.

"If it wasn't for him, we'd never have found you."

"I don't like the way he's looking at me."

"He won't hurt you."

Chad looked doubtful, but he let it go.

"Who are these guys?"

His gaze shifted from Quinn to Dane, and he frowned. Kayla drew back slightly; did he really not recognize Dane?

Quinn stayed silent but glanced at Dane. She couldn't see what passed between the two men, but it was Dane who spoke.

"I'm the guy who tries to clean up the damage you leave behind," he said.

Chad's eyes widened. "Burdette?" He looked Dane up and down. "It sounds like you, but…"

"Ten years makes a difference. Whether you're going up—" Dane looked at Chad in a similar fashion "—or down."

Chad didn't even respond to the jab—there was no sign of the old rivalry. Her brother just seemed bewildered.

"You're still around?" he asked. "I mean, you two, together?"

"For now," Dane said.

Stung by the reminder Dane's words made clear, Kayla took a step forward. Dane put a hand on her arm, stopping her. She shook him off.

"Can't you see he's not a threat?"

"What I see is the guy who ran and left you to deal with everything by yourself. Even if he is innocent—and I'm not convinced—that makes him a damned son of a bitch in my book."

Somehow his words, even though they accused her brother, made her feel better. He was angry, yes, but he was angry on her behalf, and that gave her hope.

"I am innocent!" Chad burst out. "I swear, Kayla, I didn't do it. You have to believe me."

She turned back to her brother. "Then why did you run?"

"You know why. You know the police had me tried and convicted and on my way to the death penalty."

"All you had to do was tell them the truth, that you happened to get there right after, that's why your fingerprints were in the wet blood. You got scared and ran, that's all. Anybody would have."

Chad stared at her, looking nonplussed. Then, he smiled.

To her discomfort, Kayla noticed a faint trace of his old smugness, the kind he'd shown when he'd done something he knew he'd get away with. But it vanished the moment Dane spoke.

"Well, well," Dane said. "If only you'd thought up that story at the time, eh, Chad?"

Kayla flushed, but she couldn't deny Chad's reaction when it was right in front of her. Apparently her neat little story was just that, a story she'd made up to explain what had happened. Chad's expression made it clear that it wasn't the truth.

"I'm hungry," he said. "I can't even think I'm so hungry."

Tension filled Kayla as she wondered what he would have said if he could think. Would he have gone along with her version of events? Would he have let her believe what obviously wasn't the truth if only he'd been quick enough to grab at the out she'd given him?

"You don't need to think," Dane said, "just talk. Tell her the truth. She deserves that after standing by you for ten years."

"Can't we go someplace where I could eat?"

"You buying?" Dane asked, and Chad flushed.

"We can go someplace else," Quinn said, the first time he'd spoken since he'd turned the flashlight on for her, "but if we do, I'll be obligated to call the police first. I don't feel like explaining why we let a double murder suspect leave the scene where we found him."

Chad blinked. "You're not the police?"

"No," Quinn said. "But they can be here quickly enough. So now's your chance to tell your sister the truth. Maybe your only chance."

Kayla had been watching him carefully, looking for any trace of the young, carefree kid she'd known. She found nothing. And for the first time in her life, she wondered how much of Chad's cheerful bluster had been a facade. Maybe deep down he'd been as uncertain as she had once been, only he'd hidden it so well he'd never developed the real confidence of someone who'd learned their own worth as they built it. He'd never really grown up because he'd always pretended to already be there.

"I didn't do it," Chad said stubbornly. "They pissed me off all the time, but I didn't kill them."

Kayla should have felt vindicated. After all these years of believing just that, she should have been overjoyed at hearing it from Chad's own mouth. But she wasn't. Not that she didn't believe him; she could tell he was telling the truth. But she knew that look, that hangdog expression, all too well. His appearance may have changed, but his expressions had not, and the way he wouldn't look her in the eye was an old, familiar warning that her brother wasn't telling the whole truth.

"You always were a master of omission," Kayla said. "So what are you leaving out now?"

Chad seemed surprised. That she'd called him on it? She remembered that brief flash of smugness and realized sadly that he'd been feeling smug because, as always, she had come up with an explanation for him. His little sister would bail him out again, as she always had.

"Nothing," he insisted. He glanced at Quinn. "Who the hell is this? And who's she?" he said, looking past Quinn to Hayley. "Is that their dog? Can't you get him out of here? He keeps staring at me."

Kayla expected Quinn to answer, but he said nothing. Nor did Hayley, although she whispered something to Cutter, something Kayla guessed was a keep doing what he was doing because that's what he did.

Apparently this was all Kayla's now. "They and their organization found you for me," she said.

Chad's eyes flicked to Quinn again. "You're them? The do-gooders?"

Dane went very still. Kayla saw him exchange a pointed

glance with Quinn. Quinn gave a slight shake of his head. And suddenly Dane was on the offensive.

"Is that what your partner told you? That Foxworth was looking for you? That they wouldn't give up until they found you? Why'd you come back if you knew Foxworth was here? Did he tell you to?"

Chad frowned at the rapid-fire questions and shook his head as if he were having trouble sorting it all out. She understood that; she herself wasn't sure what Dane was about here.

"He didn't say anything about any Foxworth," Chad said. "Just said she brought in professional help this time, good help, and that I should get back here so we could figure out what to do."

"Well, well," Quinn said, echoing Dane's earlier comment as he glanced at him. "Nicely done."

"Learned a lot," Dane agreed, seemingly pleased at Quinn's praise.

Kayla was feeling a bit confused herself. "Learned what?"

"That he did just come back, which makes our homeless witness accurate. That he knew you had help this time, and that it was good help. So someone's reporting to him. Which brings us to the other thing he just admitted."

"I didn't admit anything," Chad protested.

"Sure you did," Dane said. "You admitted there *is* a partner."

Kayla realized she indeed had been a bit slow.

And that once more, Chad had deceived her, had lied to her face.

What that made her, she didn't want to think about.

Chapter 32

Kayla was shaken, Dane could see that. He had to remind himself again that seeing to her, comforting her, wasn't his job anymore. At the same time, that little voice in his brain was telling him it was only human kindness to comfort someone in distress—it didn't have to be personal.

Didn't have to become…intimate.

Except with Kayla it usually did. He didn't seem to have any amount of willpower she couldn't overcome, not by trying, coaxing, wheedling. That wasn't her way. She simply was who she was, who she always had been, and she was irresistible to him.

Or had been, until her obsession had finally pushed him over a line he couldn't cross and still live with himself.

And now here she was, face-to-face with the object of that obsession, and Dane could easily tell she wasn't happy with what she was seeing. He didn't blame her; his own dislike for her brother aside, it had to be a shock to see the wreck he'd become at only twenty-eight. He barely recognized the once-handsome, charming Chad Tucker in the dirty, skinny guy with badly cut, scraggly hair and sunken eyes before them now.

And he could see in Kayla's face that she knew he was, even now, still lying to her. Or at least not telling her the whole truth. Hayley had moved to Kayla's side and whispered something to her. Dane wondered if it had something to do with him because it was he Kayla glanced at for an instant before she turned back to Chad.

"Who is it?"

Kayla's words were flat, emotionless. Chad shifted uncomfortably.

"Who's helping you?" she asked again. And then, as the conclusion he'd reached a while ago struck her visibly, she added, horror echoing in her voice, "Is it whoever helped you that night? Helped you get away?"

Something about the way she said it got through to Chad. "You do think I did it! You think I killed them, don't you?"

He was nearly shouting, and Cutter let out a warning rumble. Chad drew back, glancing warily at the dog. *Good boy,* Dane thought.

"Atta boy," Hayley said to the dog, loud enough this time for Chad to hear.

"I've spent ten years of my life trying to prove you didn't," Kayla shot back at her brother. "With no help from you. Nothing but a note every few months to let me know you were alive."

"Or to keep you dancing on his string," Dane said. "So you'd be focused on looking for him, instead of—"

He cut off his own words as Kayla's head snapped around and she looked at him. It would be better if she got to that realization on her own. And she did it so quickly he knew she'd already thought of it before.

"Instead of thinking about who did do it, if he didn't?"

"Yes," Dane said simply.

"But why would he do that?"

"Good question," Dane said.

She whirled back on her brother. "Tell me the damn truth, Chad. Or are you so twisted now you can't?"

"I didn't kill them," he insisted.

Kayla made a small, harsh sound. Dane knew her so well

he could almost follow her thoughts. She'd waited so long to hear that from her brother, and now that she had, it only emphasized what he wasn't telling her. She seemed to finally realize he'd been playing her all these years.

She turned away, shaking her head slowly, like a wounded animal. It was more than Dane could take. He glanced at Quinn, but the man merely nodded; apparently he was satisfied with the way things were going. Dane looked back at Chad.

"Then why did you try to kill your own sister?" Dane demanded.

Chad gaped at him. "I didn't! I wouldn't."

He ignored the denial. "For that matter, how did you even know where she lives now?"

Dane didn't make a move toward the man, but Chad cringed backward anyway. He seemed shrunken, a long, long way from the swaggering, cocky bully he'd once been. He would have almost felt sorry for him—if not for the thought of Kayla nearly dying in her burning house.

"I don't know what you're talking about."

Kayla whirled back. "You were there. You were seen there."

When Chad looked away, still refusing to speak, Dane's disgust spilled over. "This is pointless."

"Yes, it is," Kayla said, surprising him with both her words and her tone; her voice was a harsh, bitter thing. She looked at Quinn. "You might as well call Detective Dunbar."

Quinn nodded. "Between us we'll find whoever it is he's protecting. Just like we found him. Of course, it'll go worse for him—" he jerked a thumb toward Chad "—because he refused to cooperate, but he's already in so much trouble it won't matter much."

"Wait, wait," Chad stammered. "Kayla, you can't do that. I'm your brother."

"You don't get it, do you?" Dane asked, almost astonished at the man's refusal to understand. "You think you're just going to take off again, run?"

Chad looked at him. His words were tinged with his old bluster, but Dane saw the doubt in his eyes. "She won't turn me in."

"This is for real, Chad. It's out of your hands, our hands. You won't tell your own sister, the woman who's stood up for you for ten damned years, the truth, but I bet by the time the police get done with you you'll spill it all."

"But—"

"And they'll realize quickly enough you didn't do it all on your own," Dane said. "You're not smart enough."

Chad let out a foul curse. "You always did think you were so smart."

"He didn't think it," Kayla said softly, "he knew it. Because he is."

A stab of pain at the quiet declaration shot through Dane as he glanced at her. But she wasn't looking at him; she was staring at her brother. This time he wasn't sure what she was thinking, only that she was; her expression told him her mind was racing.

"You two are the perfect couple," Chad said, that trace of bluster growing stronger. "You always thought you were better than everyone."

Dane almost laughed at that; Chad seemed to have a very different memory of their adolescence than he and Kayla had.

"If that's the way you feel about me, then why did you come back at all?" Kayla asked. She sounded flat, emotionless. "Why the notes even? Why bother?"

Chad shifted, as if her tone had made him uncomfortable, draining away some of his regained swagger. "You're my sister."

"And that obviously means less than nothing to you because you won't even tell me the truth." She looked at Quinn again. "Make the call."

Quinn nodded and pulled out his phone. Kayla again turned away.

"No!"

Chad's regained facade of confidence crumbled like the shaky structure it had been. Perhaps had always been, Dane thought. Chad wasn't inherently mean, like some. With the knowledge of maturity, something Chad had never achieved, Dane realized that behind the bullying exterior had likely been an uncertain, timid kid. It didn't excuse his behavior, but he understood better now than back then, when he'd only been angry and scared at being a target.

And out of that had come his resolve to change that, to become someone nobody would mess with. The pact made with Kayla that long-ago day, to defy the expectations of those who judged on appearance alone, had arisen out of her brother's bullying, although she'd never known it until today. So in a twisted sort of way, he supposed he owed Chad a thank you. He was who he was today in part because of him.

Kayla looked at her brother over her shoulder. "If you're telling the truth, if you didn't kill our parents, you're protecting who did. And you expect me to keep protecting you?"

"Kayla—"

"You're not worth it. And you're surely not worth what you've cost me. The man I've lost over you is worth a million of you. Ten million. I've been a fool to believe in you."

She turned and started to walk away. Dane watched her, feeling tangled inside, proud that she'd done it, sorry for the pain that had been in her voice and shaken by hearing her declaration of tremendous love and loss in the same sentence.

The sound of her footsteps echoed in the cavernous room. For a long, torturous moment that was the only sound. And then, finally, Chad broke.

"It was Troy!" he shouted.

Kayla stopped. Dane's head snapped back. His brows furrowed.

Kayla slowly turned around.

"Troy?" she said. "You seriously expect me to believe that?"

"It was him."

Cutter was on his feet, apparently reacting to the sudden upswing in tension. For the first time the dog looked away from Chad, while Dane himself was staring at the guy in disbelief. It echoed in his voice.

"Of all the people you could try to pin this on, you pick on the poster boy for goodness and clean living? The adults' favorite 'why can't you be more like him?' guy?"

"It was him," Chad insisted. "We were both there that night, but I only wanted the money. Troy was broke, I was broke, and his car payment was due and I wanted to buy a motorcycle, and I remembered dad's stash."

"You knew about the money in his desk?" Kayla looked puzzled.

"God, you didn't?"

Kayla shook her head. "I thought it was just all the important papers—birth certificates, insurance, that kind of thing."

"Yeah, they were in there, too. Troy was looking through it all, searching for more money." Chad shook his head. "I can't believe you didn't know he kept over five grand in there."

"How did you know?"

"I overheard him telling Mom about it, in case she ever needed it."

"So you snuck into the house intending to steal from your own father?"

Chad's smugness at her lack of knowledge vanished.

"Hey, I asked him for a loan, and he said no."

"Maybe because he knew you wouldn't pay it back?" Dane

suggested. He knew a whine was about to ensue as Chad opened his mouth to protest, and he was in no mood. He cut him off with an impatient question. "What happened?"

Chad seemed distracted by Cutter as the dog began to turn in place, sniffing and listening at every angle. But after a moment he went on.

"I don't know how they heard us. I thought they were upstairs. But they walked in on us. Dad saw the money in my hand and saw Troy digging through the drawer. He yelled. And Troy freaked."

"Freaked? And killed both your parents?" Dane couldn't picture the always polite, charming Troy doing any of this. The guy had never been in trouble. He was the proverbial good kid, the one every parent wished was their own. Smart, well-mannered, polite—all those things adults treasured in teenagers.

"He did," Chad insisted.

Now if he'd said Rod, that he could believe. But Troy? He couldn't help thinking Chad was pulling this out of thin air, trying to save himself. Maybe Troy was just the first person to pop into his mind when cornered.

"Where'd he get the knife?"

Chad didn't look at him; he kept his pleading gaze on his sister. "It was him, I swear. I didn't know he'd brought a knife. I didn't even realize what was happening until it was too late. Until it was over."

Cutter growled, and Chad lowered his eyes to the dog uneasily. Kayla took a few steps back toward him.

"Why did you run?" she asked.

Chad's head came up. "Because I knew they'd suspect me. Troy told me I'd better get out of there. Because it was my idea to take the money, he said I'd take the fall. Besides, nobody would ever believe it was him." Chad flicked Dane a glance. "Because of just what you said. I was the one with a record."

"And he just stayed here? Went on with his life?" Kayla demanded.

"And you just let him?" Dane added.

"He sent me money." Chad's voice was resentful, and Dane wasn't sure who it was aimed at. Life maybe. He was the type. "He owed me for what he did."

"Owed *you?*" Dane nearly shouted it. "You were eighteen, technically an adult. Your sister was only sixteen!"

"It wasn't my fault! Once he found out about the money, there was no stopping him. Besides, he warned me to stay away, told me that they were still looking for me, that I was still the only suspect."

"And I suppose the thought that your good friend should confess and take the heat off you never occurred to you?"

Chad shifted uncomfortably, and Dane guessed it had indeed occurred to him more than once. "But he said we'd both go to jail," Chad whined, "and this way at least we both were free."

"If you call this free," Dane muttered, indicating Chad's sorry state with a tilt of his head.

"It wasn't my fault. I never—"

"You never thought anything was ever your fault," Kayla said. Dane had once thought he'd give anything to hear her say that, but there was such pain in her voice he took no pleasure in it now. "But you got our parents murdered as surely as if you'd used the knife yourself."

"I never touched them!"

"Your partner was right about one thing," Quinn said, breaking his silence. "In the eyes of the law you're equally culpable. You broke into a residence with the intent to commit a felony, and in the course of that felony, two people were killed."

"But I didn't mean for anything to happen to them!"

"And I'm sure the jury will take your good intentions into

account, right before they convict you of murder," Dane said, only realizing as he said it that he was buying Chad's story. It was too stupid, too ridiculous for him to have made it up. And it was just like Chad. His always-looking-for-the-easy-way selfishness had not only cost his own parents their lives, and nearly destroyed Kayla's, it had cost him the woman he'd loved. Restraint was beyond him at the moment.

"I can't believe this," Kayla whispered, sounding a little shell-shocked. "Or rather, I can, and it makes me sick. You make me sick. All these years I wasted, while all along you—"

She broke off as a low, threatening growl rumbled up from Cutter's throat. The dog whirled and took off at a head-down dead run toward the back of the building.

Quinn swore. "I knew something was up with him. I should have paid more attention."

Dane realized Cutter's restlessness hadn't been merely reaction to the tension. "He's headed toward the stairs," he said as the dog left the lighted area and disappeared into the shadows. "It's like a loft, and the office and storage rooms used to be up there."

"He heard something. Sensed something. And now he knows. Somebody must have gotten in when Rafe went to rig the lights." Quinn's voice turned sharp as he looked at Dane. "Get Kayla and Hayley outside, back to the car."

"What about him?" Dane asked, indicating Chad.

"Call Rafe on the walkie-talkie and give him an update. If Chad's stupid enough to run, Rafe'll take him out."

Then he was gone, running into the shadows after the dog who had known something was wrong long before they had.

"No," Kayla began when Dane took her arm.

Dane cut off her protest. "Let's go." He wasn't sure if she was protesting going or wondering just what Quinn meant by the lethal Rafe taking her brother out.

"But—"

A loud, explosive sound cut her off this time.

A shot.

Kayla gasped, then ducked instinctively. Chad yelped and hit the ground, cowering into a corner. Dane turned Kayla around and found Hayley had grabbed her other arm, and between them they propelled her toward the door they'd come in. But she still didn't seem to want to move.

"Don't you get it?" Dane demanded. "He's here. The guy who murdered your parents is here. And he's graduated from a knife to a gun."

Chapter 33

"Stay here. Keep the doors locked."

Kayla heard the words but couldn't seem to react. She was trembling—she could feel it, hated it, but couldn't seem to control it. There had been so much to process so quickly that now she felt as if her brain was trying to swim upstream through a rush of revelations she'd never expected.

Belatedly, she realized Dane wasn't getting into the car.

"What are you doing?"

"Quinn might need some help in there."

"Rafe is there."

"Yes. But he's got Chad to deal with, and obviously Troy is armed."

He took off back toward the building. She stared after him. When had her Dane become fearless? Heroic? Or had he always been, and it just hadn't been put to the test until now?

This was insane. He could be hurt—or worse. An image of Dane lying dead on the dusty floor of the old arcade nearly smothered her. The last, shaky vestige of naïveté about her brother crumbled away. She'd been a fool. And it had cost her the man she'd loved nearly half her life.

Her Dane.

Only he wasn't hers. Not anymore.

She'd been devoted to finding Chad, while for his part a few unsigned notes had been his sole effort at keeping in touch. She'd spent years searching for him, and if she'd found him earlier she would have channeled that time, energy and money into proving his innocence. Even as kids, she'd always been loyal to him, tolerating his behavior because she loved him and because every now and then he threw her a crumb of brotherly affection. Now, she doubted he even knew what the word loyalty meant.

But she did.

Loyalty was Dane, sticking with her for so long, despite taking second place to her foolish stubbornness. Loyalty was Dane, giving her chance after chance to move on, to make the life with him they'd always planned, always wanted.

Loyalty was Dane, who came running when she was hurt, even after he'd finally walked away, even after being suspected himself.

Loyalty…and love.

And she'd worn out that love, thrown it away, all for nothing. For a brother who at best had been a careless, self-centered fool and at worst a stupidly, willingly manipulated pawn who had cost the people who loved him the most their lives.

She glanced around. Hayley was in the back of the SUV, digging through what looked like a locker and occasionally stopping to speak into the walkie-talkie. Hayley apparently was serving as a coordinator.

While she sat here doing nothing, like the helpless female of some fairy tale. While the men were inside, likely dealing with a confirmed killer.

While Dane, even lacking the training the Foxworth men had, was in there.

A muffled crack jerked her out of her self-castigating reverie.

Another shot.

She'd had enough of sitting on the sideline, even though

it had only been a couple of minutes. She'd gotten everyone into this, after all. She scrambled out of the car and ran toward the building.

The moment he'd gone back through the door, Dane had heard Cutter's bark. In the echoing space it was hard to pinpoint, but it seemed to come from the back. And from above, so Dane guessed the dog was up in the raised loft. For a moment he hesitated but decided Quinn was a pro and would instinctively assess that Chad was the lesser threat and deal with the armed man first.

Dane ran back to where Chad had been hiding out. And collided with him as he darted out of the alcove.

Chad staggered back a couple of steps.

"Running, as usual?" Dane asked.

"He's got a gun," Chad said, a tremor in his voice.

"And that night he had a knife."

"I didn't know—"

"Spare me. You've put Kayla through hell for ten years. You're a coward, Chad. You always have been."

Another shot split the dark, the sound bouncing off the walls, making it sound like the crack and roll of thunder. Chad jumped, then tried to push past Dane.

And Dane indulged in the urge that had been prodding him since the moment they'd found Kayla's brother huddled here in a shameless heap, not caring what he'd done to his sister for years.

He launched a solid punch carefully aimed at Chad's lips and nose. The crunch was immensely satisfying.

Chad crumpled, wailing.

Dane left him there. And ran in the direction of the shot.

The halo of light Rafe had managed was fainter here, but after a moment his eyes adjusted and he could at least see to move, if not details and colors. He found Quinn crouched halfway up the stairs, head turned toward him. Then he saw some tension ease when he saw who was there.

"He's up there?" Dane whispered.

"Yes." Quinn's voice was even quieter. "He leaned out to take that shot, but it was nowhere close. He was just firing blind." Quinn glanced over toward the light. "Chad?"

"He tried to run when he heard the shot. I stopped him but probably not for long. We'll have to find him later." And he had no doubts Foxworth would do just that.

"Rafe's around. He won't get far. Kayla?"

"Locked in the car." Dane grimaced. "Whether she'll stay there…"

"Gutsy girl. Hard to find."

Dane couldn't deny that. And wondered if Quinn was making an observation or a recommendation.

"What now?" he asked.

"I think Cutter has a plan."

Dane nearly gaped at the man. Quinn was tough, smart and a former special forces operative, and he was trusting a dog to have a plan?

"I know, I know." Even in a whisper Quinn's wry tone was obvious. "I can only tell you that if I don't trust him, things get screwed up. If I do, things always seem to work out."

And so he crouched there, beside Quinn, waiting on a dog to make a move.

Kayla was nearly there when a shape reeled out of the door they'd used to enter. She stopped abruptly, nearly slipping on the gravel. The man started to run, half stumbling back the way she had come, toward the road.

Was it the man with the gun? Had he somehow escaped even the clever Cutter?

Then she saw the red cap. Chad. Running away as usual.

So intent on avoiding the consequences of his actions that he didn't even see her as he ran.

Without a second thought, she stuck a foot into his path and sent him sprawling.

He swore, rolled over, then finally saw her.

"Kayla! What the hell?"

Even at night, there was enough light for her to see that his mouth and nose were bloodied. The instinctive, automatic lurch of concern died almost instantly; her brother didn't care about her, never had, so she wasn't going to waste any more time worrying about him. Someone had given him his split lip and bloody nose, and it was the very least he deserved.

"You're through running, Chad," she said coldly.

"C'mon, sis, I've got to get out of here. I can't go to jail."

"You can, and you will. You're almost as responsible as Troy is."

"I'm not. I didn't know. It wasn't my fault."

"Shut the hell up, you coward. You're a useless piece of humanity, and I regret every second I spent worrying about you and searching for you."

"Hear, hear," came Hayley's quiet cheer of approval from just behind her.

She saw realization dawn on his face, realization that he'd finally lost his grip on his little sister. He rolled to his hands and knees, starting to get up.

"Oh, no you don't."

She let loose a short, quick kick Dane had taught her years ago, catching Chad hard just below the rib cage. His breath whistled out of him and he collapsed face down. Following part two of the lesson, Kayla came down hard, planting a knee just over his kidneys. He grunted. She ignored him.

"Nice job."

She jumped at the male voice coming out of the dim light

just feet away. But she calmed as she recognized the slight limp of Rafe Crawford as he approached.

"You were here?" she asked, startled. "Not inside?"

He nodded as he came to a stop and looked down at Chad. "Quinn'll handle it."

She wasn't surprised, now that she had a chance to think, that Quinn would want Hayley's, and her own, safety insured before anything. It fit with who the man was.

But that didn't ease her main worry. "Dane," she said.

"That boy'll do, don't worry," Rafe said. She had the feeling that from this man, that was the highest of praise. "And they've got Cutter," Rafe added. "It's taken us all a while but we've learned to trust that darned dog." He glanced down at Chad. "Besides, it didn't seem like you needed much help. And some things you need to do yourself."

She stared at the man. Saw a world of understanding in his eyes. And felt a small burst of pride that he had held back, trusting her to handle it. "Thank you."

"It had to be a tough call, him being your brother and all."

"I'm not sure who he is anymore. I'm not sure the brother I loved ever really existed."

Rafe only grimaced but managed to do it in a way that conveyed such empathy that she felt an easing of the pressure that had built inside her since she'd realized what her brother had become and only increased as she was forced to admit he probably had always been.

They were an amazing group, these Foxworth people, she thought. She bet each one of them had a story that would fascinate.

But much as she might want to know them all, in particular this laconic, obviously dangerous yet clearly understanding man's, right now she was only worried about one thing.

What was going on inside that building.

* * *

Dane heard faint steps above, on the landing. He wondered what Cutter was doing; it sounded like the man—Troy, he amended—was just walking around.

"Troy!"

The scrape from above made Dane think Troy had jumped, startled, just as he himself almost had at Quinn's sudden shout.

"Give it up, Troy. It's all over."

"Go to hell!"

Quinn glanced at Dane. Realizing what he was silently asking, Dane nodded. "It's him."

"What was that?" Quinn called out. "I couldn't hear you."

Dane frowned. Troy's words were perfectly clear. Then he realized Quinn was trying to lure him forward, out of the shelter of the hallway between the offices.

"I said go to hell."

"Still can't hear you. Acoustics are weird in here."

And where was Cutter? Dane wondered. He didn't expect to hear the dog's steps, but—

"Cops already know it was you, Troy," Quinn yelled. "There's nowhere to run."

"Who's running?"

There was another sound, a creak of the floor, toward the front of the loft. Quinn held out an arm to urge Dane back against the stairway wall. Dane didn't argue but pressed back, expecting to hear another shot any second. Instead, he heard a yell of surprise and a series of heavy thumps.

Troy rolled past them, somersaulting down the stairs.

At the top of those stairs, Cutter let out a woof of pure satisfaction.

At the bottom, Troy was now sprawled, groaning.

Dane looked up at the dog, who had clearly managed to

nudge Troy over the edge. Then at Quinn. The man grinned and shrugged. "Told ya' he had a plan," he said.

Then he headed down the stairs to where Troy had now rolled onto his side, still groaning pitifully.

Cutter headed down the stairs, stopping to give Dane a nudge with his nose.

"You are something else," Dane said. "I'll never call you just a dog again."

Cutter tilted his head quizzically. And Dane could have sworn he winked. But in the faint light it was impossible to be sure. And ridiculous to believe. Then the dog was gone, headed down to check personally on his handiwork.

And realizing the threat was over, Dane launched himself over the stair railing to the floor and began to run. Toward the door.

Toward Kayla.

Chapter 34

When she saw Dane burst from the building, she nearly cried in aching, heartfelt relief.

No, she *was* crying, Kayla realized. She started to wipe at her eyes, then stopped. She didn't care if he saw it. She was just glad Chad was facedown and couldn't see her; he was so self-centered he'd probably think she was crying for him.

Dane skidded to a halt. For a moment he just stared. She supposed she made quite a sight, kneeling on Chad's back, forcing him down as he flailed, trying to get up. For an instant she thought she saw something in his face, a flash of promise, or at least hope. She tried to quash it, afraid to believe.

He glanced toward Rafe, standing off to one side.

"Don't look at me," the man said. "She did it. Nicely, too. Didn't need my help at all."

Kayla saw disbelief warring with the realization that Rafe had no reason to lie to Dane. Did he really think, after what she'd learned tonight, that she'd just let her brother waltz away and go on the run again?

Why wouldn't he? she told herself. *Haven't you made it clear you'd forgive Chad almost anything?*

She noticed Dane flexing his right hand, then rubbing at the knuckles as he looked at her brother.

"It was you," she said. "You punched him."

Dane's gaze snapped to her face. There was a touch of recalcitrance in his voice when he said, "After what he's put you through for so long, it was the least I could do and still sleep at night." He glared at Chad. "And I'll do it again if he tries to get up," he added by way of warning.

Chad fell still, and his body went slack, as if he'd finally given up. Kayla barely noticed. She was too distracted by the leap of her heart in her chest. Dane had punched Chad for what he'd put her through. Was there some hope, some possibility that she hadn't completely killed his love for her?

"Quinn cleaning up?" Rafe asked.

Dane nodded, never taking his eyes off Kayla. She saw Rafe look from her to Dane, then back. He gave the slightest of nods before he spoke. Somehow it encouraged her.

"I'll just take care of this clown then," he said, indicating Chad.

Kayla stood up, releasing her brother. Rafe yanked him up to his feet and started walking him back to Quinn's SUV. When he got there, he reached in and turned on the powerful headlights, throwing a shaft of light all the way to the door of the building.

"Don't you want to go help him?" Dane asked. "I bloodied him up a bit."

"No."

He studied her for a long moment. "You finally have what you wanted."

"No." He drew back slightly. "What I wanted never really existed, did it?" she said.

"Little late realizing that," Dane said.

"Yes," she admitted. But she didn't dare voice the crucial question; was it too late?

A sound from the building turned them both around; the door opened again. First out into the swath of light was Cutter, who quickly turned to supervise the exit of the two men who followed; Quinn and a limping man cradling his right arm. Cutter then took up a position on the other side of Troy, keeping the man securely between himself and Quinn.

Until this moment, Kayla hadn't quite believed it. But as Troy gave her a sideways glance as the trio reached them, she saw it in his eyes. Not guilt, but a sort of deadness that she realized must have always been behind the charming smile.

"Why, Troy?" she asked, not even really expecting him to answer. "My parents always liked you. Everybody liked you."

"Except you."

Dane saw Kayla's eyes widen. There wasn't a trace of anger in Troy's voice or his expression, just coldness.

"That's why you did it?" she asked, astonished. "Because I turned you down?"

Troy laughed, and it was even colder. So cold Dane had to suppress a shiver. "You'd like to believe that, wouldn't you, sweetheart?"

"But why my parents? They were the ones trying to push you and me together, they liked you so much."

"All the parents liked me." The smirk on his face, even now, echoed in his voice. "It made life so easy."

The smirk widened, but Troy said no more. Cutter wasn't happy with the pause. He had moved, put himself between Troy and Kayla, a move she noted with affection for the clever dog. She resisted the urge to pet him, with the idea of not disturbing a working dog while he was working, which Cutter obviously was just now. He was watching Troy with an intensity that was almost unnerving even to her; she couldn't imagine what it must feel like to Troy.

Then again, after what she'd learned tonight, she wondered if he would even be affected.

"All this time I thought he was defending his best friend," Kayla said, feeling a bit numb, "and he was really telling the truth. He knew Chad hadn't done it."

"I'm guessing Detective Dunbar will get it all out of him," Quinn said. "He's got enough sore spots to work on. And the broken arm, of course."

Kayla saw Troy's expression change at the mention of the cop's name. "You've called him?" she asked.

"Hayley did," Quinn said. "He should be here momentarily. He'll have to look around, of course. Do a thorough investigation. Maybe call in forensics or something. Finding those bullets this idiot shot in a building that size could take some time. Probably take quite a while to get that broken arm set. Be a shame if it never was right again."

Dane and Kayla could see Quinn's wink. Troy could not, and he suddenly wasn't quite so smug. He took a step, as if to test the strength of Quinn's grip. Cutter whirled, growling. It was a dangerous, spine-tingling sound Kayla would never have imagined coming from the whimsical dog. But Troy heard it, and with one look at the dog's lethal-looking exposed teeth, he gave up whatever idea had entered his head. And went docilely as Quinn led him back to join Chad.

"Definitely an alien," Dane said.

She saw one corner of his mouth quirk upward. Something about that half-grin gave her hope. More, it gave her courage. If there was a chance, the slightest chance, now might be the only time she had to take it. She would have preferred a better place, inside somewhere, where it was warm and comfortable. But she knew things would likely get complicated once the police arrived. Statements, interviews, she knew too well how it all worked. It could be hours before she'd see Dane again.

She wasn't about to pass up this chance. She just didn't know where to start.

"I never would have thought Cutter could be so scary," she said instead.

"You should have seen him inside. He literally pushed Troy down the stairs. Felt like we were just there to clean up after he handled it."

She drew in a deep breath. "That must have felt familiar. You've been cleaning up for me for ten years."

He didn't answer and went very still. Then she heard him let out a long breath.

"We're going there right now?" he asked.

"I owe you too much to put it off."

"You don't owe me anything. Anything I did was my own choice."

"Why? Why didn't you just stay away once you left?"

He shifted his feet, looked to one side, then back at her. "It's hard to turn off a decade of feelings."

"Then don't." She stopped, aware her voice was shaking.

"Kayla—"

"I understand. I wouldn't blame you, not a bit, if you really left now and never wanted to see me again. It's no more than I deserve. I took you for granted, assumed because you'd always been there for me, you always would be."

Again he said nothing. Dane had never been one to dodge serious discussions, so it worried her that he wasn't really participating in this one. But whether he spoke or not, whether he accepted it or not, he deserved this and more.

"You were right all along. I should have known. I had a blind spot for Chad, and I always have had. I'm so sorry it took me this long to wake up. That I had to see it for myself to realize he wasn't the guy I'd built him up to be in my mind."

"Well that's something," Dane muttered.

A car pulled up behind Quinn's SUV on the drive. Detective Dunbar got out, and she heard the crunch of his steady stride on the gravel as he walked toward Quinn, who had gone to greet him. Dane looked toward them, as if in his mind he was already over there, as if he was only staying here with her out of that innate courtesy she'd always admired.

She understood that, too. She wanted to be there herself, wanted to hear what they found out, wanted to know what had been behind the night that had destroyed life as she knew it.

"I want to know, too," she said, flicking a glance down

the drive. Then she said, very pointedly, "But this is more important."

Dane's head snapped around and he focused on her once more.

"It always was more important. I just lost track of that in my blindness."

She looked at him for a long moment. In the silence she felt a churning inside, as if her fear she'd lost him, her disappointment at Chad, her anger at herself were all battling each other, leaving her shakier than she could remember since that night ten years ago.

"This would be easier," she said, barely aware she was saying it out loud, "if we were in a tree."

Something flashed in his eyes then, something startled yet warm, and the feeble hope she'd nurtured glowed brighter for a moment.

"Want to go climb one?" he suggested.

"I would if it meant you'd listen."

"I'm listening."

She took in another deep breath, as if she were preparing to jump into the cold, deep sound.

"I love you. I have loved you since the day you climbed into that silly tree with me. I knew I was too young for you, but I waited. Then that night came, and you were there for me like no one else could be. I would not have survived it without you."

Here was where he usually would have protested, told her she was stronger than she knew, even back then. That she would have managed; she would have gotten through it. But this time he said nothing. And she didn't know if that was a good sign or an awful one.

She made herself go on. "I knew you could find someone else when you went off to college, but I still waited. When you came back to visit, I wanted to ask if you had, but I was so afraid of the answer I couldn't bring myself to do it. The two years between us meant nothing to me, but I knew it did to you. That I was probably still just a kid in your eyes."

"You were never a kid again after that night."

His quiet words sent a chill through her, stirring up memories that were always there but that she managed to control most of the time. That he'd spoken at all stirred that hope again.

"I never felt like one," she agreed.

"I did meet some girls at college," he said. He'd admitted this to her before but never added any details. He did now. "Some pretty, some smart, a few both. But all of them seemed…shallow next to you. They were carefree and careless. They had no idea how tough life could really be."

Kayla swallowed tightly. "Carefree must have seemed… appealing after all my drama."

He didn't answer, which, she supposed, was answer in itself. Now that she was finally seeing the whole picture, it seemed nothing less than miraculous that Dane had stuck with her so long.

"Kayla? Dane?" Hayley's voice held a world of apology at the interruption. "Sorry, but Detective Dunbar wants us at the station, ASAP. Time to start unraveling all this mess."

Kayla didn't think she was imagining Dane's relief.

Chapter 35

It was almost over.

Dane rubbed at his stubbled jaw. He knew he was pacing, wandering the anteroom of the small holding cell, but he was afraid if he stopped moving he'd fall asleep; it had been a couple of rough nights in succession. And by the time they'd arrived here at the small police station, it had been close to dawn. Besides, it kept him from looking at Kayla, where she sat huddled on one of the hard, plastic chairs along the back wall.

He supposed the sun was up now. He couldn't tell, down here in the back of the lower level of the building with no windows. They didn't have a jail of their own, and prisoners were transported to the county facility after being booked and processed here.

It was only luck—and Detective Dunbar—who had kept him out of this place himself, Dane thought. He could easily have been sitting in there, ink on his fingertips, awaiting transport to county jail. Silently he again thanked the man's instincts or whatever it had been that had made him decide Dane wasn't, after all, the fire bomber he was looking for.

Or maybe it had been Kayla.

Her defense of you was what they call spirited, Quinn had said.

She had never doubted him. Not for a minute. It was he who had fallen down on that particular job. Maybe he was the one who needed to make that up to her. Maybe he was the one who needed to give some reassurance.

Or maybe he was just looking for a way to still make this work, to keep this woman he'd loved for so long in his life.

A door opened, and Dane stopped midstride and turned. Kayla's head came up. Quinn stepped out of the secured area, the heavy, steel door closing behind him with a solid thud. He nodded to Dane, but it was Kayla he went to, crouching beside her chair.

"Chad's talking now. Detective Dunbar made him see the wisdom of coming clean, for his own sake."

"His own sake. All he cares about."

She sounded hollow and, worse, broken. Just the bitterness in her voice made Dane's chest tighten. He hated that she could sound like that, that after ten years of searching, of never giving up, it seemed she finally had.

He hated that she could still make him feel that way. That she could make him feel that strongly.

That she could make him feel.

"What about Troy?" Dane asked.

"He's a tougher nut," Quinn said. "But he took those shots at us, so he'll be on his way to county on attempted murder charges when Dunbar is done questioning him. That should soften him up a little."

"I still can't believe it was Troy. He was always the quint-essential charmer."

"I'm no expert," Quinn said, "but I think that man's been a puppet master for a long time."

"So you think he manipulated Chad?"

"I think he's gone beyond that to controlling," Quinn said.

"Chad was easy prey for that," Kayla said, the bitter edge back in her voice. She'd come a long way in the past few hours, now seeing the truth about her brother for the first time.

"Do you want to talk to him?" Quinn asked her.

Kayla hesitated, then stood up. She seemed to sway slightly, and Quinn steadied her with a hand on her shoulder. Something sparked through Dane, something hot and unsettling. Not jealousy because he'd never seen a man more in love with his woman than Quinn was with Hayley. But that was his place. Kayla was his—

He broke off the automatic thought. No, she wasn't. Not anymore, no matter what his automatic, long-ingrained reaction to another man touching her might be.

"I want to hear his explanation," she said, sounding a bit stronger now. She looked up at Quinn. "Do you think he's telling the truth?"

"Probably not all of it," Quinn said, "but what he is telling is true, I think. He's too shaken not to. Dunbar is good."

Quinn glanced at Dane, one eyebrow lifted in query. Dane nodded; he wanted to hear this, too. Chad had cost him everything; he had the right to know what had really gone down that night and why.

Shaken, he thought after a few minutes on the other side of that steel door, wasn't a strong enough word. Chad looked like he'd shrunk to child size.

He wasn't behind bars per se—the small room was screened, not barred. But it was clearly a cell, and Chad clearly knew it. He was willing to talk to his sister, although Dane suspected it was an effort to regain her sympathy and enlist her help in saving him from the consequences of what he'd done.

From the consequences of who he was, Dane amended silently as Chad again gave them the same version of that night's events that he had back at the abandoned arcade. Kayla listened, expressionless, although Dane knew that hearing about it all again had to be excruciating. It was hard enough for him to listen to Chad's repeated excuses, his declaration that he'd had no idea, that he'd only wanted the money.

"Why?" Kayla finally said, asking again the ultimate question.

"I told you, they walked in on us. Startled us."

"Please," Dane said. He'd stayed quiet throughout the long, rambling discourse, but now he was unable to stop himself. "Troy could talk squirrels out of trees, and you expect us to believe he murdered two people because he was startled?"

"But he had the money in his hand and was reading Dad's papers. He was caught red-handed."

"Papers?" Dane asked, brows furrowing. "Even after he had the money? What papers?"

Chad looked blank. "I don't know."

"I think I do."

Detective Dunbar's voice came from the doorway behind them. The detective walked into the room, wearing the expression of a man who'd figured out a puzzle.

"I went back through the old evidence files. There was a list of the papers from the desk that were booked as evidence because of blood spatter." He glanced at Kayla, as if to see if she was okay with the blunt description. She gave the slightest nod of her head, so he continued. "The investigators at the time thought it was just a result of the fight. And because the killer wore gloves, there were no prints, even if we did go back and look with better technology now."

"I already told you Troy had gloves on," Chad said, that whiny note that had always irritated Dane creeping back into his voice. Dunbar ignored him, which made Dane like him even more.

"One set of those papers had more blood than the rest, indicating they were on top of the desk. Or closest to the attack."

"Meaning they were what Troy was holding?" Kayla asked, getting there quickly.

Dunbar nodded. "There was a void in the pattern, indicating perhaps a thumb holding them and that they were on top."

"What were they?" Dane asked.

"Insurance," Dunbar said. "Life insurance."

Kayla frowned. "I remember that. It took a long time for the insurance claim to come through because the police had the papers. Dad's attorney had to step in."

Dane remembered that, too, but he was focused now on something else. "Wait, are you saying there's a connection? Between the insurance and the murders? That makes no sense—Kayla got the money."

He didn't mention that she'd spent a goodly chunk of it hunting down her brother. Or the painful fact that she'd accused him of being after it himself. But he saw her wince and suspected she was thinking just that.

Detective Dunbar looked at Kayla. "According to those papers, you and your brother were equal beneficiaries."

"Yes," she answered.

"What did you do with the money?"

"Wasted too much of it looking for him." She confirmed Dane's suspicion about her thoughts, indicating Chad with a jerk of her head, not even looking at him.

"Including his half?"

She looked startled. "No. Of course not. I never touched his."

Dane saw Chad perk up at this. He was thankful they were separated by that metal screen, or he likely would have punched him again. As if he'd sensed it, Dunbar moved them over to the far side of the room, where Chad couldn't listen to every word.

"Chad's half is still sitting in a beneficiary account," Kayla explained.

Dunbar looked as if the number-one thing on his list had just been checked off. "Okay," Dane said, still baffled, "I get that there's a tempting pile of money there, but—"

Dunbar held up a hand. "Here's what I think went down.

Troy—and if that guy's not a pure sociopath I'll be surprised—sees the insurance papers in the desk. Realizes that with their folks dead, Chad comes into a hundred times what he had in his hand. And knows he's got Chad under his thumb."

Kayla gaped at him. "You think he killed my parents so that Chad would get that money and he could manipulate him out of it?"

"So when Troy called Chad a tool, he meant it literally—is that it?" Dane asked.

"If I'm right, yes."

"I always wondered why Troy stayed friends with Chad." It made perfect, if twisted, sense, Dane thought. Except for one thing. "But Chad ran and never collected. And if he had contact with Chad all this time, why did he wait so long? And why was he sending him money, which helped him stay away?"

"Yeah, that hung me up, too. I figured at most he'd give it a cooling-off period, until things settled, before he brought Chad back."

"But Chad was the only suspect you were looking for," Kayla said. "He couldn't have collected the money, could he?"

"Not likely while he was the suspect, and especially not if he was convicted. This state has a pretty solid Slayer Statute. But that would mean it would go to the next likely beneficiary. If Troy convinced Chad to make that him, gave him power of attorney on that account or something…"

Dunbar let it hang with a shrug.

"And he could," Kayla said. "Chad's that weak-minded."

Something in her voice, something steely and solid, told Dane she truly had reached the end when it came to her brother. He was a little puzzled; he should be glad, but he was feeling a bit numb. Had the love that had guided his life for a decade truly died, or was he just afraid to believe after having been burned so many times?

He made himself get back to the matter at hand. "So why the wait?"

"I did a bit more digging. You knew Troy's dad died shortly after the murders?"

Dane nodded. "Cancer. Troy was—or seemed—pretty devastated."

"So was his mother," Kayla said. "She just wasted away afterward. He even moved back home to take care of her. Everybody thought that was so noble of him."

"A million dollars buys a lot of nobility," Dunbar said.

Dane blinked. "What?"

"His father had a million dollar life insurance policy, too."

Kayla's eyes widened. "And taking care of his mother likely meant taking care of the money, too."

Dane's mind leaped ahead. It was crazy, but so was this whole thing. "So you think it was just coincidence that Troy's dad died during the…cooling-off period after the murders, as you called it?"

"Had to be. It's the only explanation for why they never went ahead with it. Troy didn't need the money by then."

Kayla's eyes widened. "I remember once, when his father was still alive, Troy saying how his dad's illness was sucking up everything. He said it as if he were worried about his mother doing without, but it was probably just himself he was worried about."

"Makes sense. Things must have been tight, and anything extra would have gone to his father's care. Time, attention, money, everything. A guy like Troy wouldn't take to that very well. He's got that entitlement mentality to the bone."

"So that triggered the theft of Kayla's dad's stash?"

"I'm betting if we dig deep enough, we might find some

other thefts, too. Buddy burgs, we call them—stealing from friends' homes."

"And then when his dad died and the insurance came through, he didn't need that anymore," Dane said.

"Or Chad's," Kayla said.

"He has been living pretty high," Dane said.

"And," Dunbar added, "sending money to Chad. To keep him on the string, if my theory is right. I'll put the financial guy on it in the morning, but I wouldn't be surprised if he's run through most of that money in the last ten years."

Kayla shuddered visibly. "So now he needed Chad's."

"Did Troy know you hadn't touched it?"

She nodded, her expression grim. "The subject came up a time or two when we would run into each other. It seemed casual at the time, but now I see he was checking to make sure it was still there."

"So there were two options," Dunbar said. "Chad comes back, somehow proves his innocence and collects and Troy manipulates the money out of him. Or…"

He hesitated, looking at Kayla as if not sure he wanted to finish. Dane did it for him.

"Or he tells Chad to come back knowing he'd be arrested and convicted." Kayla sucked in an audible breath. She had to be reeling from all this, Dane thought, but he made himself finish. "Much easier to just be the secondary beneficiary."

"Unless Kayla fought it," Dunbar said as Dane had just gotten there himself. "He did it, didn't he?" he asked, staring at Dunbar.

The detective looked at Dane. Then, slowly, he nodded. "That's my guess."

Kayla glanced from Dane to the detective and back, looking a little shell-shocked. "What?"

"I'm betting the insurance policy or your folks' will said that if one of you died, the other got what was left of that money. Troy would have to fight that, as long as you were still alive."

Dane saw the realization dawn. Her voice shook as she spoke it. "Troy threw that fire bomb. He brought Chad back to collect one way or another and tried to kill me. He planned it all along."

Dane would have done worse than kill Troy if he'd been able to get at him just because of the look on her face. She'd been betrayed by her brother and a man who was supposedly a friend.

And by he himself?

He shoved aside that thought as another occurred to him. "Why was Troy there at all tonight?"

Dunbar studied him for moment. "I think you already know."

"To clean up the other lose end," Dane said slowly. "Chad."

Dunbar nodded as Kayla gasped yet again. "I think he knew things were falling apart. Once he realized Foxworth was never going to stop, he decided to cut his losses. And the only person who could throw suspicion on him for the murders was Chad."

"My God," Kayla breathed. "Is he really that…evil?"

"Just how sure are you," Dane asked sourly, "that Troy's mother died of natural causes?"

Dunbar's brows raised, and he gave Dane a slight nod of salute. "I'll be looking into that," he said. "It would explain why he got so cocky, if he'd already gotten away with it once."

"My God," Kayla said again.

She swayed on her feet. Dane caught her but with, he told himself, no more personal involvement than Quinn had shown before.

It really was over. There was nothing left to do but pick up the pieces of their lives, separate them and move on.

Chapter 36

He'd forgotten they'd both come in one car, Dane thought as they arrived back at Foxworth. It would have been easier if they each had their own, but then, none of this was going to be easy.

It hit him suddenly. Where was Kayla going to go? Back to the house, which was so damaged? Maybe even still smoldering?

He glanced over at her as she slid out of the other door of Quinn's SUV. Hayley was already at the back, opening the hatch for Cutter. She and Kayla had been in quiet conversation for a few moments after they'd left the police station; had they been discussing what would happen now, where Kayla would go?

He should offer his place, he thought, but the idea of having her in his apartment, so near and yet so far, was more than he could handle just now. Maybe later, when he'd had some sleep and was steadier, he could deal, but now? No way.

Cutter jumped to the ground, and Hayley closed the hatch. If the dog was tired, as the rest of them were, it didn't show. His head and tail were up, and he trotted off toward the back of the building.

"Rounds," Quinn said as he walked around the front of the car. "He seems to think it's part of his job to inspect and secure everything whenever we've been gone for a while."

Kayla smiled at that, but it seemed halfhearted.

"He's amazing," Dane said.

"Yes, he is," Hayley said, then added with a grin up at Quinn, "and so's Cutter."

Quinn's smile at that was like a punch to Dane's gut. He'd been like that once. Happy in his life, confident in Kayla's love and enjoying her teasing him like Hayley had just teased Quinn.

"Come along, dear," Hayley said, linking her arm through her fiancé's.

"What?" Quinn looked surprised.

"Just come inside, Quinn. Now," she added when he still hesitated.

Dane didn't know what she did, but the man suddenly glanced at him and Kayla, and realization dawned; she was trying to get him to leave them alone.

"Oh. Yeah. Right."

They vanished inside the Foxworth building, leaving the two of them standing there in the growing morning light. Saying nothing.

Rafe, having parked the Foxworth vehicle he'd borrowed because they had his, came up to them. His brain fogged by weariness, it took Dane a moment to realize Rafe needed his keys back. He dug into his pocket and handed them over with assurances it was in the same condition it had been in.

"No new dings? Too bad," Rafe said. "Adds to the sleeper effect."

"Don't mention sleep," Dane said.

"We could all use some," the lanky man agreed. He turned as if to go, then turned back. "You two have something special. Don't blow it."

And then he was gone, leaving them standing there once again in awkward silence.

"We did have something special," Kayla finally said. "And I'm the one who ruined it."

"You did what you thought you had to do."

"That's no defense for what I did to you. And I'll pay for it every day I have to go on without you."

He didn't have an answer for that. And he didn't like the sound of it, put flatly into words like that.

"I love you, Dane Burdette. I have loved you more than half my life. And I will love you for the rest of it, whether you love me or not."

"Kayla—"

"So is that what I'm facing? A life spent knowing I ruined the best thing I ever had because I was such a fool?"

This was it. All he had to do was say he was sorry and walk away. Quinn and Hayley would see to her, he knew that. But he stood there in silence, letting the painful question hang in the air unanswered.

He was vaguely aware of movement out of the corner of his eye. Cutter, he thought, finishing his "rounds." The dog headed for the front door of the building, stopped suddenly and spun around to look at them. Then he started toward them.

The dog came to a halt and sat between them, looking from one to the other with an expectant expression.

"Hey, Cutter," Dane said, reaching down to scratch the ears of the dog who'd started all this.

When he straightened, as if she didn't want to get too close to Dane, Kayla crouched in front of the animal, stroking his head. "Thank you," she said to him. "For everything."

Cutter made a low sound that wasn't a growl or a woof but still managed to be commanding. Dane supposed it was how he got sheep to do what he wanted—that is, if he'd ever really seen a sheep.

The dog moved then, getting up and walking behind Dane. He looked over his shoulder at the animal, curious about what he was up to. Cutter leaned suddenly, pressing his full weight into the back of Dane's legs, forcing him to take a step forward. Just as he had with Troy at the top of the stairs. Only now, he was pushing Dane.

Toward Kayla.

Dane jerked around, startled, staring at the dog. And Cutter met his gaze with a look he would swear was impatient.

Cutter moved back between them. Sat again. And yipped.

Dane knew he was losing it then because that yip had sounded for all the world like "Well?"

The dog's gold-flecked eyes seemed to pin him, and Dane knew with a certainty that had no explanation that, in Cutter's mind, he and Kayla were supposed to be together, and he was holding things up.

"Look, Cutter, it's complicated."

The dog woofed then, sounding disgusted.

"What are you, a matchmaker or something?"

The dog glanced over his shoulder at the door Quinn and Hayley had gone through.

"Taking credit for them, are you?"

He nearly laughed then; was he really talking to—and worse, trying to divert the conversation with—a dog?

"Hayley said he picked Quinn for her. And made it happen."

Kayla's soft words brought his head up. But she was looking at the dog, not him. He looked back at Cutter's intent expression.

"I wish you could fix us, boy," he said to the dog. "I mean, the worst is over now, so the problem is over except for Chad's in trouble and she—"

"Doesn't give a damn," Kayla said, cutting him off.

"Even if that's true," he said to the dog, "after ten years, I just can't go on. But I can't give up either."

Wait. He hadn't meant to say that.

"I've always assumed we'd be together. Forever. So how can I quit on that now that the only problem we had is—"

He stopped himself this time. That was *not* what he'd meant to say. What the hell was going on?

"Look, Cutter, it's just that I got so tired of coming in second. I used to think it was making us stronger because nothing this bad could happen to us again, and if that's true then we've been through the worst and made it, and we'll always know that if there are problems in the future."

He stopped again, realizing he had somehow shifted focus in the middle of that rambling explanation, that he'd gone from convinced it was over to explaining why it wasn't.

To a dog.

"That's what you're saying, isn't it?" Kayla said to Cutter. "That we belong together."

Something in her voice, the tiniest quaver, sent a ripple up Dane's spine. A ripple that reminded him of the heat of their passion, and the deep, sweet softness of snuggling with her in the night and the joy of waking with her in the morning.

"You think I should listen to a dog—is that what you're saying?" Dane asked, aware of the sudden huskiness of his voice as the memories flooded him.

"I think you know as well as I do this is no ordinary dog."

Dane sighed. Because when it came right down to it he couldn't deny one simple fact.

Cutter was right.

He reached down and ran a hand over the dog's soft fur. "You're right, Cutter-dog. We do belong together. We have since that day I first climbed that tree between our houses to find out why that skinny neighbor girl with the big eyes was hiding up there."

He was talking to Kayla now more than the dog.

"I waited for her to grow up, I waited until I finished school, then I waited for her to find her brother."

"All good things…" Kayla said softly.

"Come to those who wait? Personally, I'm of the opinion

that good things come to those who quit just waiting and do something about it."

"You may be right. So are you going to do something?"

He gave up the pretense of talking to the dog. He straightened up and met her gaze head-on. He wasn't sure, but he thought she was holding her breath.

He'd been right about one thing. He was through waiting.

He held out a hand. Kayla took it. The moment their fingers touched, the electric jolt seared away the pain, the doubt, the determination.

Yes, Cutter had been right. They belonged together. They always had.

"Now, I think," Hayley said.

Quinn looked at her, wondering where women got that sixth sense about people and their emotions. But he knew better than to disagree with her because he knew she was almost always right.

He opened the door and leaned out. And found out that, of course, Haley was right again. There was no mistaking the passionate kiss going on for anything other than two people putting things back together.

"Cutter! Get in here," he yelled.

The dog hesitated, looked from Dane to Kayla, then gave a satisfied nod and got up. He trotted toward the building, his tail up and waving with every step like a banner carried by a victorious army.

An army of one, Quinn thought, smiling at the old saying. Whoever had begun it had probably never thought of it being one dog.

When Cutter was back inside, Quinn took another look at the two people outside, standing in a shaft of morning sunlight, wrapped in each other's arms.

"Good job, dog," he said. "Time to leave the rest to them."

Cutter woofed.

"They'll do it," Hayley said. "They came close to losing it, but they'll rebuild."

Quinn knew she didn't mean just Kayla's house. Which Foxworth had already made arrangements to have repaired.

"Have I told you lately I love you?" he asked.

"Me or Cutter?" she teased.

"Yes," he answered, glancing around for the clever animal who had brought them together.

Cutter was curled on his bed in the corner of the office sound asleep.

Resting up, Quinn thought, for his next adventure.

* * * * *

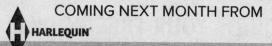

REQUEST YOUR FREE BOOKS!
2 FREE NOVELS PLUS 2 FREE GIFTS!

✦ HARLEQUIN®

ROMANTIC suspense

Sparked by danger, fueled by passion

YES! Please send me 2 FREE Harlequin® Romantic Suspense novels and my 2 FREE gifts (gifts are worth about $10). After receiving them, if I don't wish to receive any more books, I can return the shipping statement marked "cancel." If I don't cancel, I will receive 4 brand-new novels every month and be billed just $4.49 per book in the U.S. or $5.24 per book in Canada. That's a savings of at least 14% off the cover price! It's quite a bargain! Shipping and handling is just 50¢ per book in the U.S. and 75¢ per book in Canada.* I understand that accepting the 2 free books and gifts places me under no obligation to buy anything. I can always return a shipment and cancel at any time. Even if I never buy another book, the two free books and gifts are mine to keep forever.

240/340 HDN FVS7

Name	(PLEASE PRINT)

Address	Apt. #

City	State/Prov.	Zip/Postal Code

Signature (if under 18, a parent or guardian must sign)

Mail to the **Harlequin® Reader Service:**
IN U.S.A.: P.O. Box 1867, Buffalo, NY 14240-1867
IN CANADA: P.O. Box 609, Fort Erie, Ontario L2A 5X3

Want to try two free books from another line?
Call 1-800-873-8635 or visit www.ReaderService.com.

* Terms and prices subject to change without notice. Prices do not include applicable taxes. Sales tax applicable in N.Y. Canadian residents will be charged applicable taxes. Offer not valid in Quebec. This offer is limited to one order per household. Not valid for current subscribers to Harlequin Romantic Suspense books. All orders subject to credit approval. Credit or debit balances in a customer's account(s) may be offset by any other outstanding balance owed by or to the customer. Please allow 4 to 6 weeks for delivery. Offer available while quantities last.

Your Privacy—The Harlequin® Reader Service is committed to protecting your privacy. Our Privacy Policy is available online at www.ReaderService.com or upon request from the Harlequin Reader Service.

We make a portion of our mailing list available to reputable third parties that offer products we believe may interest you. If you prefer that we not exchange your name with third parties, or if you wish to clarify or modify your communication preferences, please visit us at www.ReaderService.com/consumerchoice or write to us at Harlequin Reader Service Preference Service, P.O. Box 9062, Buffalo, NY 14269. Include your complete name and address.

HRS13

Copper Lake on a pretty spring Sunday was at its best. It was welcoming. Peaceful.

It was home, Stephen realized. It had been luck that brought him here, and now he wanted to stay. He belonged.

If only Macy felt the same.

They turned the corner, where a couple of tables and chairs flanked the coffee-shop door. Stephen held the door for his girls.

His girls. He liked the sound of that.

"Did you sleep well last night?" he asked after dragging a chair to the two-person table for Clary.

He looked back at Macy in time to see her shoulders stiffen slightly. If he hadn't spent much of the past six days with her, he might have missed it entirely.

"I did. It was nice having Clary to cuddle with." She gazed across the street, then met his eyes again. "But when I got up this morning, I couldn't find my keys. I leave them on the kitchen island. I always have. But we finally found them on the mantel underneath the wedding portrait."

He faked an accusing look. "Were you planning to scratch out your faces with the keys? 'Cause I've got to tell you, car keys weren't made for destroying canvas and oil."

Her smile was unsteady. "I don't remember putting them there."

He wasn't sure why that was so important to her, but he shrugged. "You forgot. You were preoccupied. It happens all the time."

"I'm not normally forgetful."

He curled his fingers around hers. "But this isn't a normal time for you, is it?"

"No," she agreed with another weak smile.

Stephen couldn't help but wonder why the incident troubled her more than he understood. But if there was a subtle way to ask, he couldn't think of it, so he just went with straightforward. "Tell me why it bothers you so much."

Her gaze drifted away—not an obvious shift, as if she didn't want him to see her eyes, but he would bet hiding was exactly the reason. "You'll think I'm crazy. The hell of it is, I might be."

**Is Macy crazy? Or is something more
sinister at work in Copper Lake? Find out in
COPPER LAKE CONFIDENTIAL**

**Available April 2013 from
Harlequin Romantic Suspense
wherever books are sold.**

ROMANTIC suspense

Look for the second book in Elle Kennedy's
The Hunted miniseries!

Dr. Julia Davenport spends her days saving
lives, but when she stumbles upon a shocking
government conspiracy, the only life that now
needs saving is her own. Teaming up with
Sebastian Stone was supposed to help her
stay alive, but Julia doesn't expect to feel such
overwhelming passion for the sexy soldier.

SPECIAL FORCES RENDEZVOUS
by Elle Kennedy

Available April 2013 from Harlequin Romantic Suspense
wherever books are sold.

Heart-racing romance, high-stakes suspense!

ROMANTIC suspense

Available next month...

FBI profiler Mark Flynn has come to Vengeance, Texas, with a team of agents to solve three murders and a strange kidnapping. He's instantly drawn to Dora Martin, an older student and a woman who has secrets of her own—one of which puts her right in the sights of a sociopathic killer. Dora Martin has spent a lifetime making mistakes about men and bad, self-destructive choices. Given a second chance to find success, she has focused her life on education... including a rule of no men allowed. Mark Flynn instantly gets beneath her defenses with his brilliant mind and quirky habits. One of Dora's biggest secrets is that she is Professor Melinda Grayson's sister—and Melinda Grayson and her strange kidnapping are at the heart of Mark's investigation....

Look for the final book in the electrifying Vengeance in Texas miniseries!

A PROFILER'S CASE FOR SEDUCTION
by Carla Cassidy

Available April 2013 from Harlequin Romantic Suspense wherever books are sold.

Heart-racing romance, high-stakes suspense!

It all starts with a kiss

Check out the brand-new series

HARLEQUIN® KISS™

Fun, flirty and sensual romances.
ON SALE JANUARY 22!

Visit www.tryHarlequinKISS.com
and fall in love with
Harlequin® KISS™ today!